South of Sunshine

Dana Elmendorf

Albert Whitman & Company
Chicago, Illinois

To my husband and two boys—
you are my heart, my soul, my everything.

Library of Congress Cataloging-in-Publication
data is on file with the publisher.

Text copyright © 2016 by Dana Elmendorf
Hardcover edition published in 2016 by Albert Whitman & Company
Paperback edition published in 2017 by Albert Whitman & Company
ISBN 978-0-8075-7571-0

Printed in the United States of America
10 9 8 7 6 5 4 3 2 1 LB 22 21 20 19 18 17

Cover photo © Shutterstock.com
Design by Jordan Kost

For more information about Albert Whitman & Company,
visit our website at www.albertwhitman.com.

Chapter 1

You don't expect to be dumped five seconds after someone shoves his tongue down your throat. But that's what Dave Bradford just did to me. I suppose the kiss was Dave's idea of a consolation prize. Or maybe he was giving it one more try to see if there was any possibility of a spark. He'd have a better chance of lighting a wet match.

I want to tell Dave thank you for saving me from another week of spit baths before I eventually ditched him. Instead, Dave Bradford stands there—his fat slug tongue safely back in his mouth—and he gives me the whole "it's not you, it's me" speech. He has no idea how wrong he is, but I have no intention of enlightening him as to why.

Then, as if breaking up with me in the locker hallway in front of God and everybody isn't enough, he also informs me he'll be taking Chelsea to the big party Friday night. Wow. First day into my senior year, the boyfriend I've had for the last three weeks is my longest relationship. Ever. And because I'm unable to feign interest in any guy for very long, I'm being dumped for Chelsea Hannigan—*tiny tank top* Chesty Hannigan.

Dave leaves me hanging at my locker, feeling like a total loser, wondering if my kissing skills equal those of a dead fish.

I've kissed lots of boys. Well, what I think would be lots for the average seventeen-year-old girl. If we're talking, say, Becky Staggs—who has kissed every guy this side of the Mississippi—then my lip-locking would be a drop in the bucket.

My first French kiss was the single most disgusting moment of my life. Hayden Mays, my summer boyfriend before eighth grade, had pulled me under one of those big beautiful oak trees. The butterflies in my stomach had migrated to my throat. Their wings raked against my esophagus, trying to get the hell out of there. It took a full thirty seconds of teeth gnashing and tongue lapping before I could decipher why the moment felt so terribly wrong. The second Hayden set me free, I ran straight home, immediately texted him, and broke up.

I shove my backpack in my locker and shut the door.

"Finally," says my friend Van. He wraps an arm around my shoulders and marches us toward the cafeteria. "Thank God that relationship is over."

"You're such an eavesdrop whore."

Van sticks his tongue out at me. "Dave may be a hottie, but I was worried you were going to drown in all that saliva." He makes an exaggerated slurping noise, and I laugh.

That's Vander Elgin Lovelace for you, all jokes to wash away the hurt. He's been that way ever since preschool. Not that I'm sad Dave dumped me, but Van knows how hard I worked all summer to rally up a boyfriend, a charade that's getting harder and harder to keep up. Now I'll have to go to the Goodman's annual kick-off-the-school-year party without a "boyfriend" again.

It's a legacy party that's been a tradition in our small Tennessee town for ten years. Thirty if you count the previous two generations of strapping Goodman boys. Three sons each generation—that family has some serious XY dominant chromosomes.

It started with Andrew's grandfather's barn dances. Then Andrew's father and uncles hosted cornfield parties. Now it's a bonfire bash by their family lake, unchaperoned. Andrew, the third and last Goodman boy of this generation, is the grand host. And anybody who's anybody is going.

Van and I both grab salad bowls. "Nice tats on the shoes," I say, complimenting his airbrushed Chucks—which I'm pretty sure is his third customized pair of Chucks he's punked up. But Van, with his deep-purple skinny jeans, vintage Poison T-shirt, and black blazer, wears them like it's the latest punk trend. His messy layered hair screams Johnny Depp.

"Thanks. I like the clawing tiger." Van roars and mimics the slashing paw of the image on his shoes. His smile glistens when he bares his teeth.

"Look," Van says, pointing to the spill of chocolate pudding on the counter, "a love note."

In an attempt to clean up a drop of pudding, someone had inadvertently smeared it into the shape of a heart. Hearts abound in nature. Love notes from the universe, asking you to pay attention. I take out my cell phone and snap a picture of it to add to my collection.

Van plops four cherry tomatoes on my salad. I hate cherry tomatoes, but Van loves them, and the lunch lady in charge of the salad line is a tomato nazi. She only allows four per salad. Like our Podunk high school will go in arrears over an excess of produce consumption. Van smirks at the lunch lady as she scans his card.

We plunk down onto the barstool-style seats attached to the lunch table. Van calls the stools "orange butt mushrooms." They're one of the "mini upgrades" our school made over the summer, because what school wouldn't benefit from butt mushrooms over new library books.

"Eeeeee!" Sarabeth squeals as she sits down across from us. "Four more days!" She wiggles on her butt mushroom.

Sarabeth Anne Beaudroux's local family lineage dates back to the early eighteen hundreds. Her family owns a historical yellow colonial home in the heart of Sunshine—as in "Sunshine, Tennessee. A good place to be." (According to our clever, catchy, and completely lame city limit signs.) Her home has the oldest, grandest oak tree in town, with a rope swing to boot. And she is the epitome of a southern peach—all charm with a pinch of scandal and intrigue. Shampoo commercials have got nothing on her blond shine.

"Whatcha gonna wear, Kaycee?"

"Definitely not plaid," Van answers before I can. A death stare beams from Sarabeth. On cue, Andrew Goodman—in his light blue plaid shirt—sits down next to Sarabeth, pecking a quick kiss on her cheek just before he tucks into his lunch: two cheeseburgers, a glop of spaghetti, and a mountain of dinner rolls. I wonder if he plans on trucking in his dessert.

"Haven't decided," I say before Van cares to elaborate on plaid. "Maybe just a T-shirt and shorts." I know what's coming next—a sour face, a grunt in disgust. I want to remind Sarabeth of our childhood days in her Granny's creek bed, catching crawdads and riding horses. Where plaid shirts, jean overalls, and muddy waders were our wardrobe of choice. That is, until one kiss from a cute farm boy at eleven—after that it was dresses and pink for Sarabeth. Thank goodness all that pink didn't go to her head, or we wouldn't still be riding horses in that old creek.

"Ugh." Sarabeth and Van exclaim in unison. Though they butt heads occasionally, they have a united front against my all-natural look. My jeans, T-shirt, and lip gloss kind of style drives their fashion genes insane.

A herd of plaid cattle fill in behind Andrew. "Seniors!" bellows Charles Buck, who likes to call himself Chuck the Buck. He high-fives his best bro, Andrew. Their thick hands make a loud clap. Chuck the Buck spreads the wealth and high-fives everyone at the table. I'm even a little caught up in being Kings of the Cafeteria. Heck, Kings of the School! I high-five him too.

Andrew stretches his palm across the table to give Van some senior love, but when Van reaches his arm out to reciprocate, Andrew yanks his back and slicks it over the side of his hair. "Not happening, daffodil." Laughter moos from his audience.

"Asshole," Van mumbles. I hope I'm the only one who heard.

"Are we ready to kick some Viking ass next Friday night, boys?" Andrew asks. Chuck and the other thick-necks sit to graze at the same time. The heels of my feet rise slightly off the floor as the weight of meat tips the table off balance. Next to me, I hear Van snicker.

Andrew, who was saying something about the upcoming football scrimmage, stops shaking one of his *three* cartons of chocolate milk and glares at Van. The laser vision dares Van to make one smartass remark. I nudge Van's knee with mine, a plea for him to keep silent. It's bad enough Van's first act as council president was to convince the student body to help fund our struggling art program instead of customizing the football player's practice jerseys with their last names. We don't want to piss off Andrew any more than we have to.

Van keeps his trap shut, miraculously.

The boys at the jock end of the table talk about the rival schools they will face this season. Sarabeth leans over to me to discuss more important stuff. "I was thinking you'd look cute in my white summer dress, with the cherries." Her southern drawl makes it sound like "chair-ees." Her voice is whisper-sweet and breathy. "You know—the sexy one with the ruffle neckline that hangs off the shoulders." A small grunt comes from Andrew. Sarabeth shoulder bumps him with a giggle, acknowledging his caveman approval.

"Let me guess, she can borrow your cowgirl boots to wear with it too? Cliché." Van rolls his eyes, wiping the smile off Sarabeth's face. "I think you should wear that slinky orange one-shouldered dress we got at Spitx."

Sarabeth forks a cucumber. "Oh, so she can wear your hoochie-momma hot pink pumps and sink her heels into the cow pasture?"

"I borrowed 'em from your momma," Van snaps back.

"Guys." I throw my hands up in surrender. "Shut. It." I shake my head at Sarabeth. She promised me she wouldn't goad Van. Van humphs, and I elbow him in the ribs.

"I have some really cute cut-off jean shorts," I say to Sarabeth. "And a glittery lips Rolling Stone strapless top." I look at Van. "Okay?"

Sarabeth picks at her salad. Van spears one of my tomatoes. Their lack of protest says they silently approve. I don't get their constant need to jack up my style. My social life certainly isn't suffering from it.

"What about her *hair*?" Sarabeth asks Van, as if I'm not sitting right here.

"I am not getting lowlights again," I say before they can suggest it. Last time they decided to experiment on me, I had these god-awful black streaks that made me look like I had a yarn wig on top of my wavy sandy-colored hair. We had to bleach it three times before the color stripped away.

Never. Again.

"Does anyone still have their graded copies of Mrs. Engel's tests from last year?" Melissa clunks her tray on the table. Her fraternal twin sister, Misty, swings in beside her. More of our normal crew joins us. Everyone talks shop, from whose teacher sucks worse, to who's going with whom to the party. The I-don't-have-a-date-to-go-with void grows a little bigger. Not that I could show up with my kind of date anyway.

"Hey, did y'all meet the new girl yet?" asks one of the M&M twins.

There's a new girl?

"I hear she's like an Amazon," says one of the plaid cows.

"A Brazilian Amazon, if you like them slightly browned. But dude, she matched Andrew point for point in b-ball this morning," says plaid cow number two.

Andrew nods, almost admiringly. "She has a wicked jump shot." Resident football, basketball, and golf pro Mr. Goodman is not threatened by a fellow athlete? That's a shocker. Must be because she's a girl.

"You know what Harry found out?" asks Chuck the Buck.

"Pipsqueak Harry?" Sarabeth laughs. "Figures he'd molest the new girl before she's even had lunch." Harry's height deficiency landed him a position as the school's Wildcat mascot instead of front point guard for the basketball team.

"He says that back at her high school in Boston, she already had college recruiters from UT Knoxville and Notre Dame scouting her out. When she was a junior, no less."

Andrew whistles an impressed approval. "That lucky bitch."

Not much happens in Sunshine. Besides Nashville's Baptist Youth Conference or family vacations to Florida, most of us never meet out-of-towners. A new student from Boston is like a celebrity in our midst.

Sarabeth's gasp refocuses my attention. "*What* is your boyfriend doing cozying up to Chelsea Hannigan?" She nods across the cafeteria.

"Ex. Dumped." Van so eloquently updates her in two syllables.

Mouth agape, I gawk at Van. "Hag." I smack him.

Sarabeth's puppy dog eyes are sympathetic. "Aw, honey. Again?" Her hand pats mine.

"Not *again*." I yank my hand away in protest. Sarabeth cocks a brow. Van clears his throat. "Chris Wiggins did not dump me. Nor did Milton Ross Jr."

Both were earlier attempts at securing a boyfriend until I was so grossed out I couldn't fake it anymore and *let* them slip away. It's a small town. The well does not run deep.

"Oh gawd." Sarabeth scrunches her nose and turns her head in revulsion. "He just slimed her. And what is up with her hair? It looks like a cat's been licking on it."

Everyone watches the Dave and Chesty make-out hour. Happy it's her and not me getting the spit bath, I laugh and turn to check out her hair.

There—just beyond the tongue fest—standing like a Roman column, is the new girl. She has full pouty lips and smooth eyes under sleek, arced brows. Mink brown hair, off-the-neck short and voluminous on top, curves over her head pompadour style. The sides are back smooth, vintage biker chic. The sleeves of her Boston Marathon T-shirt bunch at her shoulders. Athletic shorts give way to her oh-so-long gorgeous legs.

Flanked on each side of her are LaShell Hayes and Tawanda Shaw, two of our all-state regional girls basketball champions. She's not really going to sit on *their* side of the cafeteria, is she? While laughing at something LaShell says, the new girl sits down with them, unfazed by the criticizing stares for sitting outside her group. I wish I didn't care what people thought.

Before taking a bite, she scopes the cafeteria. Her confident air radiates. I'm completely thrown off kilter. Everything about her vibe, her look, her *everything* screams fresh, different, and alluring. Just like an obsessed fan, I find myself wanting to know more about her.

Her eyes scan me from head to toe and then lock with mine. *Did she just check me out?* An easy smile curls her lips, and she tips her chin up. I'm caught in the awe that is the new girl.

And then I realize…I'm staring.

Blood rushes to my face, and I whip back around. A clammy sweat breaks over my skin, and I stare directly at my salad and hope to God no one sees me blushing. This is not good. I clamp down on the part of me that wants to escape, and command it to stay hidden. Before I can go over the edge into a full freak-out, I see Andrew jerk his head to acknowledge the new girl in return. Instantly, I feel like an idiot. Of course she wasn't checking me out. I breathe.

But I'm a little disappointed too.

The last thing I need is for the new girl to think I'm star-struck. I vow right here on the spot to avoid her at all costs. Even if it kills me.

Chapter 2

After history on Friday, I hustle my butt to the library. The librarian, Mrs. Bellefleur, asks one student to be her aide each year. The last two years she's picked me. She *loves* me. The job is only on Fridays, but it gets me out of sixth period—Social Media in the Digital Age—which is a fancy name for computer class. Not only do I get to skip my brain numbing computer class, I get to help pick what books we add to the library, and it has never been so popular. I've even seen Chuck the Buck reading.

The buzz in the hallways about tonight's party amps up my giddiness. I surely hope the new girl isn't going to be there. With any luck, lake parties will be too backwoods for her.

"Eek!" I squeak when Van gooses me. The stack of textbooks I'm carrying slides dangerously to one side. "Vander Elgin Lovelace!"

He falls in step alongside me. "Oooo. What's up with you? And why are we running?"

I puff a breath to move the bangs that have fallen into my eyes. "I'm on my way to the library. Mrs. Bellefleur says if I can get all the books done early, I can—"

"Skip school?"

"No. I can return the Community Swap books back to the public library."

"And skip school," Van says a little too loudly as we pass the principal's office.

"Shh. I'm not ditching school," I say softer. Technically, I'm not. The public library and Sunshine High have a check-out-a-book-return-it-anywhere policy. The idea is if you make it convenient to return the books, students will read more. It works, sort of.

"You have that woman wrapped around your little finger."

I grin. "It's not my fault Mrs. Bellefleur has a turd for a husband, and my reading suggestions rekindle the forgotten sixteen-year-old in her."

To avoid the main flow of traffic, Van and I cut through what everyone calls Taco Hall because it's where the Mexicans hang out. Ugh. Some people's sense of humor is downright awful at this school.

"Hey, so...do you think you could ask Sarabeth to co-chair on the Homecoming Parade Committee with us?" Van doesn't look at me when he asks this. "You know, because she's got a great eye for design."

"Ha! I knew you liked her style. I don't know why y'all are so fashion competitive. You're both destined to be voted best dressed." Van perks at this thought. We round the corner just before the library. "And yes. We're cutting early to get pedicures; I'll ask her then."

"You hate when people pick at your feet." He grimaces.

"I know, but girl maintenance is necessary for the single greatest party of the school year." I stop just outside of the library. "I've gotta go. Sarabeth told me to be at her car in fifteen minutes." I turn to walk away.

"Guess you don't want to hear how lunch went."

I freeze. I can't believe I forgot. It's not unlike Van to migrate in the cafeteria from table to table; he likes to work his popularity. And there's only so much plaid the boy can take. Today, he ate lunch with the new girl.

The girl who has made friends with everybody in school.

The girl who lived for two years in Zimbabwe.

And the girl I have successfully avoided all week.

My heart pounds in my throat. Self-preservation tells me to keep walking forward and to blow him off with a simple, "Tell me later. I'm in a rush." Survival instincts have served me this far in life. Surely I can live through the new girl epidemic.

But the dark little secret I've hidden away and locked up tight peeks its ugly head out. Despite my better judgment, it wants to be fed.

I turn around, cool and easy. "Lunch? What…were the Tater Tots extra crispy today?" I'm too casual, too nonchalant. And Van knows he's got me.

He just stands there, quiet, with a schmuck-face grin. I want to strangle him and kick my own ass for letting him bait me.

The halls start to clear, and any second the sixth period late bell is going to ring. I'm dying to know what they talked about. I'd tongue Slug Boy again if it meant Van telling me, but I will not break down and ask. I will not break down and ask.

I will *not* break down and ask.

The bell rings as my lips part open to betray me.

"Andrew invited her to the party." Van waggles his brows and starts to strut away.

Before I can stop myself, I step in front of him, cutting him off. "He did? What did she say?" Andrew invited the new girl? I'm glad to hear her new-girl popularity trumps her winter tan, but dang it, this is just going to make it harder to avoid her. And even harder to continue to deny who I really am.

"She said 'Sounds cool.'" He cops a swagger tone for the last words.

"What does that mean? Is she going or not?" A thousand excuses for bailing out of this party pop into my mind. Not a single one of them would fly with Van or Sarabeth.

"I'm late." Van shimmies past me. Halfway down the hall he calls back to me, "She asked if *you* were going to be there." He disappears into the art room.

My tongue catches in my throat when I try to swallow. *She asked about me?* Why? Surely she doesn't know I'm...not like the other girls at school. How does she even know who I am? I've done a superior job of avoiding her this last week. And as luck would have it, I don't have a single class with her.

Up until now, I thought that was a good thing.

I shake out the frenzy of nonsense growing in my head and rush into Mrs. Bellefleur's office. She's sipping a cup of joe from her favorite mug. Red letters across the black cup read "Vampires suck in Forks, Washington."

Upon seeing me, she clunks down her mug. "Oh, your pedicure." I try to shush her, but she fans away my concern with her hand.

On the book cart she shows me which books need to be put away, which need repair, and how to handle those, but I don't hear a thing because sitting at one of the library tables is the new girl. And she's not alone.

Chesty Hannigan giggles her bubbly ditzy laugh. That girl will flirt, kiss, or screw anyone. The only reason she gets away with this behavior is because her family owns a local chain of funeral homes, making her family the second richest in Sunshine. Obviously she's taking a break from making out with my ex to hit on the new girl. They look like they are having fun, and for some reason, I want to smack Chelsea. And not because she's dating Dave now.

The new girl—whose name I found out is Bren Dawson—laughs too. She holds her finger horizontal under her nose, a big bushy mustache inked onto it. It sounds like she is doing a Principal Cain impersonation, and it's actually pretty accurate. I can't help but laugh too.

Mrs. Bellefleur looks at me. My cheeks flush, and I wipe the grin from my face and grip the books I don't remember picking up. "So, I should repair these books next week?" I ask, hoping I've recalled the conversation correctly.

"Yes, honey. Just stack them in that pile for now, so we can clear this cart for returns." She pulls the rest of the books from the return box under the desk.

Like a drone, I walk the books to the shelf where she directed me, all the while my eyes trained on the giggle-fest that is Chesty Hannigan. I strain to hear what she's saying. The books don't quite fit on the crammed shelf, so I have to shove them in. Then I hear a mousy squeal.

I jerk my head up. Bren is holding Chelsea's hand, studiously drawing a mustache on her finger. Chelsea holds it up to her face and giggles again. *Vomit.*

"Miss Hannigan?" Mrs. Bellefleur barks to Chelsea.

Everyone's attention snaps to Mrs. Bellefleur. Bren's eyes flick over to me.

"Is there a reason you're lingering past the bell? Or do you think you can find your way to class without a detention slip? Miss Dawson, I believe you have work to do."

Slowly, Chelsea gathers her books—taking her sweet ass time. Bren opens up one of her textbooks and makes a show of studying. Chelsea looks sheepishly at the new girl and whispers something that makes her smile. Bren slips another glance at me. I drop my gaze to the books.

The freaking skank *finally* leaves.

"Well, Kaycee, you'd better get to shelving if you want to get out in time to return these books to the public library." Mrs. Bellefleur winks.

"Yes, ma'am." I hurry the squeaky-wheeled cart behind the wall of shelves and shove the books into their proper places.

In no time, I finish the history and science sections and make my way over to the reference books. What I should be doing is bashing my skull in with this six-inch-thick dictionary for being like the very zealots who stalk the new girl. And yet here I am, obsessing over her like the freaking paparazzi.

I stretch up on my toes to slide a flimsy atlas onto the top shelf. I'm just a hair too short. I step on the bottom shelf to boost myself up just a teensy bit more—

"Can I help you?" Bren's voice catches me off guard, and I slip. My chin bounces off the wooden shelf, and my teeth jab my bottom lip. Books thunder downward as I fumble and catch myself. The tangy taste of copper bitters my mouth.

"Oh man." She lurches toward me. "I'm so sorry. I didn't mean to startle you."

I reverse back like a cat avoiding water. "It's okay. No worries." My teeth tingle.

At the end of the row, I catch Mrs. Bellefleur watching us. As soon as she sees me staring back, she busies herself with some paperwork and smiles at her desk.

"Hey, I'm Bren." Her voice is velvet smooth. I become caramel, warm and gooey. I hesitate before shaking her lingering palm. Static pulses zigzag throughout my body; quickly I yank my hand back. An unreadable grin edges Bren's lips.

"Hi. I'm Kaycee. Kay-c-double e." I reply with my standard introduction. Her brow frowns. "The spelling...sorry. K-a-y-c-e-e. As in

Kay-c-double e." Shut up, Kay-duh-cee. Repeat yourself much?

Her lips widen into a smile, baring a perfect row of shiny white teeth. "Cute," she says.

"I try," I say with a bit of oomph in my voice, and then semi-curtsy. What the heck is wrong with me? I've always been able to block this part of me, and one gorgeous girl with amazing eyebrows and a blinding smile will not change that now.

Will. Not.

Bren thumbs over her shoulder. "Mrs. B said you were in a rush. So I offered to help you put the books away."

Oh, Mrs. Meddling Freaking B. What on earth made her do that?

Together we pick the books up off the floor. I try real hard like to ignore her fresh scent of ocean and spice. This is my opportunity to tell her how lame the party is going to be tonight and convince her not to go. "By blue blay—" I blubber like a baby. My now fattening lip bulges against my tongue.

Bren starts to laugh and looks up at me. "Oh." Her face falls. "Your lip." She gestures to the corner of her own mouth.

I dab my lip, and a smear of blood smudges my thumb. "Oh man, I'm bleeding like a stuck pig," I say, which comes out sounding like I have a lisp. Nice.

"What?"

"Nothing." I wipe my mouth and hide my crimson face. "Um, let me just show you how the books should be put away and then—"

"Pssst, Kaycee." Sarabeth calls from the end of the bookshelf. "What is taking you so long? I'm tired of waiting. You ready or what?"

"Yeah. Just a sec." I sigh in relief for the chance to escape all this closeness. I give a hearty pat to the books left on the cart. "Okay, all I have left are these paperbacks. They're on the honor system. We organize them in alphabetical order by author's last name on that shelf over there." I point and speak extra loud because this is all about the library biz, nothing else.

Sarabeth motions me with her hand to come on.

I scoot around the cart extra quick as I pass Bren. I thumb my back pockets and bounce. "Think you can handle it?"

"Not a problem. I can handle quite a bit." Bren pops up a brow.

Swallow. "Cool." I swivel around and scurry toward Sarabeth. Omigod, is she flirting with me? Or maybe, Kaycee, she's just the super friendly type. Freaking relax.

"See you tonight," Bren calls from behind. Sarabeth cuts a weird look to Bren then me. I clear my throat and smile.

"Finally. I thought you were going to keep yakking all day," Sarabeth says as we sneak out the side entrance toward the parking lot. "Look at your lip. What the heck happened?"

I'm wondering the same thing myself.

Chapter 3

Main Street cuts through the center of town with the courthouse dead in the middle. Shops border a square around the historical judicial building. On the east side is Kappy's Diner—a home-style food place—and Hot Flix, the video store Van's parents own. On the corner is Mother's Merle Norman shop, where she sells their makeup brand alongside her clothing boutique.

When I pass the diner, Mr. Bobby greets me from his usual hitching post at the bistro tables. He's been a permanent fixture in Sunshine since forever. Back in the mid '60s when he ran the *Sunshine Review*, he made local history when he hired black journalists to report on the Civil Rights Movement, a risk not many white business owners took back then. People like him are the reason I want to teach American History someday.

He's also the sweetest old man I know despite my mother's opinion about the color of his girlfriends.

"Nice tootsies, toots," he says. The breeze lifts his soft white hair. He smoothes it back down over his bald spot.

I stop in front of Mr. Bobby's table to wiggle my shiny new colorful pedicure.

"What's them there sparkly things?" His shaky finger points toward my toes. Tiny crystals center the flowers on each big toe.

"Rhinestones. Fancy, huh?" I eye the limp purple flowers lying on the table. "Any luck getting Ms. Doris Carver to fall in love with you yet?"

"Nope. Asked her to Sunday lunch. She said she was thinking on it. Don't worry," his old voice revs. "I wooed her back in the day, I can do it again." He winks.

"I'm sure you will, Mr. Bobby." I wave at Van's mother in Hot Flix as I pass. The sound of the door chime in my mother's boutique announces my entrance.

Baby powder and a heavy musk choke the air. Why do old ladies find it necessary to bathe in perfume that puts hair on your eyeballs? A gaggle of ladies ooo and aah over the new clothing that's just come in.

Mother spies me. Refined ash-brown hair curls just below her ear. Starch keeps her blouse and skirt crisp. Her eyes scan my T-shirt and shorts. I immediately know what the scowl on her face means. Remembering her audience, Mother lightens her expression.

"Kaycee," she says, almost too cheerfully. As she approaches me, the scowl returns. "I thought I asked you to wear the khakis and blouse I just bought you." It's a harsh whisper in my ear. "And what's wrong with your lip?"

"Bit it." I turn away so she can't see my flushed face. The only reason I own khaki slacks is because she bought them. The floral blouse, with its scarf-tied-into-a-bow collar is something my grandmother would wear. No, thank you.

"Paula, can you help me decide between the black sandals or the coral?"

"Be right there, dear," Mother says to Mrs. Jones, then turns back to me. "And what is that crap on your toes?" she asks from the corner of her mouth. "Is that something that Van fellow put you up too?"

"No, Mother. Van doesn't get his nails painted, contrary to what you believe." I love how she refers to him as "that Van fellow," as if he hasn't been my best friend since the beginning of time.

"Well, it looks *ghetto*." She whispers the last word as if it's a sin to say it.

Ignoring her, I drop my book bag behind the makeup counter and get to work helping old Mrs. Perkipsky pick out clip-on earrings for her drooping lobes.

* * *

These old ladies with their thickly rouged cheeks and lipstick-stained teeth have worked me to death. With a pile of clothes on one arm and two boxes of shoes under the other, I glance at the clock. Twenty minutes until close, and then time to go to the party. I'm still trying to decide if this knot in my stomach is dread or excitement.

I hand the clothes from the dressing room to my mother and kneel down to help one of the ladies slip a loafer on to her knotty, corned feet. I spend a moment or so wrestling with her foot before I notice the collective hush. I turn toward the door just as it closes, and the most gorgeous creature I have ever seen saunters in. Immediately, I recognize the firm sculpted brows and sultry eyes. This has to be Bren's mother.

"Good afternoon," Mother greets her. Her eyes greedily devour the woman's regal appearance. Mrs. Dawson is tall and swooping with the grace of a macaw. The other women lean to get a better look-see as if polarized by her presence.

"Hello. I wonder if you carry remover for makeup." Every syllable is short and crisp. Her accent, whatever it is, is light. Her skin is bronzier than Bren's. Rose liner defines the sharp arc of her lips, which are not plump like Bren's.

The low buzz of chatter returns as Mother leads Mrs. Dawson over to the makeup counter and shows her one of Merle Norman's products.

One of the ladies from my church says it first. "She looks like she's got a little *something* in her." There they go whispering about sins again. The mentality of some people around here grates on my nerves.

"She looks like a Mexican."

So every Latina is automatically a Mexican? These women are so clueless.

From the five women in the semi-circle that's formed around me, comments and opinions jump around.

"What's Larry Beaudroux hiring Mexicans for?"

"Her husband is not a Mexican. She is."

"What is he then…Puerto Rican?" Mrs. Jones's southern accent makes it sound more like Pordo-ree-can.

Where in the heck is she getting that?

"Her husband ain't no kind of 'can,' because I've seen him. He's a handsome fellow. I wish I could catch a husband that looked like him."

Mrs. Jones scrunches her nose at Ms. Rita's plump figure. "Huh. You'd have better luck catching a meal at a buffet than a husband like that." All the women cackle, except for Mrs. Rita.

"Are you starting to get a little hot tamale fever there, Rita?" One of the ladies mocks her and fans herself.

"I don't like wetbacks."

"Shhh!" A sharp shush cuts the women off mid-sentence. All eyes land on me. Did that come from my mouth? Frozen in the wake of the silence, I await their reprimands. I don't know what I was thinking shushing my elders like that.

To my astonishment, the ladies turn their conversation back to the shoes and clothing.

Mortification is what I was thinking. If Bren's mother heard them I would be so embarrassed. I've known these church-going women all my Sunday school days. They have always been this way, but I've never had the nerve to say anything before.

Mother bags up Mrs. Dawson's products, and it's not until the door closes behind her that I get the scoop. According to Ms. Rita, Larry Beaudroux—Sarabeth's dad and the biggest factory owner this side of Tennessee—hired Bren's father to save the machinist plant. The power tool company sold its manufacturing rights to a plant in Mexico. If Mr. Larry doesn't get a contract with a new factory to establish itself in Sunshine, a lot of people will be out of jobs. Mr. Dawson has ties to several countries, and it's rumored that a Japanese auto company is considering our small town for its main production plant.

"Great, they're importing Japs into Sunshine now." Mrs. Jones screws her face into a more soured expression.

"I hear they're paying him a pretty penny to set this all up," my mother says.

"What's a pretty penny?" Mrs. Perkipsky asks. That's exactly what I was thinking.

There's a staged pause before my mother answers. "Five. Hundred. Thousand. Plus a ten percent finder's fee."

"Where'd you hear that?" I blurt out.

"From Nancy at the beauty shop. You know her sister's neighbor works in the human resource office at Rally Tools."

I consider the source. Ms. Nancy does have her nose in every nook and cranny of Sunshine. She's probably right. The women continue gabbing, asking one another if they saw "the size of her rock" or "the fine leather on her purse." I guess Mrs. Dawson's financial status trumps her ethnic background. Pathetic.

Oh shoot. I'm late meeting Sarabeth. I pull Mother aside. "Um,

I'm supposed to meet Sarabeth for the Goodman party, but if you need me to stay late and close, I can." Right now, my mother is my only saving grace to bail me out of this party and avoid those things I desperately need to avoid. Though it would be the first time in four years I've missed the party, and I would look like a complete loser if I didn't go. Of course there's also that part of me that doesn't want to keep avoiding "those things" anymore.

"Oh, you're going to the *Goodman* party with *Sarabeth Beaudroux?*" Mother intentionally over-pronounces their names loud enough for the ladies to know I'm friends with some of the wealthiest families in town, as if it elevates our meager social status by proxy. "Well you don't want to be late for that. Go. Take off. Skedaddle. Momma's got plans anyway."

Fantastic. The one time I need my mother to be the slave driver she usually is, she decides to be nicey-nicey and let me off. And I bet she has plans with Mr. Billy Arden. Ever since his divorce, he's been sitting in the same pew as us at church. Something is definitely up with those two.

"And if any of them unsavory kids show up, I expect you to come on home," she hollers at my back as I jet out the door. "Unsavory" is code for nonwhite and poor. I'd like to point out to her that we're half unsavory based on the tiny size of our bank account.

On the way to my car, my cell beeps with a text from Sarabeth.

Where r u?

Running late. R u ready?

Another beep. Gurl, they better have fire extinguishers out there bcz I'm smokin hot n this dress. Andrew better be ready for a good time, esp if I'm going to be getting my drink on.

I laugh out loud. Maybe I'll be having too much fun to even notice Bren. My only hope is that by some miracle, she will not be at this party, and I won't have to deal. What was up with her asking Van about me? I don't even know what to make of that. Then again, she seemed pretty flirty with that I-Can-Handle-a-Lot comment and her glorious smile and stuff.

Oh God, if she's at the party, she's probably going to want to talk— which means a whole lot of her up in my space.

A clammy sweat breaks over my body. An unsettling feeling in my gut whispers things I'd rather not think about. Things I'm certain I filed away in that never-going-to-go-there box. Next to my car, I bend over and do the whole head-between-the-legs routine to keep from throwing up. I inhale and exhale long, deep breaths. I've kept this part of me a secret this long; I am not going to ruin it now. That voice of reason speaks up, the one that tells me I'm over-thinking shit again. I remind myself that there is absolutely no reason I can't be polite to the new girl without going all fangirl on her.

Or I could just never talk to her, ever.

Because that's worked out for me so far.

Chapter 4

Orange and purple hues cover the sky as the sun sets. The Goodmans' lakeside property rests on their two hundred acres out in the middle of nowhere. It's home to some of the best horse trails around. Andrew and Sarabeth picked me up in his four-by-four truck. The last time I drove out here in my silver Honda Civic, it got stuck in the mud. My mother was pissed.

Freshly cut field grass pokes my ankles when I step out of the truck. The dry smell of hay fills the sticky country air. Next to the lake is a huge pile of wood and cardboard boxes stacked on top of a hundred-pound bale of recycled paper. It's going to be a big blaze tonight. Five-gallon water buckets sit near the lake's edge in case things get out of hand.

There's a table covered in snacks with coolers tucked underneath, full of beer I'd guess. Andrew's mother, with sun-leathered skin from farming, walks over. Her faded jeans bunch on top of her work boots. She wears her usual plaid shirt—plaid runs in the family.

"Andrew," she calls.

"Yes, ma'am." Andrew straightens to attention, pausing from pulling out a sleeping bag from the back of his truck.

"Garbage bins are at the end of the table. Do not throw your cans in my lake," she says. He gives a firm nod. She turns to Sarabeth. "If they can't drive, they sleep in the back of their truck. Ya hear?"

Sarabeth "yes ma'ams" too. It's the one rule everybody respects because nobody wants to get busted by the sheriff for drunk driving.

Trucks roll into the field, and more people arrive as Andrew's mother leaves.

"Girl," Sarabeth hollers, "you ready to get your drink on?" Her arms stretch out wide. She has a wine cooler in each hand. I take one.

The ice-cold bottle feels good against my bottom lip. It's not as swollen as it was earlier, but it still hurts when my teeth graze it.

"Yeeee-haw!" Chuck the Buck hollers as he turns his truck radio to max volume. Two huge stereo speakers vibrate and boom in the truck bed, playing "Sweet Home Alabama." A few yards away flames burst into life as they consume the gallons of gasoline on the wood stack. Sarabeth plays hostess and passes out wine coolers to all her girls. That's when I stop and take a casual glance around the lake.

She's not here yet.

"Boo!"

I jump. Red wine cooler runs down my hand. "Vander!" I turn to him and lick the drink off my knuckles. He's cute as can be in his fedora hat, fitted white tee, and slouchy faded jeans. A leather band cuffs one wrist and a white bandana wraps the other. "Aw, you'd make Mr. Depp proud."

"Check it." Van grabs my hand and makes me do a dog-and-pony-show spin.

"Likey?" My strapless top bands my chest, blouses out, and gathers around my waist. On the front, the Rolling Stones' big mouth glitters and sparkles in the firelight.

"Nice Daisy Dukes." He tries to pinch my butt cheek, but I squirm and spin free, spilling more of my drink.

I'm laughing and licking wine cooler off my wrist again when I see a black two-door BMW pull up. Limo-tinted windows and chrome fat rims. A sound system so tight, the blare of music can be heard from the outside. It is not the type of car people from around here drive.

Vander butts shoulder to shoulder with me. "Did you see that sick shit parked in the school lot this week?" he asks, barely moving his lips.

"Um, hell to the no," I mumble back.

A sleek door cracks open and a white pristine sneaker drops to the ground. Bren stands. That hair. God, how does she make it swoop over the top of her head like that? The way she runs a hand over the slicked sides, I wonder if she has a comb in her back pocket. A white tank shows off her sculpted shoulders; the lace of her lavender bra strap peeks out the side. Some lightweight pants, all slack, hang low on her hips. I check to see if there's any more matching lavender. She has the whole "I'm cool" package wrapped up tight.

"Drool much?" asks Van as he nudges me.

"It's a sick ride." I shrug, not looking him in the eye.

"Yeah, right. You're admiring the car." He rolls his eyes.

"Ew." The indignation jumps out of me reflexively. My stomach knots.

Van gives me a soured look.

"Whatever," I say, brushing him off.

Sarabeth comes up and slings an arm over my shoulder. "Kaycee says y'all are looking for another homecoming co-chair. Guess it would be kind of fun to combine our super powers." She smiles and scans Van's attire. "Nice hat, Vander."

Finally, this might be the one thing that unites them.

"Ugh, Bren's here." Sarabeth scowls in Bren's direction, where she's making small talk with Andrew and a few other guys. "Now all Andrew will do is talk sports all night. Is she seriously wearing a ribbed tank from the men's department?"

A flame of anger licks across my skin, but I force myself to turn away. "Hey, the M&M twins are here." And I move toward Misty and Melissa by the bonfire. Van loops his arm through mine and swings me in a U-turn back toward Bren. *Breathe. Breathe.*

"Maybe we should say hi to Bren. We wouldn't want to be rude." There's *way* too much shadiness in his voice. And I'm feeling *way* too vulnerable to tempt this. I can't let myself cave.

I spin us around full circle and weasel my way out of Van's grasp. "I will later. I want to catch up with the twins."

"What are you running from?" Van calls out behind me.

I'm not running, I mouth back at him. Damn, it's getting harder to fight these survival instincts. And what's worse, I think Van sees I'm weakening.

The twins catch me up on who's already wasted, who's making out, and which boys they've already called dibs on. Jesus, people, the party just started. Somehow I seem to have Bren in my sights no matter who I talk to. My Bren-tracking abilities are annoying the crap out of me.

Sarabeth and I mingle through the crowd. Van keeps giving me *that look.* I keep pretending not to notice.

Bren doesn't get more than a few feet anywhere in this party before someone stops her to chat. I maneuver myself to better hear what she and Andrew and Chuck are talking about. It's about the finals from last year's basketball game. There's no more than a lazy "cool" or sultry "yeah" when she replies. But there's something about her self-assured ease that's drawing.

"*What* are you doing?" Sarabeth's voice startles me.

"Nothing." I straighten up from my hunched position. Discretion and eavesdropping are not my forte.

"Give me that wine cooler. You're acting weird." She snatches the bottle from my hand.

As she walks away, it takes me a moment to find Bren again. Finally, I spot her. A girl from my political science class and her boyfriend are asking Bren about Zimbabwe. Bren says her dad was some kind of peacekeeper there. He brought in foreign mining technology that bettered the tribe's working conditions but was cheap enough for the companies to pay for. It's the most I've heard her talk. I'm surprised at how liquid-smooth her voice is, like everything is no big deal.

Hello? Zim-bab-we.

Sarabeth snags my elbow and drags me off toward a row of truck beds. The gap between Bren and me grows.

Some of Sarabeth's fellow varsity cheerleaders stand around talking. "Hey, did y'all hear that Bren spent the summer down in Cuba? How cool is that?"

"Yeah, that's where her grandmother lives," says another girl.

"What about that sweet ride? Is she scared to park it at school?" Melissa asks.

Sarabeth speaks up. "No, they had it shipped down from their place in Boston. It just got here today." Astounded, I look at her. When did she talk to Bren?

Conversation bounces between the girls, and they talk about everything—from Bren's full-ride basketball scholarships to college, to her world travels, to her amazing collection of 1950s movie posters. Everyone is obsessing over her, not just me.

"Did you know they don't own a television?" asks Misty.

"How does anyone *not* own a TV?" asks Sarabeth.

"After they came back to the states from Africa, her parents just never bought one. They're, like, into books and stuff. Weird." Misty makes a face.

Someone needs a beer refill. Sarabeth decides to check on Andrew to make sure he's not puking. Everyone scatters. I'm tight on Sarabeth's heels as she walks. All of this Bren-information swims in my head. Why haven't I heard any of this before now? A full-ride scholarship? Wow, that's like, amazing. I wish I had a scholarship of any kind. Unless we win the Tennessee lottery, I'll be headed to community college. And after college, somewhere far away from here the second I can afford it.

And someone saw her poster collection. *Someone saw her poster collection!* Which means they were in her house. In her bedroom. Who else has been to her house? It occurs to me I don't even know where she lives.

There's this thing brewing inside, and it feels suspiciously like envy. There's no one to blame but me. In my efforts to not seem overeager, I've not only avoided Bren, I've avoided anything Bren-related.

People thicken around us, and it's hard to keep track of Bren with Sarabeth's fluttering. Someone laughs behind me, and it sounds vaguely Bren-ish, but it's just some junior I don't know. I turn back around—

"Oomph." Sarabeth shoves me back. "Geesh, Kaycee."

"Sorry."

"You've been breathing down my neck all night." She wipes a hand across her neck as if to clear the moisture. "Shoo. Go play." She flaps her hand in a sloppy, overdramatic wave. She turns back to her conversation with the girls.

Van steps up next to me. "Yeah, Kaycee. Go play." His eyes dart to Bren. Then he stares me down…with *that look* again.

"I'm going."

"Then go," Van says when I don't move.

"I'm going." And I stand there.

After a few seconds, Van makes a frustrated noise and stalks over to me. This time he manhandles my elbow and forces me to walk with him. "You're being a big chicken," he says. "If it will make you feel better, I'll stay by your side the whole time. There is absolutely no reason you can't talk to her like everybody else."

He's right. In fact, my blatant avoidance might scream something else entirely. So I willingly let him drag me.

Across the crowd, Bren stands in a group, sipping a can of diet soda. It's always easy to spot her because she towers above everyone else. Her head falls back as she laughs at some goofball. I want to be that goofball. I look over at Van again, to be sure.

"Everything will be fine," he says and gently squeezes my elbow.

We bob and weave through swaying bodies. I avoid a red plastic cup before it sloshes all over me. The closer we get, the louder the thundering is inside my chest. Bren tips up on her toes. Her eyes pick through the crowd, searching. When they find me, a huge smile breaks across her face. I exhale.

"Hey, guys," Bren says, smoothly. "How's that lip? I'm really sorry."

"It's fine." I wave my hand. "Stop apologizing. It was my fault. I'm as skittish as they come." I fidget with my back pockets and wait for Van to fill the conversation.

"Oh. Look at that." Van checks his phone. "Sarabeth texted me. Chip emergency. Gotta go." The lying traitor abandons me on the spot. I didn't hear his phone so much as vibrate. He is *so* going to pay for this. I turn back to Bren.

Those little flirty moments seem to fuzz and blur, and I'm not sure if they ever really happened or if they were just my imagination. God, I hope I didn't misread her signals. I've never allowed myself to act on these feelings before. For all I know, I could be standing here, about to make a complete ass of myself.

Her purple bra is totally visible under her white tank, and I force my eyes up to her face. "Sooo, how's your first Sunshine High party go—"

A commotion erupts behind me and before I can continue, I am shoved from behind. My body falls against Bren's, and she spins us out of the way. Her ocean and spice scent weakens my senses. I have no clue what's happening. All I know is I want to take a swim in these waves.

"Piggyback race," she says.

"Huh?" I look up at Bren—and get a *good* look at those lips. The top of my head doesn't even touch her chin. She nods to the side, not taking her eyes off me.

Two jackasses—big enough to flatten a small child—race through the party with guys who are even bigger riding on their backs. Beer splashes from the riders' cups. People swat the racers' butts as they pass and cheer them on, while the racers squeal like pigs. I laugh. That's when I feel Bren's fingers lightly caress my arm where her hand still lingers. A thrill shoots through me.

Okay, this is not my imagination. And the scary thing is, it's the best feeling *ever*.

All the pretending, avoidance, and lying to myself about what I am starts to melt away. For once in my life, I'm going to do something I've never allowed myself to do. To want something I've never allowed myself to want before. And I want it with Bren.

Abrupt laughter from nearby snaps my thoughts into awareness about the whole public witness thing, and I ease away from her fingers. "Bet you don't see that in Boston," I say. She laughs and shakes her head. I scan for witnesses.

"No. But in Zimbabwe, a tribe we lived with liked to play a game called Fat Cricket," she says. When I don't catch on she explains.

"Cricket, the English baseball? Except with Fat Cricket, all the adults have a kid riding piggy-back while they play, making everyone heavy and slower. The little ones love it." She revels at the memory.

"Wow. Zimbabwe, huh." I snuff my nose and puff out my chest. "I went to Canada once." She rewards me with a big smile. "Yep. Found me a whole Canadian dollar at the zoo too. I went screaming to my mother, 'It's a check! It's a check!'" I wave my fistful of invisible money in the air. We're both laughing now. "I thought I was rich."

There's this gleam to her smile that's infectious. I want to keep telling her my stupid childhood stories so that smile never goes away.

Then it dawns on me. "Hey, wait a minute. You're from Boston, right? But I don't hear you saying 'cah' or 'wicked good' or 'frickin' killah.'" Someone bumps me and I step out of the way, closer to the bonfire.

"Well—" She has to speak up because the music just got louder. "I don't think we've lived anywhere long enough for me to pick up an accent." She's right. I don't hear any inflection or drawl. It's just clearly spoken words that pour out like warm sorghum.

"Your mom has one," I say. Bren cocks her head. "Uh, she stopped by my mother's shop today to pick up some stuff." I feel like I'm yelling now. "She's really beautiful."

Why did I say that? The flames of the bonfire heat up my backside. Sweat trickles between my shoulder blades. I fan the back of my shirt.

"You want to move away from the fire? The noise?" she asks.

No. Yes. I follow her lead. Instead of going to the truck beds where everyone else is sitting, we walk in the opposite direction. Away from the music, the flames, and the chaos of farm boys who've had too many beers. Bren flips a water bucket over and offers one to me. I sit.

She positions her bucket right next to mine. It's a low seat, so when Bren sits, she's all granddaddy longlegs. Her knees jut past her armpits. She checks herself out, nodding in satisfaction. "Comfy," she says sarcastically. A deep huff chuckles out of her.

"I can see that." I grin. "If you'd rather sit over on the tailgates with the others—"

"Nope. I prefer to be over here with you," Bren says. Her sureness sends a wave of tingles all over my body. The firelight barely reaches us, but it's enough. I can see Bren's eyes studying my features. It's too much to bear her gaze, so I look out toward the lake. Not a single coherent thought comes to mind.

"Nice toes," Bren says after a short silence.

"Thanks. My mom thinks they look *ghetto,*" I mimic my mother. "But I think they're beautiful."

"Me too." But she's not looking at my toes. My face heats up. Get it together.

"So…your car—glad to have it back?"

"For sure."

"Don't park that thing in the main school lot. It'll get dinged in a heartbeat. I can't wait to hear what Mr. Bobby says after you roll through town in that. He'll think it's 'swaggy.'"

"Is Mr. Bobby that old guy who always hangs out in front of Kappy's Diner?" The way she squints when she asks a question is so cute.

"Yep. He's out there every day either sipping on coffee or munching on a bag of pork rinds."

"What are pork rinds?" Bren's face is a mix of curiosity and horror.

"You've never had pork rinds?" She shakes her head. "Oh, you haven't lived until you've had pork rinds." I explain what the crunchy goodies are, and Bren turns pale.

"Fried pig skin. That sounds disgusting." She laughs. It's all gruff.

"Hey, don't knock it till you try it. Mr. Bobby says they're 'da bomb.'"

"Da bomb? Swaggy? Who talks like that anymore?"

"Only Mr. Bobby. He tries to be 'hip' with the kids. I heard him telling the preacher's wife the other Sunday that she was his Woman Crush Wednesday."

"No way." Her whole body shakes from laughter.

I tell her how his newspaper supported the civil rights movement back in the day and enlighten her on a few colorful Mr. Bobby stories. By the time I tell her about him going to Black Hair Planet and having the girls put cornrows in his hair to impress his Ms. Doris, tears are welling in both our eyes.

"He's a white man with a comb-over!" Bren chokes through her laughter.

"I know! But the man has got a sweet spot for that woman and will do anything to impress her." My sides hurt and my cheeks ache from laughing so hard. God, her smile is amazing.

"Well, hello." Van draws out his hello like he's just caught my hand in the cookie jar. Sneaky rat, I didn't even see him come over.

I straighten on my seat. "Vander," I say just as pointedly.

Bren springs to her feet. "Dude, you want my bucket?"

"No," Van and I say at the same time.

"Seriously, take it. I'm getting a leg cramp." Bren stretches. Van takes the seat, and I narrow my eyes at him.

"What's with all the giggles?" he asks, with way too much insinuation. I kick his foot, then glance at Bren. She's busy looking at something over by the cars.

"You would not believe the moons I've seen tonight," Van says, changing the subject.

"Moons?" Bren turns back to us.

"Big and hairy and one was attached to Chuck the Buck, the big fat—"

"Oh, that is gross," I say. Bren cringes too. "Seen it. Don't need to relive it again. Thank you very much."

Van pinches the bridge of his nose and shakes his head. "I think I'm scarred for life."

"Who was he mooning now?" I ask.

"Hey," Bren interrupts before Van can answer. "Be back in a sec." She takes off before I can ask why.

"One of the M&M twins commented on his butt crack showing," Van starts, but I'm watching Bren. She's walking past the bonfire toward the trucks, with purpose.

"And he says"—Van pauses to control his laughter—"'If you like my crescent, you'll loooove my moon.' He dropped his tighty-whities so fast our eyes were violated before we knew it. Ha, ha—what are you looking at?"

There's a crowd gathering over by the cars, so I stand. "Something's going on."

Van pops up next to me. "Ooh, is somebody fixin' to open up a can of whoop-ass?"

I shush him. The party chatter dulls to where the music is awkwardly loud. Van and I start walking toward the commotion. So does everybody else. On the other side of the crowd, I catch a glimpse of Andrew standing with his fists clenched tight by his sides, his face pinched in anger. I can't see who he's pissed at. Chuck the Buck pushes into the middle, concerned.

"Oh no," Van says. "There's a fight." We move quicker.

Great. There's got to be fifty-something people here, and the biggest guys who could potentially stop a fight are the drunken ones causing it. Van and I pick up our pace, but so does everyone else.

"Who is he fighting?" I ask.

"I don't know," Van says with as much frustration as I'm feeling.

I hold on to Van's shoulder, and he leads us through the thick mob of bodies. He shoves people to the side and clears a path for us.

We emerge at the front of the pack and my heart drops. Andrew is seething like he's nine kinds of pissed off. Directly in front of him stands Bren. Why does she feel the need to involve herself? Seriously, she probably shouldn't be drawing any unwanted attention. She plants a hand on Andrew's chest, and he knocks it off with force.

Oh shit. This does not look good.

Chapter 5

I lurch forward. Van snags my elbow and slowly shakes his head.

"My bad. I didn't know," says Bren. She throws her hands back in surrender.

Didn't know what?

"They didn't come to crash your party. I invited them." Bren gestures behind her.

I didn't even see the ten or so people standing there. It's her basketball buddies, Tawanda and LaShell. I recognize Terrance Carver, LaShell's boyfriend, who subbed as quarterback after Andrew busted his knee last year and cost the Wildcats the championship. The other faces I don't know by name, but I've seen them at school.

A girl next to me mumbles to her friend. "Why'd she invite *them*?" The disgust in her voice is thick. "Don't they have their own parties to go to?" She crinkles her nose.

"Yeah, in the hood." Her friend snickers.

I turn toward the both of them, and the words "stupid" and "bitch" are very close to escaping my mouth. It's pathetic that Sunshine hasn't advanced past the sixties. These girls don't even know them. Especially LaShell because she works her butt off in the college prep courses, and these two skanks skim by in remedial English. Second of all, LaShell doesn't live anywhere near "the hood." Her daddy is some big lawyer over in Memphis, and they live in a huge house out in the country. *Idiots.*

Vander nudges me. My attention pans back to Bren and Andrew. Now they are talking in low voices, and I can only hear every other word. Some old school "Baby Got Back" is thumping in the background. I wish somebody would turn the music off.

Andrew points to Tawanda and LaShell. "Those two can stay. But everyone else has to go."

Terrance moves forward. "Why you gonna play me like that?" He barely comes up to Bren's shoulder, but he's a stocky fellow.

"You"—Andrew stabs his finger in the air—"cost us the championship."

"It was *one* game. How was I supposed to live up to the Goodman legend?" Terrance has a point. Those Goodman boys have sports soldered to their DNA. Sunshine High's Trophy Hall should be renamed Goodman Hall with all the gold-plated plastic they've earned.

"Hey, man," Chuck says to Andrew. "We don't want this to get out of hand. They're not here to cause any problems."

Andrew takes another swig of his beer and his posture softens, but he doesn't say anything. For once, I think alcohol might be helping to defuse the situation.

Bren looks at Terrance and eyes him up and down. She says to Andrew, "Bet his jump shot sucks too." The tension breaks slightly when both of the boys smile.

Chuck puts an arm around Andrew. "Come on, give the little pit bull some love." *Ha!* Terrance *is* thick and stocky like a pit bull. "Can't we all just get along?" That gets a chuckle out of everyone. Chuck makes a ridiculously sappy puppy-dog face and nudges Andrew forward.

There's a bit of reluctance and hesitation before Andrew takes one long look around at his audience and then reaches out his hand to Terrance. They shake. The gesture releases a universal sigh. Maybe there is some hope for this town.

Someone turns up the music, and a hip-hop dance mix blares. "Awwwww, hey." Tawanda bounces to the beat. Her groove causes a chain reaction amongst her friends. The electric buzz is infectious.

Van swings his hips, and I join him. Sarabeth grabs Andrew, and their pelvises lock together, pumping to the base. I do a little wiggle dance with Van.

Chuck jumps into the back of his truck and points the spotlight on his roll bar over everybody, flickering it on and off like a strobe light. The crowd does a collective "Ooh." I turn to see the excitement. Bren busts out with a pop-and-lock, then leans to one side and waves her body from head to toe. *Holy shit.* If it wasn't for the fact that she was six feet tall, and, well, a girl, I'd swear Michael Jackson rose from the dead.

Everyone forms a semicircle around her, cheering. Her pelvis snaps up and down. She grabs her invisible fedora and glides backward out of the center of the circle, gesturing to LaShell as she exits. LaShell and Tawanda erupt into a stomp routine, but all I see is Bren.

Her skin glistens, and her chest heaves up and down. A stray hair hangs down her forehead like Superman's curl. It's a thing of beauty.

Bren cracks up, and I focus back on the circle. Chuck the Buck bounces in the center. His belly jiggles up and down while he's riding the pony, then he flicks his tongue between the V of his fingers. *Gross.* The M&M twins shove him out of the way and do something…uncomfortably suggestive for two sisters. And what do you know, Van and Sarabeth clasp hands and do a swing dance. They look so freaking cute together.

Casually I let my eyes skim back over to Bren. I'm transfixed by the lines of her face, her defined jaw line, and high cheekbones. I'm tired of watching her from afar. I want to see her up close, touch her, and let her touch me.

It's scary and freeing all at once to allow myself to look at Bren like this. But she's different than any other girl I know. Bren is breathtaking. Magnetic.

Bren catches me watching her. It sends a shiver down my spine. She nods her head toward the dancing and raises a brow. But I don't know if I can do it. Her wide smile urges me to go ahead. I think, yeah, I want to do this.

My feet propel me into the middle of the circle. At first I do my typical little ragtime ditty—I shake the hem of my invisible skirt with one hand while propping a pinkie on my lips with the other. Then I pause to the beat of the music and drop my body limbo-low to the ground and snap back up. Everybody roars in surprise.

Pipsqueak Harry jumps in after me and does his leprechaun/Charlie Chaplin thing, and everyone starts to boo him. Until Tawanda and LaShell move in to bump and grind on him like a Harry sandwich. The height difference is hilarious, and he loves every minute of it.

We're in a haze of gray where things no longer fit into the tight, compartmentalized area of black or white.

Across the crowd, through the bonfire blaze, Bren watches me. My smile falters for a second. I try to focus on the dancing, the fun. Anything but those sultry brown eyes that have me pinned.

In that moment, I realize I can't fight it any longer. I can't keep kissing boys and pretending I'm something I'm not. I can't keep lying to myself. This ain't some kind of new-girl girl-crush. This is a crush-crush. And I'm terrified. It's not so much the fall that scares me, but the repercussion of the bottom I will inevitably hit.

Chapter 6

Okay, so I know I said I was ready to plunge into that ocean, but it's not as easy to get your feet wet as you'd think. Especially when said ocean rolls in beside me at our table at lunch on Monday. It feels oh so right to like Bren, and pretending to like boys is no longer an option, but I have my mother's reputation to maintain—not to mention my own.

It's a torturous hell to be Switzerland.

As Bren sits down at our table, her beachy scent taunts me. And what the heck is that spice? It's driving me mad.

She tips her chin in a hello to all the boys. Sarabeth gives a quick wave and cuts a worried look in my direction. Before I can understand what she's concerned with, she's smiling and talking about cheerleading stuff with Misty.

Bren stabs a few green beans with her fork. "That was one sweet party, Andrew."

"Dude, where'd you learn to bust a move like that?" Chuck asks in awe.

"I think she's got a little black blood in her," Andrew says, chuckling.

Bren shakes her head, and her bronze skin shades a little darker on her cheeks. "Naw, man," she says to her food. "It's just...you know, something I do."

"Yeah, I do lots of things too." Chuck bucks like a bronco in his seat.

"I bet you do," Sarabeth says. "Like eat your momma out of house and home." Everyone cracks up.

"Them's fightin' words. Don't be talking 'bout my momma like that." Chuck fakes like he's going to jump Sarabeth. "Yo Momma" jokes whip across the table.

"So, you always in the library on Fridays?" Bren knocks her leg against mine. My pulse ignites.

"Yes. You?" My voice peeps. I clear my throat.

"Yeah. Study hall. I took most of my required courses in Boston. College prep stuff and whatnot. I still need one more English class and another science, but the rest of my classes are fluff. Like drama." She scoops up a bite of potatoes.

"What else are you taking?" What I really want to ask is, *Can you write down your class schedule so I can stalk you easier?* She names off her classes. Of course she has PE. She's the one person in the whole school who actually *wants* to take PE. I tell her what I'm taking—in case she wants to stalk me. She doesn't think it's boring at all that I'm in AP History.

LaShell comes up behind us. "B-ball after school?"

"You know it," Bren says. A fist bump seals the deal.

"You going to bring white boy?" LaShell nods toward Andrew and smiles.

Andrew looks up, not smiling. "I don't play with a bunch of girls."

"Aw, it's a sex thing. I see," says LaShell with a shaky smile.

"No." He tilts his head. "Five days a week till sundown, I'm gonna be out on that field"—he points with his fork toward the football field—"making the Wildcats proud."

43

"A'ight. Football's cool." LaShell reaches to fist-bump Andrew. He stares at his food, acting like he doesn't see her hand reaching across the table. The silence is amplified by the scraping of forks against plates; it's awkwardly loud. My face flushes with shame as I stare at my food like everyone else and wait for her to walk away. When she does, Andrew shakes his chocolate milk and eyes Bren with a long scrutinizing look.

Whatever happened over the weekend did not translate into today. I glance around the lunchroom. The clear dividing line between the blacks and the whites, the haves and the have-nots, still separates the cafeteria. Just when I think this school might be dangerously close to becoming *tolerant*, the sobriety of daylight nips that shit in the bud.

* * *

Midweek I race to the gym and change into my workout clothes. PE does not suck this week. Next week and for the rest of the year, there will probably be suckage and then some, but this week, it's all about volleyball, my favorite sport. As for other things not sucking, Bren sitting with me at lunch all week also did not suck. Or that her science class is down the hall from my AP American Government class, and she walks me there every day.

The challenging part of all this Bren activity is figuring out how to keep my personal space. The slightest nudge from her scatters butter-flies in my stomach. And as much as I like being around her, I'm worried about people noticing how much we're hanging out.

The class bell rings, and everyone starts warming up. I arc my body and nail a perfect serve.

"Nice," a voice compliments me. Her voice. I close my eyes so I can absorb it in my bones.

I pivot on the balls of my feet toward Bren. "Young lady, aren't you supposed to be in English lit?" Walking toward her, I check to see who might be watching. No one is within earshot. Grunts and smacks echo throughout the gym. I step past the edge of the bleachers, hoping for privacy.

"Mr. Wallace gave me a pass to skip so I can talk to Coach Wilson about basketball tryouts." Bren props her hand up on the edge of the bleachers next to my head. I'm thrown off-kilter.

"I—I bet Tawanda and LaShell are happy about that," I say. She smiles at my stuttering.

A whooping holler calls our attention toward the gymnasium. Halfway up the climbing rope, Charlotte Wozniak is scrambling up like a chimpanzee.

I knew Charlotte when I was a little girl. Ms. Veda used to babysit us during the summers. The girl I see before me today does not even remotely resemble the sweet creature I knew back then. Now, she's got business-in-the-front-party-in-the-back hair. Camouflage and plaid are the only types of clothing she owns. Everybody in school knows she has a girlfriend, and I'm not talking girl-who's-a-friend either. No one cares because she's from the trailer park, so it's not like they expect her to act any differently, which is a sad point of view. Jacinda, her girlfriend, used to date a black guy from the neighboring county. Both Charlotte and Jacinda are perfect outcasts for each other. Forever exiled from the social circles.

We're supposed to be working on our volleyball form—which Charlotte stinks at—so she's climbing the rope instead. Strands of hair from her mullet are plastered to her sweaty face, and her homemade middle finger tattoo mocks us from her shoulder. She slaps the metal beam at the top and slides down military style. After she lands on the ground, she tags Bren with her eyes.

My territorial instincts kick in, and I lean in front of Bren to block Charlotte's view. Bad move on my part.

Charlotte's hands hit the wooden floors, and her heels fly up in the air. She walks upside down across the gymnasium. It's a circus side-show long past its prime. Surely Bren is not impressed by such antics.

As the thought slips into my brain, Bren says, "Wow, that's..." Shock and confusion twist her face. "Disturbing. I feel a strong need to call my mom." She widens her eyes at me, smiling.

I release the tension from my shoulders and laugh. "Yeah, seri-ously." I stare over my shoulder at Charlotte, wanting to grunt some ape commands to let her know to back off.

Charlotte stands right side up and spins a volleyball on her finger, probably about to balance it on her nose. Great, not only do I have Chesty Hannigan moving in on Bren, I have to worry about Charlotte now too. But then Charlotte smiles and flashes me a thumbs-up. The way she's nodding her head, it's like she's encouraging me to make a move on Bren. I swear that girl ain't right.

"You should have seen her do-si-do during square dance week. I had nightmares for a month." When I turn back around—Smack! A sting pegs me in the back, and I tumble forward into Bren's arms. It's an awkward tangle of limbs, but I retreat fairly quickly.

"Wozniak, get control of that ball," Mrs. Eastman barks. She is the epitome of a PE teacher: stocky figure, spiked hair, and a man's voice. Charlotte smiles huge, like she meant to push us together. "Dawson, are you going to flirt with my pupils all day or do you have somewhere to be?"

Bren beams. I want to crawl in a hole and die. "Gotta go," Bren says. And I'm left with a circus ape, a drill sergeant for a teacher, and twenty sets of eyes trying to figure out who's flirting with whom. So much for my rocking week.

Chapter 7

In the back corner of the library, Van and I scrunch down behind the shelves and sit on the floor—it's the corner where I catch stray lovers kissing at least once a month. We've come back here for a super-secret meeting. Planning the float for the homecoming parade is some serious business here in Sunshine. As senior class president and one freaking amazing artist, Van's in charge of the homecoming float—I'm just here to reaffirm his ego. Mr. Peterson gave him permission to skip computer class because he actually believed Van when he told Mr. Peterson that his dog had eaten his homework—which, for computer class, is a USB drive—one that Van's parents are now supposedly rushing their dog into emergency surgery to have removed.

"I can't believe he bought that." I widen my eyes.

"I know. It got me out of not doing my homework *and* going to class." Van pulls out a fat file folder. "I'm probably going to hell."

"Most definitely." I pull out my fraying notebook, crammed full of notes. "Did he really say that he could recover the data?" I snicker.

"Yeah. But I told him not to get his hopes up. Stomach acid can be seriously destructive." We both bust up laughing.

"Shhh." I hush him as I hear Mrs. Bellefleur a few rows over.

"Come on, you're her pet." He sits cross-legged. The toes of his black and white zebra striped Converse peek out from under his knees. "I have a get-out-of-jail-free card by association."

"Stop saying that. You never know what mood Mrs. Bellefleur will be in. If she's been reading Nicholas Sparks again, our super-secret meeting will be off."

"What super-secret meeting?" Bren peers over the top of the short bookcase I'm leaning back against. Shocked, I look up at her, and she smiles down at me. My insides go every which way.

"Did you invite *her*?" Van asks loud enough for Bren to hear, but he's only kidding. I kick him anyway. Bren chuckles as she comes around to join us. The space barely fits two of us, so we have to bunch together tight to make room for her, which means there is touching, glorious and nerve-racking all at the same time.

Bren adjusts her long legs three or four times before she can get comfortable. "So what's the big secret?"

"Nothing," Van and I say together. Tight lipped are we.

"Come on, guys, tell me."

"Uh-uh."

"No way." We both cross our arms and make our best tough cop faces. Van needs to work on his, but I rock it.

"Why not?" she asks.

"Because," Van says.

"Because," I parrot. But I'm not sure why we can't tell her. Not that we aren't going to tell her, but still. "Why can't we tell her?"

"Becauuuuuse—" Van pauses and slips a glance to Bren, as if he's trying to come up with a good reason. "Because she *says* she's from Boston, but I've never heard her say 'cah.'"

"Good point."

"But I told you —"

I lean into Van, cutting Bren off. "You never know, Van, she could be a rival Tomahawk or Boll Weevil." He nods at my clever assumption.

"Boll Weevil?" she asks.

We both look at Bren. "Do not underestimate the Boll Weevil," Van starts.

"They can destroy an entire cotton field in less than a week. Serious predator here in farm country."

Bren laughs. "Yeah, if you're a Hanes T-shirt." Even though what she says is giggle-worthy, Van and I look at her with blank, serious faces.

I roll my eyes back to Van. "I don't think we can trust her, even if she takes the Oath."

"The Oath," Van says ominously, slowly nodding his head in agreement.

Adamant protests fly out of Bren. She promises to abide by the Oath. Van and I have our own little conversation, ignoring her. We pretend not to trust her and muse about her being a spy for one of the underclassmen. We keep her in the dark for a little longer, then Van says, "Fine. If you agree to say the Oath, we will tell you."

Bren nods her head, all eager.

"I, state your name." I hold up my right hand and Bren and Van do too. "Put your hand down, dork. Only she has to swear." Van drops his hand.

"I, Bren Dawson."

"Promise to respect and never belittle, make fun of, or disindumb-edify the secret."

"Is that even a word?"

I bite my bottom lip to try and keep a straight face. "If it's in the Oath, it's a word."

"Don't question the Oath." Van backs me up. Bren repeats the vow. Van jumps in. "No matter what phallic symbols may result from our work."

I crack and start giggling something fierce. Some of the "masterpieces" the students make do look suggestive. "What he said," Bren says.

I add, "And I promise to abide by this oath and keep secret the events discussed at the super-secret library meeting forever henceforth."

"Amen," says Van.

"Amen." Bren drops her oath hand. "What's the big secret?" she asks.

It's painfully hard to focus on what Van is saying with Bren so close to me. Van tells her about our homecoming football game. It's the biggest Friday the Wildcats have all year, with a big game against our rival, the Cairo High Syrupmakers, a crowned queen, and a huge parade beforehand. The big super-secret is the design of our float for the parade. Each class has to create a float, according to the theme. The whole town, including the elementary school and middle school, comes to watch the parade. Today the student council announced the theme: Tennessee Treasures. The winning class gets the Friday before Thanksgiving break off.

"Cool," Bren says. "Who judges?"

"Well, that's the tricky part," I say. "About half the votes comes from the teachers here. Principal Cain picks five teachers, but he doesn't tell the students who he has picked until it's over, so we can't sway their vote or bribe them."

"But the other half comes from the elementary school, kindergarten through fifth. Each grade level gets one vote. That's six more votes," Van finishes.

"Eleven votes in all. We're talking very close here. And the way to win the kids' votes," I say, pausing dramatically, "is by throwing the most candy during the parade."

"Wow," Bren says. "Scary how you guys have this calculated down to a science. And you're bribing kids with candy. That's just awful."

"It's war, Bren honey." Van pats her arm. "It's not always pretty."

"Okay then, how does one go about building a float?"

"Well, let me show you." Van opens his file folder with fifteen years of float pictures and designs from previous winners. We're explaining to Bren the technical aspects of the structure, what the teachers prefer in design, and the importance of the materials, when something tickles my knee. Bren's pinky stills when I dart my eyes in her direction. Van just keeps on talking, unaware.

Maybe it was by accident—like her pinky just twitched—and I wanted it to be something more? Then Bren reaches for my knee, and I jump, shoving the file folder up. The contents dump out into Van's lap.

"Hey, watch it, McCoy." Van picks up the jumbled mess. Bren holds a single photo in her hand, and I realize she was just reaching for the picture Van was handing her.

I safely tuck my knees into my chest and tell my brain to get a handle on all this wishful, fantasy touching nonsense.

"Anyway," Van gives me a what's-your-problem glare and continues on with his ideas.

My fetal-tight body doesn't help. The moment I start to relax, Bren rearranges her legs. The toe of her shoe taps mine, and I flinch at the contact. Float photos and schematics go flying once more.

"Jesus, Kaycee." Van slams down the folder. "You're twitchy as a squirrel. What's wrong with you? You got ants in your pants?" He jams the stuff back in the folder.

"Sorry. Leg cramp." I rub my calf and *do not* look at Bren, but in my periphery I can see her big fat grin.

"Hey," a harsh whisper comes from overhead. Above me, Sarabeth stares down at us. "Isn't the float committee supposed to be meeting in the choir room?" Yes, the choir room. Space, glorious space. I jump to my feet.

"Some super-secret meeting this is," Bren says with a smile and stands.

My eyes stay down, and I shimmy out of the tight corner. I catch up with Sarabeth just as the final bell rings.

From behind I hear Van ask Bren, "You coming?"

"Nope. Shooting hoops with the team. Later." Ways are parted.

I need a Valium, or rather something non-pharmaceutical to calm my jittery nerves. Stupid Kaycee. How could I have let my feelings off the leash so easily? I have no idea how I'm supposed to rein them back in.

After our official homecoming parade meeting, I wait against Sarabeth's black Jetta. It's her turn to drive for carpool. Directly behind me on the driver's side door, she and Andrew share a very public display of affection. A tiny piece of bitterness flakes off me, jealous I can't have public moments like that with Bren. Not if I ever want to show my face in Sunshine again. Or at home for that matter.

The metal door to the gym crashes open, and a sweaty Bren emerges with a basketball wedged under her arm. She holds the door open with her other arm, and Chesty-freaking-Hannigan walks under it, bobbing her head all coy. Chelsea walks Bren to her car, parked two rows over from Sarabeth's. Ridiculous cooing and giggling make me want to gag. Chesty leans forward in Bren's line of sight. The valley between the mountains Hu and Mongous is exposed.

What a display. How sickening. I already handed her Dave, what else does she want?

Bren looks up at me. The soured look on my face gives away my disgust, and I cover it with a wobbly smile. Bren bends over and whispers something in Chelsea's ear that makes her slap Bren's arm flirtatiously.

After another minute of "check out my boobs" from Chesty, Bren jumps in her car, which forces Chelsea to say good-bye.

As Chelsea walks away, she sees me brooding. My arms tighten around my book, and I give that skank the hairy eyeball like nobody's business. She does a little whatcha-gonna-do-about-it shrug.

"You okay, Kaycee?" Sarabeth asks as she opens her car door. Andrew's halfway to his truck.

I straighten. "Yeah, I was just…thinking about how much work I need to do on this stupid English lit paper I have."

Sarabeth's eyes glance over to Bren's car and back to me. "Football game isn't until later tonight. We could squeeze in a quick ride. How about we take the horses down to Nance Creek? Get out in the country for a bit. The fresh air will help you clear your head." Sarabeth may not always know my secret thoughts, but she knows when my heart is heavy. And she knows just the trick to fix it.

"Yeah," I agree, "Let's go." I put on my happy-go-lucky smile and hop in the car.

Inside, I seem to have lost my happy and my go-lucky.

* * *

The soft clip-clop of hooves echoes in the valley of the creek. This late in the year, the summer has dried up most of the water. Sarabeth rides her painted pony, a gift from her parents. My horse is an old gelding named Rambo. He would have been off to the glue factory years ago if such a thing still existed.

"Is everything okay with you?" Sarabeth glances my way.

"Of course. Why wouldn't it be?" I keep my eyes focused on the rocky creek bed in front of us.

"Well, it's just…lately you've been acting different." She keeps slipping small glances my way, making me as nervous as a cat in a room full of rocking chairs.

"Different? Different like how?" I'm trying my best to sound surprised by her comment. All the while, my raging heartbeat clogs my throat.

"I don't know. You seem jumpy lately. Distracted even."

A shaky laugh escapes my lips. "Oh, you know me, I've always been antsy."

"I guess. But you'd tell me if something was bothering you, right?" Without looking, I can feel her staring at me. It's like she's waiting for me to tell her something.

I push down the fear rising in me. "Yeah. It's cool. I'm fine."

"I worry about you. And I just don't want you to lose focus and get any silly ideas or anything."

I put on my best happy smile. "Oh please. Don't worry about me. I leave all the silliness to Chuck the Buck. I'm fine. Swear. Nothing different here. Same ole me I've always been." It's the truth. I've been who I am since the day I was born. I'm just not sure how much of who I am she's aware of, but I suspect it's more than I give her credit for.

She pats the thick muscular neck of her horse. "Yeah. I know."

Does she know? She's not saying anything directly, but I think she has a good idea of why I'm acting so "distracted." I don't know how she'd handle it if I told her the truth about me. A part of me wants to trust her. Talk to her. But how am I even supposed to talk openly to her when I'm just starting to be honest with myself?

I have to find some way to work this out. Find someone I can talk to, someone I can trust. Someone who gets it. Because this freaking back-and-forth pull of denial is killing me. If I don't figure this out soon, my Bren opportunities are going to be gobbled up by Chelsea Hannigan. I am not going to hand Bren over so easily.

Chapter 8

As you drive down Main Street, it's hard not to notice the two-story painted brick wall on the backside of Hauser's Pawn Shop. A giant Sunshine High Wildcat rips through the wall like it's shredded paper. Painted below is the high school's current football schedule and scores. We creamed the Vikings last week. The Wildcat's colors have faded over the years, but the image still screams *Friday Night Lights*. I park my car at the base of the wall and walk up to Hot Flix, Van's family-owned video store. I plan on spending my Friday night with him instead of going to the football game with the rest of the town—and, probably, Bren with Chelsea. Ugh.

Hot Flix smells like fresh popcorn from the vintage style popper in the front window. The theater carpet is bright blue with colorful confetti sprinkled all over it. Behind the counter, a giant flat screen hangs, playing mostly—if not always—Johnny Depp. It's probably the only video store still open within a hundred-mile radius. Those DVD vending machines just haven't taken over Sunshine like people expected. I think folks around here still like the old-fashioned way of doing things, preferring human contact to a hunk of metal and plastic.

In the back are two doorways curtained in black. Curtain number one leads to the office and bathrooms. Curtain number two hides the porn closet. It's the shame of Sunshine. You have to be eighteen to enter the closet, and a number-coded system keeps video covers from ever seeing the light of day. It also happens to be—at ten bucks a rental—Hot Flix's bread and butter.

So much for shame.

"Hello, sweet pea," Van's mom says to me as she emerges from curtain number one.

"Hello, Mrs. Betty."

Van's mother has the face of Mrs. Claus. Thin silver spectacles perch on top of her nose. Gray and blond blend together in Mrs. Betty's beauty-shop styled hair. I have never seen her in anything but a dress, vintage style with a slim waist and buttons down the front. Mrs. Betty gives the biggest hugs, as if you're about to go off to war and she'll probably never see you again.

After she releases me, I flop down on the plush sofa. Worn stretched-out fabric covers the most comfy couch I've ever lain on. Van's mother moved it in here so his lazy friends could hang out with him at work. I suggested Mother put one in at Merle Norman—the suggestion went over like a lead balloon.

"You kids going to watch Captain Jack tonight?" she asks all giddy.

Lord, I hope not. "Not sure what the big guy has planned for us." I cut Van a look. He sees me, but he's helping a customer. "You and Mr. Lovelace got a hot date?" I ask, forcing myself to be social, though all I really want to do is mope.

She giggles. "Oh no. He wouldn't know 'hot' if he touched an oven. I'm going over to Craft World to buy a whole bunch of paints. After seeing your pedicured toenails the other day, I got an inspiration for a *big* project." She winks.

The last time Mrs. Betty got an idea for a big craft project, she knitted thirty-two dog sweaters for the local pound. Homeless pups never looked so posh in their vibrantly colored chenille sweaters.

"Be good, kids. See you later, hon." She waves bye to Van.

"Well, Mr. Perkipsky," says Van, "if you liked *Little Shop of Horrors*, you'll love *High School Musical*." *What?* I do my best not to snicker.

Van is the guru of movies. You can tell him a few movies you love, and he can name off ten more that you'll like equally as much. He's got a ninety-nine percent accuracy rate—pretty impressive. The old man thanks him for the rental and leaves.

I bury my face in the crook of my elbow. "*High School Musical*, really?"

"Hey, the old man has a musical fetish. He doesn't care what they're about." I hear Van pecking away on the computer. "Are you going to the football game tonight?"

I shake my head.

"You didn't go last week either."

"Neither did you," I growl, though he actually has a social life. I was avoiding certain people.

"Huh." He works quietly while I wallow in my misery. "What do you think about our float idea? Picking several iconic treasures of Tennessee to feature on our float instead of one will be pretty epic. I just hope we can pull it off."

"Yeah."

"Did you hear that the freshmen are building a giant-sized ball of cotton? It's supposed to be something grand like what you'd see in the Rose Bowl Parade. Sounds cool."

"Uh-huh."

"Sophomores have some big secret. The juniors are doing a giant songbook with sheets of music for the song 'I Wish I Was in Dixie.'" He sings the last part. "Bo-ring."

I grunt.

More pecking. "You're going to work on the float next weekend, right? Bren said she'd be there."

The sound of my sigh is a cross between a dying moose and a deflating balloon.

"What's wrong with you? You sound pathetic."

A week of watching Chelsea mauling Bren will do that to a girl. At first Bren seemed to encourage her advances, but by Wednesday, Bren seemed...annoyed? Or maybe that was wishful thinking on my part. In sixth period today, Bren tried to talk to me, but Dewey Decimal won out.

"Do you think Chelsea Hannigan is a lesbian?" I vomit the question.

"Wow. Okay. We're going there today. Um, I'd guess she's bisexual, and please, God, don't tell me you're in love with her."

I peek out from under my arm. "Chesty? Please, Van, give me more credit than that. Not her."

"Phew," he blows out a breath. "Oh..."

"'Oh,' what?" I scowl at him.

"I didn't say anything."

"Yes you did. You said 'oh.'" I sit up and narrow my eyes at him. "What does 'oh' mean?"

"You know what it means."

And I do. I can't pretend I don't because he's right. This isn't about Chelsea. It's about Bren. The thing with Van and me is, we have an unwritten don't ask, don't talk about *it* policy. He's comfortable with his *it*. His parents know about *it*, but no one talks about *it*...or me being *it*, for that matter.

Van's parents have always been a touch on the squirrelly side, especially Mrs. Betty, so it's like everyone expects him to be different.

Also, he's never hidden his flair for fashion or downplayed his love for theater or art. He's never had to hide who he was because everyone just knows. It's like as long as he doesn't dip into Sunshine's pool, no one cares where he swims.

Me, on the other hand, an ordinary girl with good conservative upbringing—why, if I came out, it might threaten their logic that gays aren't well-bred people. Pair me up with another well-bred person, and we might get the crazy idea to marry like regular folk now that the Supreme Court has made it so easy. Oh no, we wouldn't want to disrupt their conformed lives.

Another customer comes in and halts our conversation. I lay back on the couch. For me, the first time I realized *it* was the day Charlotte Wozniak kissed me. Now, the thought of that happening brings bile to my throat. At the time, we were nine going on ten. I blame an inattentive Ms. Veda and an overdose of *Days of Our Lives*.

Ms. Veda took care of Charlotte and me over the summer. After *Dora the Explorer* went off, the five hours of soap operas began. Cat fights, scandals, and make-out scenes got the better of us. Now, I'm not blaming TV for being *it*. I'm just saying it was the first time I suspected…*it*.

Under a tented sheet draped over the couch, Charlotte laid one on me. Sparks flew. It was only our lips smashed together, and our heads twisting side to side, but it was still a kiss. When we came up for air, the first words out of my mouth were, "Let's do it again." We didn't get more than three or four kisses in before the sheet was ripped off of us—Ms. Veda's expression of horror scarred me for life.

"Are we going to talk about this, or are you going to do your usual *not* talking about it?" Van asks once the store is empty again.

I exhale a huge breath, like the fizz of a soda bottle that's been shaken up. "How do you deal…with being, you know…"

Van just sits there. He chews on his bottom lip as if he's trying to figure out how to tell me the circus has denied my application for employment. "Do you remember that episode on *SpongeBob SquarePants* when SpongeBob gets really rancid breath from eating a ketchup-onion-and-peanut-plant sundae, and everybody in town avoids him, so Patrick thinks it's because he's ugly and teaches SpongeBob how to be proud of his ugliness?" Van asks in one long breath.

I stare blankly. "I...don't watch *SpongeBob*."

"Gawd, Kaycee." Van hangs his head down and flops against the counter, exasperated.

I jump to my feet and flail my hands wildly. "I don't know what you're saying. You think I'm ugly?"

Van lifts his head. "SpongeBob says, 'I'm ugly, and I'm proud.'"

"What?"

Van slaps the counter and straightens his spine. "You want to talk about *it*?" he says through gritted teeth, making phantom quotes in the air. "You're going to have to say the word, Kaycee. Say...'lesbian.'"

"I did." But I know he's not talking about my Chelsea question.

"How do you expect anyone to accept you if you can't accept yourself? I know what you are. You know what you are. Not saying it doesn't keep you from being one. So just admit what you are. Say, 'I'm a lesbian.'"

If looks could kill, I would turn Van into a bloody pulp, pooling on the floor. We have an unwritten rule for Christ's sake! How dare he break the rule? I don't ask him about the guys he sees when he disappears over to Midland City or Lawrence on a random Saturday night.

Survival instincts tell me to walk out that door and leave. Just go.

But it's like imaginary glue has adhered my feet to the floor. I crash back down on the couch. "You don't talk about your 'friends' in Lawrence." I cross my arms over my chest and glare out the front window.

"You don't ask." He simply shrugs, but his point stabs.

Minutes of long, anguished silence pass. More customers come and go. Van checks a few DVDs into the computer, dusts the shelves, and opens up the mail. Not once does he look at me or acknowledge that I'm still sitting here.

"Lesbian," I mumble.

"Huh? What was that?" Van cups his ear and strains his neck.

"Lesbian." It's not much louder, but I know he hears me.

"Say, 'I'm ugly, and I'm proud.'"

I can't help but laugh. "I'm ugly, and I'm proud." I shake my head at him.

"Say, 'I'm gay, and I'm proud.'" His eyes plead.

It's just five words. They won't kill me. But they will make things different. Heck, I'm already different. I can't make these feelings stop. Lord knows I let many a boy put his tongue in my mouth to make these feelings stop. I don't want another boy's tongue in my mouth for the rest of my life. Ew.

I bury my face in my hands. "It's just easier to keep doing what I'm doing."

Van sighs and comes over to sit beside me. "But wouldn't you rather do what makes *you* happy and not everybody else?" Van rubs my back.

"I don't want people to hate me."

"People are going to hate you, gay or not. There's no stopping it. Trust me, I know. But it also opens the door for people to love you. People like Bren."

My heart sticks in my throat. This constant battle to keep myself in check gets harder and harder. Always trying to rein in my urges—and puberty sure as hell isn't helping with that. Tears well up in my eyes. I take in a breath and hold it.

I look up at Van with my red-rimmed eyes. He wipes the moisture off my cheeks. "I'm gay, and I'm proud." I sniff.

Van sweeps me into his arms. He's telling me things like how proud he is of me and wasn't that easy and we'll figure this out. And I wonder if my mother will say these things to me one day. Will she hug her arms around me tight like Van is doing now?

I clear the snot from under my nose with my sleeve.

"That's disgusting." Van hops up. "Let me get you a tissue."

I chuckle and accept his tissue. "I don't know what to do."

"Just be you."

"But what about my mother?" I dab a stray tear.

"Baby steps. We're not there yet. Let's get you comfortable with the idea first, then we'll figure out our next move."

"How'd you tell your parents?"

He shrugs apologetically. "I didn't ever really have to. They just kind of...always knew."

"And they're okay with it?"

"Mom couldn't care less either way. Dad, on the other hand, he's still processing it. I think he's holding out, hoping I'll grow out of this like I did my unicorn collecting days."

"I can't believe you used to collect unicorns. That's, like, so...gay." I exaggerate rolling my eyes.

"I know." He yanks me up off the couch. "Now that that's over with," he wipes my cheeks one last time, "let's figure out how we can get Chesty Hannigan's paws off Bren."

"Oh my God, you see it too. It's ridiculous how she just *throws* herself on Bren." I hurl myself onto Van and make a gagging sound.

"Sickening." Van detaches me from his chest with two fingers. "Let's start with letting Bren know you like her without shouting it to the world. And when you're ready to be more vocal, I'll teach you how to sing."

Van nestles down on the couch with me and schools me in the art of flirting on the sly. It sounds like a plan I can live with. When I start to freak out about what could happen if somebody sees me, or what might happen if people at school find out, or how I'm going to ever tell my mother, Van reminds me that we'll deal with today, today. Tomorrow we will deal with when it gets here. One day at a time.

"Like alcoholism?" I ask.

Van pats me on the head. "No, honey. Gay is not a disease, despite what some bigots around here might think. All I want you to focus on is letting Bren see the most beautiful side of you. Everything else will just follow."

The thought of opening that door for her makes the pit of my stomach all warm and fuzzy. "I don't know if I can do this by myself. Will you go with me?"

"Let me get this straight—you want me to be the third wheel on your first date with Bren?"

I throw my arm over my face again. "When you put it like that... yes. Just hang with us. Let me get past this...whatever," I beg. Van sighs. "Please?"

His second sigh is more resigned.

"If you do this, I promise to watch an entire afternoon of Johnny Depp movies without complaining."

He points his finger at me. "That means no gagging when I comment on how talented he is, and no rolling of the eyes when I replay a scene." I nod vigorously, and he says, "Okay."

"Yes, yes, yes." I sit up, clapping. "Oh, wait. We can't do it tomorrow night. Sarabeth asked me to sleep over and finalize float plans."

"It's fine. I have a date anyway." A sly grin spreads across his face.

"Ooh, what's his name?" It's a simple question—one I should have asked long ago but never did. The freedom to talk openly now seems to deepen our friendship to a whole new level.

"Arthur."

"Arthur?" If my scrunched up face didn't speak for itself, my skeptical tone did the trick.

A stray couch pillow whacks me in the head. "Oh, because 'Bren' is such a hot name."

"Oh, but it is. It just rolls off the tongue and makes you want to visit Costa Rica." My phone beeps, pulling me back from the tropics. "It's Mother. She wants to know if Hot Flix has 'turned into an Econo Lodge.'"

"Tell her that if Hot Flix decides to change businesses, we would be a five-star resort, not some cheap-ass motel."

"Yeah, let me get right on that." I text her back, telling her I'm stopping by Sonic before I head home. "Because that'll make her love you more."

"Well, she can't love me any less."

"True. But I better go. So, Sunday works for you? Or do you have another hot date?"

Van walks me to the door. "Sunday...you, me, and Long and Tall."

I smile. Bren does have some great legs. I just hope I can keep my nerves in check long enough not to look like an ass.

Chapter 9

"I don't get why you're always hanging out with that boy," is the first thing out of my mother's mouth when I get home. I don't go for the bait. "Why didn't you do something with Sarabeth tonight?"

I let out a big sigh. I put my keys on the entry table by the giant Holy Bible. It's always laid open to Psalms. "Friday night. Football season. She cheers." I've explained this to my mother a thousand times the last few years.

"You could have gone to the game."

"I don't want to be the lone dork, sitting all by myself in the stands." I toss my Sonic sack on the oak table and fix myself some iced tea.

"What about Misty or Melissa? Can't you sit with them? They seem like good girls."

If she had any idea how many boys they were macking on at the party, she wouldn't be saying that. But their family owns the local dry cleaners, so they're obviously "good girls."

I really don't want to have this conversation again. I sit and smooth the nonexistent wrinkles on our checkerboard tablecloth. "Mother, I don't know why you have such a problem with Van," I say, but I really do know. But if she's not willing to call a spade a spade, then I'm going to make her dance around it. "He's a good kid. His parents are nice as can be. His mother runs the Ladies Ministry group over at their church." I bite into my cheeseburger.

"I didn't say I had a problem with Van. I'm just saying if you keep hanging out with him, you might start acting—"

My deer-in-the-headlights expression cuts her off. Just how is she going to finish this? I know she knows about me and Charlotte's soap opera reenactments. Ms. Veda's good Christian self had to tell her. And I got a serious talking-to from it, all about what the Bible had to say on the matter, but I always assumed Mother wrote it off as experimenting kids being silly. Now I'm not so sure.

"—Tomboyish," she finishes. It's a political answer, dodging.

I don't comment because she and I both know that I do not act like a tomboy. Maybe my favorite color isn't pink and I can't stand shopping and high heels, but I love other girly stuff. Like collecting butterflies and watching the babies at the church nursery.

Mother busies herself cleaning the kitchen while I finish my burger and fries in silence. "Oh," Mother says as an afterthought, "some girl named"—she squints to read the paper—"Bren called. Why didn't she call your cell?"

My entire being freezes. Why is Bren calling me? Is she home from the football game already? While I'm trying to control the panic/freak-out building inside my body, I gulp, gulp, gulp down the rest of my tea. Mother waits for me to finish. Calmly I put the glass in our dishwasher, thankful we are the only McCoys in Sunshine's tiny phone book. "She's new. The Dawsons' daughter. She doesn't have my cell number," I say, snapping the dishwasher shut.

Casually, I grab the slip of paper from Mother's hand with Bren's number on it.

"Yes, yes, yes. The Dawsons. That's right, her mother came into the store the other day—she looks a little Hispanic or something but really put together. I hear her husband is right handsome. Larry Beaudroux is paying him a lot of money to replace Rally Tools. If he can keep the factory jobs here, all of us shop owners won't go out of business." Mom turns to me just before I close my bedroom door, nodding her head. "You should call this Bren girl." As if the brilliant idea just came to her. "See if she wants to do something."

"I think I will," I say. She glows at the idea. "Maybe we can do something after church on Sunday." This tickles her pink. I close my bedroom door and rest my entire body up against it, letting the message sink in.

"Yes!" I leap from my door to my bed. The brass headboard claps against the wall. I refrain from dancing around the room, singing, "Bren Dawson called me."

It's not easy.

"What am I gonna say?" I whisper to myself. Ten different scenarios of how the conversation could go fly in my head at once. My fingertips drum over my lips. She could just be calling about an assignment. But why call *me* when I'm not in any of her classes? "You're not asking her on a date, Kaycee. You're just asking her to hang with you and your good ole buddy Van, and if she wants to make out, that's okay too." I squeal and do a manic wiggle-dance in my bed.

I arch my back and dig my hand into my pocket for my cell phone. My finger pauses on the first number. What if my mother's right? What if after all these years of hanging with Van, I act like a tomboy? I clasp the phone to my chest. Does Bren like girly girls? Because I'm most definitely not Chelsea Hannigan. But I'm not Charlotte Wozniak either.

Headlights from the cul-de-sac behind our house light up my room with a yellow glow. The butterfly collection on the left wall screams girl, unless it also screams bug-collecting boy. For the record, I have never murdered a butterfly. I've only picked them up off the ground or out of a car's front grill, which does not sound feminine in the slightest. Photos and images of accidental heart shapes cover my bulletin board. Girl. Just below that on my dresser sits a vintage ammunitions box filled with my love of American history, including mini-balls for muskets, Civil War buttons, and miscellaneous military trinkets my grandpa found with his metal detector. Boy. Plum purple duvet. Girl. Blue walls. Boy. Seashells from Florida. Girl. Pocketknife that I don't carry on my person but still own. Boy. My eyes roam around the room labeling every item girl or boy, and the end result is fifty-fifty. Gah. How frustrating.

I'm sure Sarabeth has some boy crap in her room. There's pink and lace and teen male posters, and oh, oh, oh! There's a Muscle Machines auto magazine on her nightstand, which is probably Andrew's, but since I don't know for sure, it's Sarabeth's—because yeah, she has a secret muscle car fetish I don't know about.

I'm stalling.

Breathe.

Dial.

It's ringing.

"Hello?" Bren's voice is sleepy and husky. So cute. Wait, did I call too late? My digital clock reads past eleven.

Breathe.

"Hello?"

"Hey, Bren. It's me, Kaycee. You know…Kay-c-double e." I'm going for the remember-you-said-I-was-cute angle.

"Oh, hey," her voice perks. *Score.*

"Did I call too late? I can call you later." Though I've spent all my courage on this one phone call, so it may be a while.

I hear shuffling on the other end. "No. No. I just crashed early. Shot some hoops after school, then went for a run before the football game."

Gah, I knew I should have gone. "The game, cool. Who'd you go with?" Jealous, much? "And how'd they do?" I hurriedly add. I already know they won. Chuck the Buck honked and screamed their victory in the Sonic drive-in tonight.

"They massacred them, forty-two to six. I felt sad for the Dixie Opossums. You should have heard the crowd. There were a few rabid fans who kept screaming things about roadkill."

"You should hear them when they lose. It's brutal," I add. She laughs. I make a mental note that she didn't say who she went with. "My mom said you called tonight?" *Please don't be about school, and for God's sake, don't ask me what Chelsea's number is because it's 555-never-gonna-tell-you.*

"I, um," she starts. Did she just sigh? "Was just calling to see if you wanted to do something, sometime."

Yes! I hammer my fist in the air. *Can you feel that, Chesty?* That seals it for me. She's not interested in going out with Chelsea, not if she's calling me. Maybe Chelsea was annoying Bren this week. The library. I thunk my hand against head. Maybe Bren was trying to ask me out in the library this afternoon, but I was so busy pouting I blew her off. *Stupid, Kaycee.*

Stop, stay in the moment, and reel in the crazy. Bren only asked to "do something." I can "do something" with my mother, but that doesn't mean it's a date.

"Is that a no?" Bren mistakes my silence.

"No. Yes. I mean, that'd be cool. I'd like that. Actually, Van and I are hanging out at the video store Sunday afternoon and watching a Johnny Depp marathon until his mom gets done with the big church revival uptown. If you want to join us..."

"Oh…yeah, sure."

Does she sound disappointed? "I'm sure he'll be busy with customers and whatnot." And what is that supposed to tell her? "We might even take Van's new twenty-two out and shoot some cans." I slap my hand over my face. Where did that come from? Well, gosh darn, Kaycee, why don't you show her how country you can really be? Next thing you know, you'll be taking her frog gigging or crawdad fishing or snipe hunting. *This is how us rednecks do it, Bren.* I search the buttons on my phone. Is there a rewind on this thing? A do-over button? Something?

"What was that?" I put the phone back up to my ear.

"I said, the only time I ever shot a gun was skeet shooting on a cruise once. I'm game for anything."

My shoulders relax a bit. No more hillbilly comments, Kaycee. "Great. How about we meet up at Hot Flix just after lunch? You know, it's the store down from the diner where Mr. Bobby drinks his coffee every day."

"Yeah, yeah," she says. "Good."

Guess that's all there is to say, but I don't want to let her go.

"It was nice talking to you—"

"What'd you do tonight—"

We talk over each other and then laugh.

"If you have to go…" Bren says.

"No. Not at all." I revel in the fact that she doesn't want to get off the phone either. "I, um, hung out with Van up at the store. We just talked shop." And other stuff.

She asks a little about Van. I tell her I've known him since I was four. She comments on his flair for footwear. I share my hearts in nature theory and tell her about how Sarabeth loves the outdoors as much as I do; this seems to always shock people about Sarabeth.

I hint that Sarabeth might not be fully clued in on my dating preferences—though I don't think she's clueless either. When Bren doesn't really respond, I ask about her close friends. Most of them she talks with via email or old fashioned snail mail as pen pals, depending on the country, but she's never settled long enough to have a Van or a Sarabeth. We talk about everything under the sun—basketball, volleyball—and laugh at Charlotte Wozniak's primate instincts. I say nothing about soap operas. I find out Bren's terrified of spiders—*wussy*. I tell her about the squirrel phobia I've had from the time a baby squirrel living in our attic found its way into our house and attacked me twice in one night.

"Are you joking?" Bren's laugh is breathy and deep.

I recount the whole story. I can tell by the strain in her voice she's tearing up with laughter. "It was running across the walls!"

"No." She gasps in disbelief.

"Yes. The walls were covered in that grass-cloth wallpaper. You know, that textured stuff." My cheeks are sore from grinning.

"How did you get it out?"

"I whacked it with a broom, of course."

"You killed a baby squirrel? I'm horrified."

"That was no innocent creature, Bren. Don't let their chubby cheeks or fluffy tail fool you. They are the spawn of Satan." We're both chuckling now. "I'm serious. I still sleep with my closet light on." She laughs harder.

I'm amazed at how easy it is to talk to her. Van hates chatting on the phone. Usually Sarabeth and I talk about who said this or that and what we're doing over the weekend. Not this "tell me your worst nightmare," or "what's your favorite holiday and you can't say Christmas," kind of talk.

"Earth Day," says Bren.

"Ugh. You're such a humanitarian. I was going to say Halloween because of the candy, but I hated dressing up when I was little. I'm going to go with the Fourth of July. I'm a sucker for patriotism and American history. And I don't care how old I get, fireworks feel magical, you know?"

"Yeah, they do," Bren says through a yawn.

It's after two. I don't want to get off the phone, but it's hard to keep my eyes open. "I'll see you Sunday." I yawn back at her.

"See you Sunday." She says it like she's just taken a bite of warm chocolate cake and the flavors are melting in her mouth.

There's a pause before we hang up, where we can hear each other breathing, then I tap the hang-up icon.

Excitement builds in me like a spring. "Yes! I've got a date with Bre-en. I've got a date with Bre-en," I whisper. The light on my phone flashes. Panic jolts me upright, and I double-check to make sure I hung up. It's a photo text from Bren—a picture of a Chinese lantern. In the background on the wall, the corner distorts the lantern's shadow into the shape of a heart. I exhale. The phone buzzes in my hand.

This was on my wall after we hung up. Thought of u.

I stare at it a moment longer, then text her back a <3 and post her picture on Instagram. I put my phone on my nightstand, get up, turn the closet light on, and crack the door.

Back under the covers, a tiny light inside of me refuses to die. It grows a little brighter.

Chapter 10

"Does my hair look all right?" I ask Van, who's down under the counter gathering the movies from the drop box. "I tried to make it look effortless, wavy at the ends like I just came from the beach. It's the best I could do with the rain."

"How long did it take you to do that?" He stands with an armful of DVDs.

I yawn huge. "Like two hours."

His mouth makes an O when he sees me. "Um, she's not going to be looking at your hair with a shirt like that."

I tug at my T-shirt. "Too green?"

"Too tight."

"I just washed it. Should I go home and change?" I'm scrunching and pulling at the front. Van swats my hand.

"Leave it alone or you'll make it all wrinkled. Nobody likes wrinkled boobies." He stretches the shirt out all over with even pulls to keep it from clinging so much. "Better." He gives me a big ole shit-eating grin.

"You want me to pose for a picture or what?" I shove him out of my face, blushing. Another yawn escapes.

"Why are you so tired?"

"Friday night, I stayed up till two talking to Bren." I gloat and beam. Of course it was forever before I fell asleep. "Last night, Sarabeth had me up just as late, finalizing plans and organizing the supplies for the float." I wanted so bad to tell her I had a date with Bren, but I couldn't be certain how she'd react.

Van scrutinizes me. "That explains the eye luggage."

"Great. Hopefully Bren will be so focused on my tight tee, she won't notice my carry-on."

"Don't worry, you're still an adorable tart. What are we going to do?" he asks as we plop down on the couch.

"I told her we'd be watching a Johnny D marathon."

Van gives me the stink eye.

"I shouldn't have to suffer this alone." I pick fuzz off the pillow. "Besides, it's raining and more than half the town is at the tent revival in the Walmart parking lot."

For one week every year, the five biggest Baptist churches in Sunshine convene in one place. It's a good old soul cleansing and parishioner recruiting day. Anyone who doesn't want to go to hell will be there. Of course the catfish fry and baked goods sale also bring in the sinners. Needless to say, it makes for a very empty video store.

The front door bells chime. Long and Tall walks through the door. Bren shakes the raindrops from her hair and finger-combs it back again. Dots of rain wet her kelly-green V-neck tee. Preppy-fit white shorts make her long tan legs even longer. I love the chunky white Michael Kors watch she wears; diamonds crust the rim.

She is so not dressed to be shooting tin cans off a fence post.

When she smiles at the sight of me, it's one of those mouth half-open, half-closed kind of smiles. I smile back. Inside my stomach has its own cheer section and right now it's doing the wave.

Unconsciously, Bren adjusts her watch on her wrist like it's a nervous tick. "What's going on, guys?" She towers over us.

"Not much," I say, trying not to sound so bubbly. Van and I scoot to one side, and I pat the empty spot next to me. It's never occurred to me how low this couch is until Bren sits. Her knees stick up higher than the cushions.

Bren points to the sixty-inch screen behind the counter. "That flat screen—"

"Rocks." I complete for her. She nods in agreement.

"Are we really doing a Depp marathon?" Bren asks.

"Yeah, are we?" I plead to Van with my best puppy-dog eyes for mercy.

"A double feature at first, then I'll let you know how I'm feeling."

I whisper to Bren. "Don't worry, he fast-forwards a lot."

Van aims the remote. We could watch every Johnny Depp movie from now until the cows come home, and I'd be fine with it as long as it meant being next to Bren.

Van snuggles down into the couch. "This one is my favorite. More of a cult classic than a blockbuster." The doo-wop song starts, and the title flashes *Cry-Baby*. Fifties-clad students line up to get their immunization shots at school. All the classic characters are identified, preppies vs. greasers. Johnny Depp emerges, kicking and fighting as he protests getting a shot. My jaw drops when I get a good look at Cry-Baby's hair.

On the sly, I cock my head toward Van to see if he's thinking the same thing I am. His eyes flash at me, wild with awareness. I mouth, *No!*

"Say Bren—" Van starts, but my elbow to his ribs interrupts him.

"Huh?" she asks.

"Have you ever noticed—"

"You want some popcorn?" I sit up.

"—that you and Cry-Baby have the same hair," he finishes.

I palm my face and burrow into the couch cushions. He did not just say that out loud.

"Really?"

"No," I say. Even though I know it kind of does. "See?" I finger her soft hair. "It's not all greasy and slick. Her hair is gorgeous." My touch releases the ocean. She smiles at me. The urge to smell my hand gnaws at me. I bury my possessed hands under my thighs.

Van has the dang TV paused now, pointing at it. "Except you don't have that piece hanging over your forehead. But you do have that whole bump 'n' swoop thing in the front working for you." His hand waves a demonstration.

I close my eyes and pray for the analyzing of Bren's hair to be over. "Stop, Van. You're embarrassing me."

"What? I'm just saying…"

The couch shakes from Bren's laughter. "Hey." She pats my leg and leans over to my ear. "Don't worry, I'm not sweating it. He's just jealous he doesn't have 'The Do.'" The touch of her hand on my bare leg echoes throughout my body. I huff a laugh. She slumps into the couch at an angle, smug and content. Her hand stays in that undecided zone, not quite on my knee but more next to it, as if she hasn't committed either way.

Van is in his own world, pausing the movie at different scenes and breaking down the anatomy of Cry-Baby's hair. He posts side-by-side pictures of Bren and Cry-Baby on Instagram. My mortification grows.

"How do you make it do that?" Van just keeps on going. "Is it a natural cowlick or something? Or do you use product?"

"Van, you're killing the movie here. Let's just watch it," I say. He presses play.

I'm trying to look at ease, but my body refuses to relax. Bren's pinky finger nudges my knee. I risk a glance. Bren cuts a look over to me, a small smile lights her eyes. Now I wish Van wasn't here.

My other knee bobs up and down as I keep checking the door for customers, ready to pop up for a bathroom break if someone comes in. When I force myself to stop checking the door, I kind of chill out a bit. The drizzle of rain and gray sky outside helps. I lean into Bren's shoulder to anchor my nerves. She reciprocates. Her height and my lack thereof curve us together with a snug fit.

* * *

Clap! I startle upright.

"Wake up. Let's do something," Van declares. For a second, I'm disoriented. Van stands before me, cupping his hands together. Behind him the credits roll. "We haven't had a single customer. With the revival going all day, I doubt we will."

I'm still trying to orient myself when I spy a wet spot on Bren's shoulder, and my hand goes to my mouth. Nice one, Kaycee.

"Did you drool on her?" Van is anything but tactful.

"Vander." I rub my hand over my face. Not only am I jumpy as a cricket, but I've slimed her. Bren's not asleep, but one more JD movie and she'd be out too. I yawn and stretch. "What do you want to do? It's raining." Another yawn.

Bren rallies herself. "Let's do something local."

"Well, yeah," Van says. "I'm not driving anywhere in this rain."

"No. I mean something fun you guys do that I've probably never experienced. Like cow tipping."

Van rolls his eyes. "Nobody cow tips, Bren. They only do that in the movies."

"Chuck the Buck does it." I remind him.

"Chuck the Buck is dumb as a box of rocks," says Van.

I can't imagine a girl who's been to Zimbabwe, Cuba, and God only knows where else, finding anything we do in Sunshine fun.

Van starts to shut things down in the store even though it's only three in the afternoon. "We could get my dad's truck and go mud-ding," Van offers. I give him a flat no. "What about Skeater's Skates?"

"Sounds…scuzzy?" Bren's astute observation is correct.

"It is," I say "It's this disgusting old roller rink where we skated as kids, but the rednecks took it over. Unless we want to risk getting our asses kicked, I say no."

"Where's your bathroom?" Bren walks toward curtain number two.

"No!" Van and I holler at the same time. "That's the porn closet," I say. "Go over there." She goes where I direct her with a very wary look on her face. "I'll explain later," is all I offer.

"Cuddle city up in here," Van sings once Bren has disappeared to the back.

"Shut up, Vander." But I'm grinning from ear to ear.

"Bowlerama? Arcade? Lawn darts?" Van suggests.

"Lame. Juvenile. And, hello, it's raining," I say.

Van thinks a moment, then he gets that look in his eye. "I know. Let's play Cat and Mouse."

Bren returns from the bathroom, ready to go. "I have no clue what Cat and Mouse is, but I'm game."

"Oh yeah." I'm up on my feet, fetching my cell phone from my pocket. "I'll call Sarabeth. And have her call Chuck. You call the M&M twins." While I'm dialing, Van rushes to shut down the store.

I look Bren dead in the eyes. "Oh, you just wait. You haven't lived until you've played Cat and Mouse."

Van nods in agreement. He flips off the lights. In the dark, my smile fades. Oh God, I'm actually doing this and there's no backing out now. What if someone sees us? I hope Bren doesn't expect any kind of touchiness in front of the others. What have you gotten your-self into Kaycee Jean McCoy? Van locks the doors to the video store.

* * *

Rain cascades down in sheets off the car wash's roof, creating a curtain of water. "You see," I say to Bren, "the beauty of hiding in the car wash is no one expects you to park in an exposed stall. But they forget the car wash doesn't have gutters, and on rainy days, you get the perfect cover."

Bren nods, impressed. The three of us are cramped together in the bench-seat of Van's 1969 frost green Chevy Nova, restored by his father's handiwork. I am very aware of everything that is Bren. Soft arms, beachy scent, and her hand that has taken up a little more space on my knee.

"So, we just sit here…and wait?" She's lost her enthusiasm from earlier.

"Trust me." I waggle my eyebrows. "We won't be waiting for long."

"Meeeeooooow." The CB radio crackles. "Big Kitty's ready for some dinner. Who wants to be lunch? Over," Chuck calls out to us mice.

Van snatches up the mic, but before he can speak, Sarabeth replies. "Bubblegum and Camp Counselor Drew are ready and raring to go. Ten-four."

"We're using CBs, not cell phones?" Bren whispers to me.

"Bren, honey," Van says, "we need to hear where everybody is so we can know if Chuck's getting close. Besides, you don't get cool handles on the phone."

"Carolina Hot-pants here." Misty calls out. "I'm sitting back and munching on some cheese. Copy that?"

"Ooh, Misty must have a good hiding spot," says Van.

Bren frowns so I explain, "She's telling us she has all the time in the word if she's sitting back having lunch."

"The Snooki Bandit is tucking out of sight as we speak. Hey, jerk." We hear a horn honk. "Save some room on the road for me. Sorry, guys," Melissa says. "Copy and over and out and all that." Static keys through the mic.

Van triggers his mic. "Copy that, Big Kitty. Mad Hatter, Pixy Stix and…" Van pauses, puts the CB to his chest. "Who do you want to be Bren?" he whispers.

She shrugs and looks at me. "Boston B-ball?" she suggests.

"Uh-uh." I look at Van. "Long and Tall." He's nodding an "oh yeah" with me.

"And Long and Tall are snug as a bug in a rug. Copy that?"

All the mice call in one at a time with vague hints to where they are. Bubblegum sees water. It's a trick clue with all this rain. "I bet Sarabeth is over by the water tower," I say to Van. He nods in agreement.

Rain pounds the corrugated tin roof of the car wash. "It's loud in the barn," is the clue Van offers.

While the others give their clues, Bren asks, "What's up with the 'Camp Counselor Drew' handle? It sounds creepy."

Van wrinkles his nose. "It is. The first summer Sarabeth and Andrew met, they hooked up at Football & Cheer camp. I suggested he use Mr. Heisman or QB on the SB—Sarabeth Beaudroux." Van glances sideways and snickers.

"Vander, you're such a sleaze." I shove him.

"I see me some gravel," Carolina Hot-pants calls. Van grabs up the mic and chats in code to the other mice, teasing Big Kitty.

Bren squeezes my knee. "Pixy Stix?"

My cheeks blush. "Van picked it. He says I'm so sweet, I give every-body a toothache," I say in my best doofus voice. "Cliché, right?"

"Much better than Long and Tall. Sounds like one of those cheesy cocktails with an umbrella and a chunk of fruit," she teases me.

"Uh," I mock offense. "You don't like it? Cause Boston B-ball is so much better. Besides, your legs are pretty awesome."

"Thanks." Bren smiles and looks down at my hand—which hap-pened to be wrapped around her arm. "I like you getting comfortable around me." Her eyes scan my face, linger on my lips.

"Me too." It's barely a whisper. I try not to let my eyes stray to her lips, but they can't help themselves. She has the perfect amount of plump and pucker to model her lips in a *Covergirl* ad. Bet they're soft too.

Headlights flicker past the other side of our veil of water. Chuck's big ole four-by-four zips past the front of the car wash. Brake lights flash. His tires squeal to a halt.

"Go, go, go, go, go!" I smack the dashboard. Van throws the Nova in reverse at the same time Chuck does. We whip out the back side of the car wash with a Hollywood spin. When Van floors it, I latch on to Bren's arm, tighter than tree bark. She clamps down on my knee.

"Go left down Maple Street. Quick." I yell. Seat belts click. I look over my shoulder. Chuck's roll-bar lights snap on. His truck tips a tad as he takes the turn too fast.

"Aren't we found?" asks Bren, confused by our running.

"We have to be trapped in his headlights for a full three seconds before we're officially caught."

"Watch out, Mad Hatter," Chuck roars over the radio. "Your ass is grass, and I'm the lawn mower." We all bust up laughing. My stomach bobs as we take a hill too fast. Bren grabs the oh-shit handle. We zigzag through neighborhood streets, barely keeping out of Chuck's lights.

"Why are you getting on the highway, Van? He's going to catch us," I say.

Van's Chevy three-fifty engine block roars to life, getting a taste of asphalt. "Trust me." He white-knuckles the steering wheel.

Chuck hangs tight on our tail. "You're mine, Pixy Stix," he says in a maniacal voice.

The Nova's pedal is pegged to the floor. Rain pelts the windshield. Wipers flap. Up ahead, I see redemption: Dead Man's Curve. "You will be slowing down," I say to Van. It's not a question. I squeeze Bren tighter.

"Yes, of course." Van grins. "But he'll have to slow down *way* more than me unless he wants to tip that high boy over."

We barrel down, getting closer to the curve, and bam! Roll-bar lights blind us in the rearview mirror. Chuck counts out over the CB. "Three, two—"

We take the curve before he gets to one, and sure enough, he takes it a bit too fast. I hold my breath as his truck leans too long to one side. Then his tires catch hold and he fishtails on the wet blacktop. His tires slip off the road. Mud spits out from behind his wheels. He's stuck.

"Wahoo!" we scream a victory cry. I madly stomp my feet on the floor. High fives are given all around. I pick up the mic. "Pixy Stix here. Looks like we have a jack-knifed Kitty on Dead Man's Curve, and these three blind mice are safe and sound. Copy that?"

"You should have known better than to take on a Nova, Chuck." Andrew laughs over the airways. "I mean Big Kitty."

"Holy crap." Bren jolts forward in the seat. "That was freaking awesome." She shakes my leg violently, her eyes bright.

"I told you," I say. "Leave it to us country bumpkins to find entertainment in anything."

Chuck is nowhere to be seen. Curses bark over the CB about the mud sucking him down into the shallow ditch. Van circles back toward town. My heart is still reeling in the moment. I open my mouth to suggest our next hiding place—

Blue lights flash in the rearview mirror.

I key the CB. "Damn it. We've been red lighted by a brown paper bag."

"Copy that," Camp Counselor Drew says. I turn the CB off.

"What's that mean?" Bren asks.

"A cop in an unmarked car," I say. Van pulls the car to the shoulder and kills the engine. Raindrops peck the roof, making a hollow sound in the silence of the car.

Back behind us, the cop exits his vehicle, and I recognize his bulky frame immediately. "Jesus, this is just great," I say. Van gives me a puzzled look. "It's Billy Arden. The big gorilla himself." Van mouths a silent *oh*.

Billy Arden—as in the cop who prides himself on being a hard case. The same Billy whose sole goal in life is to bust high school students for weed and underage drinking. Billy, Larry Beaudroux's cousin and my mother's secret boyfriend who she thinks I don't know about.

Billy sidles up to Bren's window. Her long arm turns the crank to roll it down. Gray skies loom overhead, but Billy keeps his mirrored aviators on, spritzed by the rain. His nostrils flare. "License and registration," he says and leans down to peer in the window. Both his huge, hairy-knuckled hands grip the doorframe. I pass over Van's papers, and that's when Billy says, "Kaycee Jean McCoy, is that you?" *Now* those sunglasses come off.

"Yes, sir." I straighten to attention at my full name. His eyes move from me to Bren then to our hands—hers still resting on my leg, mine clinging to her arm. Simultaneously Bren uses that hand to cough, and I rub my sweaty palms on my shorts. "Were we speeding, Officer Arden?" Speeding, reckless driving, running stop signs, and ten other infractions at least.

"You were doing sixty-eight in a fifty-five zone." He glares at Van. "Y'all in a rush to get somewhere?" He locks Bren in his sights like he's trying to figure her out. The whole right half of her body is getting soaked from the rain sprinkling down. A clap of thunder rumbles the sky.

"No, sir," Van says. "Just wanted to hurry and get home before the storm gets worse."

Rain drenches Billy's tan shirt, but he drums his fingers on the vi-nyl of the door, letting his silence torture us.

It works.

He stands back up with a sigh and scribbles in his booklet. Even my mother's secret relationship can't get us out of a speeding ticket. I'm almost tempted to mention my mother but stop for fear of making things worse.

"I better not catch you speeding on my highway again," he says, and hands the ticket over to Van.

"Yes, sir, Officer Arden," Van says.

But he's not listening to Van. He's eyeballing the road behind us. Headlights brighten in the rear view as Chuck the Buck's truck slowly rolls by. Just as he passes on our left, he shoots his gun fingers at us. *Dang it. We're it.*

"Yes, sir," I say, holding out my hand for the license and registra-tion. "Won't happen again, I promise."

He hands it back with another warning, and we all nod obediently.

* * *

"We're lucky he only wrote us a ticket," Van says as he puts the car in park in front of the Quick Stop.

"I know."

"At least you won't get in trouble with your momma, because then she'd have to fess up to doing the nasty with him."

"True." Even though I'm grateful for that part, I wonder if Billy will say anything to her about how cozy Bren and I were. I try to imag-ine a scenario where he might write it off as something other than two people groping each other, but my mind draws a blank.

Van pauses in the car doorway. "Kaycee, peanut brittle?" I nod. Van points a finger to Bren. "Anything?"

"Gatorade." She bucks her pelvis up to pull some cash from her pocket. The door shuts after Van takes her money.

Do I think Mother would actually say anything to me? She has gotten pretty good at dodging the subject so far. Maybe she really does just think I'm a tomboy. She won't think that after Billy talks with her, though. A part of me wants to explain myself to him, but what would I say?

"Hey." Bren squeezes my hand. "What's worrying you?" Her beautiful eyebrows frown at me. Her brown eyes melt my soul. "That cop, you're worried he's going to say something to your mom." I nod. "So your mom doesn't know."

"No." Which comes out harsher than I intended. "Sorry."

She weaves her fingers with mine. With her free hand she traces the number eight continuously on the back of my hand. "Not all parents can be as open-minded as mine." Her admission surprises me. "Yep, my parents are pretty awesome. Of course, there was a brutal fight at my Tia Lola's wedding. Involving a ten-year-old me in this horrid junior bridesmaid's dress—lace upon lace upon lace." She sticks her tongue out, gagging.

I'm smiling now. I cannot picture Bren in any kind of dress.

"Mom bribed me with a new basketball hoop if I promised to wear it. But when my cousin Louis made fun of me as we were walking down the aisle, I dove—flowers and all—and whaled on that poor kid."

"Omigosh, Bren." Laughter shakes my body. "I cannot believe you kicked your cousin's butt in the middle of your aunt's wedding."

"He called me 'la cabra en un vestido.' Which means 'goat in a dress.'" I'm rolling with laughter now. "Nobody calls Bren Dawson a 'la cabra en un vestido' and gets away with it." She stops laughing and gives me a mock-serious look. "I knocked his molar out."

"That's awful. And you gave me crap for killing satanic rodents. I think we're going to change your CB handle to Cabra en un Vestido."

"Absolutely not. Long and Tall works just fine." She shakes her head, smiling, and sighs. "After that, I guess my parents just knew. By the time I was almost thirteen, we had 'the talk,' and when I asked detailed questions about girls and what it felt like to kiss them, we had another kind of talk. I don't think it surprised them. I'd never really been the classic girly type growing up. After that, they were open doors to anything I had questions about."

"Wow. I don't see my mother doing any of that." I stare at my lap. "My mother's like this neat and tidy, everything-fits-just-so, kind of woman. Sometimes I wonder if going against the grain is really worth it, when everyone else expects me to be this certain person."

When I look up, Bren's fierce gaze burns through me. Her leg bobs up and down, and she stares at my lips. "I'll make it worth your while." She leans in and presses her lips to mine, keeping them there for the longest, most glorious two seconds of my life. She smiles against my mouth, then pulls away. "We'll figure it out, together." There's conviction in her gaze which makes me believe her.

From my periphery I see Van coming out of the store. Bren does too. She leans back just as Van opens the car door.

"Brrrr." He shivers. "It's wet and cold out there."

I couldn't disagree more. My entire body has been set on fire.

"Colder than a witch without her metal bra on?" Bren asks.

Dead silence fills the car. Van and I eye each other. On cue we erupt in laughter.

"What? I heard it from Misty, I think. Did I say it wrong?"

"Yes." Van pulls out of the Quick Stop, dying with laughter. "It's 'colder than a witch's titty in a brass bra.'"

Bren shoos her hand at him. "Close enough. I almost had it."

"Almost only counts in horseshoes," Van says and turns the CB back on. "Hey y'all, guess what Long and Tall just said." Van repeats Bren's mix-up. They roast her Yankee butt like nobody's business.

"You guys," she knocks my leg with hers. "I wish I'd never said anything."

"Hey, you know what my momma says about wishing," I say to Bren. "Wish in one hand and spit in the other, and see which one gets filled up faster." Van and I guffaw like a couple of donkeys.

Bren cozies up with her door, but she's laughing too. Van says over the CB, "Y'all she's getting pissed now. You better stop."

Chuck the Buck breaks through the radio. "Tell her it's better to get pissed off than pissed on."

Sarabeth adds, "That Yankee probably doesn't know whether to scratch her watch or wind her butt."

I break in over the radio waves of insults. "Hey hey, act like y'all got some raising. Don't be ugly."

There is a fumble with the mic and Camp Counselor Drew jumps on. "Hey, Chuck the Buck would know something about that. He looks like he's been hit with the ugly stick."

Chuck mouths off a lame comeback. Southern analogies sling back and forth. They cut Bren down in good humor. When she finally gets a word in edgewise, she says, "I don't even know what language you guys are speaking. What the heck is a 'coon's age' anyway?"

We erupt in laughter, and she hugs her side of the car.

"Ugh." She covers her face, laughing too. "All this mockery for one, tiny error. One." She shakes a single finger. "You guys are ridiculous."

We repeat "ridiculous" over and over with British accents, not that she sounds like that, but it's funny to see her squirm.

"Aww, come on Bren." I tug on her arm. "We're just messing around." She pulls away, faking mad. "You want to be that way, that's fine." I cut my eyes at Van.

"Finer than a frog hair split four ways," we say in unison.

"You people are going to hell." Bren gives me a fake glare.

"Now that's the spirit." I hook arms with her. "Now, say, 'y'all.' Come on now."

She does—with zero twang—but she indulges me. Even though we're all goofing off and having fun, her words do not slip my mind. *We'll figure it out…together.*

I hope that's exactly what we do.

Chapter 11

Today is a big day. Andrew and the boys finished framing out the float. The plan this morning was to pick up Sarabeth after breakfast. If I'm already running late, I know she will be for sure. I hurriedly blow dry and scrunch my hair. By the time I pop into the kitchen for a bowl of cereal, Mother is already in there, cooking away.

A huge pot of sauce simmers on the stove, fresh basil and mushrooms on the cutting board. Two bottles of wine sit next to the loaf of French bread. Somebody's planning a sleepover with Mr. Billy. It's silly they hide their relationship. But I know how my mother thinks. It just wouldn't look Christianly to date someone two months after his divorce. I wonder what our Baptist preacher would say about the wine.

I bite my lips to keep from letting a grin escape. "It'll be a late night, so I'm staying with Sarabeth," I say.

"I figured so. Don't stay up too late and miss church in the morning."

"I won't." But we always do.

"What about that new girl, Bren? Is she going to be there?" The question comes out of left field. Mother casually stirs the spaghetti sauce, but her eyes keep dancing back to me. I don't answer right away.

"Because, you know, I really don't know her family all that well. I'm not sure if I want you hanging out with her."

That confirms it for me. Freaking Billy Arden ratted me out to Mother, and she knows. *She knows!* I knew this whole dating Bren stuff was a bad idea. Whatever made me think I could hide it from Mother was beyond me. This sucks. Now how am I supposed to see Bren? I slurp down the milk left in my bowl. When I come up for air, an idea hits me. "No," I say, while I put my bowl in the dishwasher. "I heard she has a date with Mark, Jenny Littleton's son." The lie slips out as easy as breathing.

"How nice." Mother perks. "He's a right sweet boy." Relief softens her entire posture. I grab my keys. "Don't forget we have the bake sale after church tomorrow. Don't be late."

I kiss her on the cheek like a good girl. "Don't worry, Mother, I won't."

* * *

Out in front of Sarabeth's house, floral vans and catering vehicles fill the driveway and block the street. From the side gate, I see Mrs. Beaudroux signing for deliveries and directing her staff where to set up the tables. Crates of stemware and fine china clank as they are carried to the back by the Beaudroux's maid—degraded with a cliché fifties uniform for house maids.

I wait for Sarabeth to load the rest of her stuff in my car, float decorations and whatnot. I check my Instagram. Bren posted another picture of an accidental love note—a pothole in the asphalt in the shape of a lopsided heart. A huge smile breaks across my face. It's our way of saying "I miss you" to each other as publicly as possible.

"Whatcha grinning at?" Sarabeth asks as she gets into the car.

Quickly I lock my screen and shove my phone in my pocket. "Eh, just a stupid text from Van. What's up with the big shindig?" I redirect the conversation.

"That?" She looks up from her cell to the house. "They're having some big dinner with these Japanese bigwigs." She goes back to texting.

"For the factory?"

"Yeah."

"Are they with an automobile company?" I ask, as we pull away.

"Yeah, I think. Who cares?" She shrugs, not taking her attention off her phone. Anybody whose livelihood depends on it cares—like my mother's boutique. Things like that don't concern Sarabeth. If the factory shut down tomorrow, their family would keep on thriving. Old money goes a long way in Sunshine. The only reason her daddy is fighting so hard for it now is because he's working on his brownie points for when he runs for mayor next year.

"Are Bren's parents going?" I peer around the corner where I'm about to turn, as if I'm Miss Cautious Driver. Sarabeth's pause and stare do not go unnoticed.

"No." She's texting again. "It's just an introduction thingy. Did Van say he picked up the purple glitter for the irises? He knows we're gonna need like twenty bottles of the stuff, right?"

"Yep. Rode with him over to Memphis yesterday to get the last of Craft World's stock."

Sarabeth's phone beeps. She giggles. "He's so bad."

"What?" I smile.

"Andrew wants to know if I'll...you know." She makes the universal gesture for blow job. "I told him to meet me behind the barn."

"Ew. You *like* doing that? I could never—" The comment leaps out of me before it registers what I'm implying.

"Well, duh. Don't you? You act like you've never gone down on a guy before."

I shiver in disgust. "I haven't." Again, the mouth with a mind of its own talks without thinking.

She lowers her phone to her lap. "You and Dave didn't...play around that night you stayed at his house until two in the morning?"

That particular evening, Dave's parents were out of town. He drank beers on his couch while we watched lame *South Park* reruns. We did that until he passed out, and I fell asleep. At two in the morning I woke up with his beer-breath mouth snoring in my face. Sarabeth made her own assumptions—which I never bothered to correct. She doesn't even know I hated kissing him. "He drank too many beers and couldn't get it up, remember?" I glance over at her to see if she's buying it.

She chews on the inside of her lip. "Huh. Whatever. It's fun."

We drive in silence for a little while, heading out into the country toward Andrew's house. The float is being built in one of their farming sheds, down the long winding drive by his home. It'll stay there until the morning of the parade. It's a good twenty minutes away from town and not worth anyone's effort to drive out to vandalize.

Once we're out of city limits, the houses become scarce, and the roads wind around every which way. I get to thinking, if she does that for him, does he do *that* for her?

"Well, of course he does," Sarabeth answers the question I'm mortified that I actually verbalized. "Haven't you ever—" She stops herself.

She knows I'm a virgin, and I know she's not. But all the other stuff in between, I may or may not have embellished about here and there—or flat-out lied about. I keep my eyes on the road ahead, but I can feel her looking at me. My face flames.

"Yeeeah," she says slow and easy. "I guess you haven't. It's really... um, awesome actually. I mean, hey, Andrew and I have been dating for over two years now, so of course we've done tons. Don't get me wrong, in the beginning it was horrid. Not like the freaking movies, at all."

"Hmm," is the most I can say, pretending to be laser-focused on the winding road, but my ears are wide awake.

Sarabeth describes their first time. I do my best not to cringe. Lucky for me, Sarabeth and modesty are not friends as she describes the sexual things they do together. For the first time, sex actually makes total sense to me. She complains about certain things Andrew does to her and raves about others, and I find I'm taking mental notes. Not that I have any intention of doing those things with Bren anytime soon, but these are activities I've never allowed myself to ponder—before now.

* * *

When we arrive at Andrew's shed—thoroughly sex-educated—only three cars are parked in the field next to it. The huge building lies about a football field away from Andrew's house. Their combine tractor is parked on the exterior, saving room for the float inside.

"Hey, baby," Sarabeth greets Andrew with way more attentiveness than I'm comfortable witnessing after our conversation. "Go on inside, Kaycee. I'll be in in a sec."

"Oh, come on, let the girl watch. She might learn something." Andrew bumps his pelvis against Sarabeth's.

"Disgusting." I shake my head and go inside. Squealing giggles and male grunting fade off in the distance behind me.

Wow. Inside, I quickly notice that the skeletal structure of the float is the most complicated we've ever attempted before. The Grand Ole Opry serves as the backdrop, with the Tennessee state flag on the sides and Elvis himself standing in a bed of irises in the middle. Toward the front, the gates of Graceland frame the thrones for the homecoming king and queen. Van's overall design is freaking amazeballs.

"Where do we start?" I ask Sarabeth once she and Andrew *finally* make their way inside.

Sarabeth hands out orders to the few people who are already here. As more seniors arrive, she and Van put them to work too. For co-chairs, they work together way better than they'd ever admit. My eyes dart to the door every time someone enters, hoping for Bren.

Purple and plum glitter cakes Van's fingers, and I try to help him scrape it off.

"What is *she* doing here?" Sarabeth's sour tone brings my attention to the door.

Bren strolls in with long easy strides. One hand smoothes her wind-blown hair. I thrill at the sight of her.

"I invited her. You're cool with that, right?"

"She did swear to the Oath." Van elbows me. We both laugh at our own private joke.

"Humph." Sarabeth eyes the both of us with skepticism. "I expect to get some work done today."

My face screws into a what's-that-supposed-to-mean look. She chats it up with Bren all the time. Maybe she's getting jealous of how much time I'm spending with Bren? Or worse, maybe she's nervous about why I'm spending so much time with Bren in the first place.

"Hey, guys." Bren smiles.

Every single touch, flirty word, and unsaid thought from the last week floods my nervous system, and I want to pull her into me.

"Hey," I say, bobbing on my heels, thumbs securely hooked into my back pockets.

"I like your nails." Her eyes scan me from my head to my perfectly polished toes. Considering the tortuous *hell* I'd had to endure to have someone dig, scrape, and scrub at my feet, the gold starbursts I'd had painted on my toes better have been worth it.

We stand facing each other, in a sea of senior peers. It's as if there's an invisible barrier between us, forcing us to be…cordial. We take a collective breath. "You want to help me put on the tinsel?" Absently my hand tucks my hair around my ear, and my hip sways to one side like a coy schoolgirl. Geesh.

"Sure—"

"Bren." Sarabeth strong-arms her. I forgot Sarabeth was standing there. "Andrew is having trouble securing the float lighting. He needs someone tall to hold it up. Can you help him?" She points to Andrew at the back of the float.

"Absolutely," Bren says, apologizing with her eyes to me.

Sarabeth helps me tuck the tinsel through the wire framing at the front. "I've noticed Michael watching you." Sarabeth nods behind me. I turn to see a scraggly boy, whose waist is so narrow he makes all the girls envious. His family owns the local gas station. But as alluring as free gas may be to most, I can't get past the spit-slicked hair or the shiny skin.

"He looks"—I take another gander at him to confirm—"oily."

"What about Jimmy?"

"Jimmy? The same Jimmy who can't seem to keep his pants up and who has worn the same curled-brim baseball cap since our freshman year? His family owns a pig farm. Oh yeah, that's just how I imagined myself, someday—a pig farmer's wife." I growl. "What's up with you pushing me so hard to tie up with someone? I'm cool with singlehood." I ready myself to point out my obvious losing-Dave-to-Chelsea heartbreak, even though my only heartache is that Chelsea has moved past Dave and onto Bren. So have I.

"Humph," she grunts. "Look, I just want you to be happy and to not make any choices that will ruin your future. You do want a boyfriend, right?"

My face goes beet red. There's a lump in my throat.

Sarabeth turns away, unable to look me in the eye. "Okay, maybe the boys in Sunshine aren't prime picks. But it's our senior year, Kaycee. If you don't secure a boyfriend by college, then…then…you'll be lonely. Maybe you'll find someone there, though, who knows?" She pauses and looks over at me. I keep plugging away on the decoration. Girls around here might look at college as an opportunity to find a husband. But this girl plans on getting her degree in history, then getting the hell out of Sunshine.

"I know it's a long ways away, but after college, Andrew and I will probably get married. Don't you want to get married? Our farms could be right next door to each other. We could have as many horses as we wanted. Wouldn't it be cool if we raised our kids together? They'd grow up to be besties just like you and me. We could teach them how to ride. We could tell stories to our grandkids about how we fell in love and married our high school sweethearts. Doesn't that sound perfect?" Sarabeth reels in her painted scenario, sounding almost desperate for me to agree with her.

"Sure," I say, a bit sharper than I mean to. Yes, I want a happily-ever-after, but it won't be one like Sarabeth—or my mother for that matter—envisions. It will be years before Sunshine embraces the gay marriage law, and our Baptist church probably won't ever. I *would* love to have kids, but how would this town treat them? The thing that really bugs me is it seems like Sarabeth is trying to enlighten me on what I'll be missing if I "choose" a gay "lifestyle," as if the perfect vision of marriage requires a husband. Or maybe she's poking and prodding to get me to fess up? Like if I answer no to all of the above, then that seals it—I'm a lesbian. Because you know, being a lesbian means I never want to get married or have children. *Ridiculous.*

I'm tired of talking white picket fences, so I change the subject, handing Sarabeth another garland strand. "You think Bren's dad set up a good match for the factory?"

"He better have, considering how much my daddy's paying him. Why are you always so concerned about Bren? You have other friends you can talk about, right?" She huffs.

"You know what," I say, tossing the garland down, "I'm going to go work on Elvis." She shrugs her indifference. Between her playing matchmaker and her moodiness over Bren, I'm fed up.

The M&M twins have recruited two of the best seamstresses from home ec to make Elvis' infamous white costume. A few other kids manipulate the male mannequin to resemble his classic pose. After I stand around for a while, I realize I'm not needed here, and I go over to the iris assembly table.

Van has production under control. He puts me to work cutting out the shapes. "You just suck at gluing and sprinkling, honey," he says. I stick my tongue out at him. From across the room, Bren catches my eye, and I smile. Just about the moment I'm going to nod for her to come over and make flowers with me, Sarabeth puts her on another task.

It's hard not to suspect she's doing this to keep us apart. It's like she knows I'm falling for Bren, and she's doing her damnedest to keep it from happening. This is what I don't understand—Sarabeth loves me and wants me to be happy, but she's pushing me in this other direction. It's like she's trying to steer me away from making the wrong choice. What she doesn't realize is that it's not a choice.

* * *

Three hundred flower petals later, my scissor hand cramps. "I need a break." I stand and stretch my aching back.

Van leans over to whisper in my ear. "Can you take over? I've got to go."

I raise a brow.

"Meeting a friend in Lawrence," he grins. It does my heart good to know he's meeting Arthur. "Supervise but don't touch a thing. You flunked art in preschool, remember?"

"You will not let me live that down will you? And for the record,

U is for Unsatisfactory, not flunking. Now go and have fun." I shoo Van toward the door. I scan the float area for Bren. When I don't see her slaving away for Sarabeth, I get a little nervous, thinking maybe she left without saying good-bye. The bathroom door opens, and Bren steps out with a wad of paper towels wrapped around her hand.

"Holy crap," I say and walk over to her. "Did you cut yourself?" I pull her hand closer for inspection. It's warm in mine. Her scent of ocean and spice makes me want to run my fingers through her hair.

"It's just a scratch. The chicken wire snagged my palm." The second I remove the paper towel, blood seeps out.

"You need a Band-Aid. A big one." I spy the office over by the front entrance. "I bet they have a first-aid kit in there," I say. She dares a glance at her hand. Her face pales. "You going to be all right?"

She looks anywhere and everywhere except the direction of her bleeding palm. "Uh-huh."

"Uh-oh. Come sit down." I drag her over to the office by the hand I'm still holding. Through the glass window separating the office from the work area, I can see a first-aid kit mounted to the wall. Bren eases herself down into the chair, applying pressure like I told her. I grab the supplies from the box.

"You are such a wuss." I chastise her as I pull out the supplies I need. "Scared of spiders and the sight of blood, I bet you make your momma proud." She manages a smile at that.

Wound cleanser bubbles over the cut. She seethes through her teeth. It bleeds worse than it is. It's a haggard scratch but not deep.

"At least I'm her favorite daughter," she says.

"Only daughter," I mumble and giggle. "It's not too bad. We won't need to Medivac you to Vanderbilt." I make a show of rolling my eyes. I fold a small piece of gauze over the scratch and lay the extra large Band-Aid over the top.

Bren leans into me. She speaks in a low voice. "I've missed you today." The tip of her finger traces my kneecap, and I melt into her touch.

I sigh softly and finish applying the Band-Aid before I look up at her. Those sultry brown eyes of hers bear down on me. "Me too. I loved the asphalt heart you posted on Instagram today."

"Found it on my run this morning. When can I see you…alone?"

I glance out into the shed, then back to her. "I—I, maybe—"

"Tomorrow." It's not a question.

My fingers smooth over the edges of the Band-Aid, and my eyes stay there. "Okay." My heart soars. "I have to do this church thing with my mom, but afterward." I take another peek out the window. Bren says something in response, but I don't hear her. I'm focused on Sarabeth. Across the shed she's eyeing us up good. Her head is cocked at a curious angle. Determination spurs her into motion. She strolls our way. I clear my throat and scoot back. Any suspicions Sarabeth may have had were probably just confirmed.

The shift in body language causes Bren to look out into the shed about the time Sarabeth gets to the office door. "Y'all done loafing or what?" She eyes the space between Bren and me. I cannot imagine what's going through Sarabeth's head. I have a pretty good idea she's no dummy.

"Bren cut her hand. I was just helping—"

"Well, I could use your help gluing on the sequins," Sarabeth says. Her voice is soft, unsure. She glances over Bren's bandaged hand. "Bren, Andrew could use your help—"

"I should go." Bren stands. "Um, it's almost six, and I promised my parents I'd be home for dinner."

"Oh." I stand too. It feels like it's an excuse to leave because of Sarabeth's obvious irritation. "You sure?" I don't want her to go.

"Geesh, Kaycee. If the girl needs to go, don't hassle her about it." Sarabeth actually looks relieved. She starts to walk off. I want to ask Bren if she's okay, but Sarabeth pauses, waiting for me to go with her, overprotective like a mother hen.

"See you later." I ease out of the office past her. The urge to look back overcomes me. The metal doors squeak shut behind Bren.

"Finally, I thought she'd never leave," Sarabeth says.

"What does that mean?" I stop dead in my tracks.

"It *means* you've been hanging with her all week," Sarabeth whispers. "Then she shows up here and becomes a distraction. Now that she's gone, maybe you'll get some work done." Sarabeth starts to glue the large diamond rhinestones onto the gold spray-painted thrones for the homecoming king and queen.

"I have been working." I glue a few gems up myself on the traced outlines. "You're always messing around and kissing on Andrew." I throw back at her.

"You're comparing my boyfriend to your *friend?*"

I fumble and drop a few of the gems I'm holding. My hand shakes a tiny bit when I go to pick them up. "She's everybody's friend." I wish I could keep my mouth shut and stop talking before I say too much.

"I don't get why everyone is all gaga over her." Sarabeth slaps on the rhinestones.

Hmm, let me see. She's tall, athletic, beautiful, intriguing, worldly, philanthropic, and, oh, did I mention beautiful?

"She's a lanky basketball star. Whoop-de-do," Sarabeth says, whirling her finger in the air. "Every day she plays *b-ball* with LaShell and those girls. If she keeps hanging with them, people are going to think she dates black people." A few seconds of silence passes, and Sarabeth says, "And Zimbabwe—Africa really isn't that cool. I mean seriously, we have our own black people here. What's the big deal?"

At this point, I stop gluing. I stare at the girl I call my best friend. The girl I've been riding horses with since we were six. The girl I played dress-up with, danced in my pj's to One Direction with, and who I made pinkie promises with under the covers. This person before me now, it's as if I've never met her.

If I'm being honest with myself, it's not the first time I've seen this petty dark side of Sarabeth. Before, I always blew it off because I wasn't the one under scrutiny. Now it's hitting so close to home, it makes my skin itch.

Sarabeth pops on sequin after sequin. "What's with that hair? And the clothes? She looks like a gangly greaser with a jock wardrobe. She'll never land a boyfriend looking like that."

"Her hair is not greasy." The repulsion comes out of me before I can stop it.

Sarabeth glances at me. "Well, you've got to admit her wardrobe isn't the most girlish."

"I like the way she looks. I like her hair too. There's a lot about her I like." My tone sharpens.

"Please don't tell me you're going to chop all your hair off and do that ridiculous wave up top. Being a clone doesn't suit you." The Bren bashing continues, but my mind goes numb.

Where is all this coming from? My heart races as I replay every touch exchanged between Bren and me. This last week I've been super careful around her. I mean sure, sometimes Bren's knee would press against mine at lunch, but that wouldn't look suspicious to anyone. She walks me to class, but so does Van. She makes me laugh, but she makes everyone laugh.

Sarabeth has no right to say these things. It's almost like she's—

"Are you jealous?" My mouth decides to act on its own again.

"What?" Sarabeth seems shocked by my question. "I'm not jealous.

It's just that…you need to be careful. People are starting to talk, you know." She fiddles with a stubborn sequin.

My blood starts to boil. The thought of anybody scrutinizing my personal life and thinking it's any of their business is getting under my skin. Especially since this scrutiny is coming from my best friend.

"You've been spending a lot of time with Bren lately." Sarabeth is trying to be casual, but she's failing. "There are a lot of questions about her."

"What do you mean 'questions'?"

"Well," she starts but refuses to look at me, "you know how Chelsea Hannigan is and, well, it just doesn't look good." Now she looks at me. "I'd hate people to think you were…you know."

My stomach drops to the floor. Air refuses to enter my lungs. The thud…thud…thud of my hearts pounds a slow beat in my ears. Is the room spinning in a slow whirl or is that just my head? I manage to take in an even breath. My surroundings move back into focus. Chelsea Hannigan is a lot of things; I don't want to presume which attribute Sarabeth's referring to.

Sarabeth gapes at me, uncertainty washes her face pale. She averts her eyes. "You don't want to look cheap, like Chelsea," she says softly. Something inside tells me that is not what she was going to say. Just as the thought enters my head, Sarabeth snaps back to her chipper tone. "Because that girl tries way too hard all the time." She laughs nervously and slaps the rhinestones onto the throne like nobody's business. "I heard she slept with Terrance. That's why he and LaShell broke up for a while. You know what else I heard?" Sarabeth steers the conversation to gossip. "I heard that Keira Hauser girl is dating that weird dude in your lab class. You know, the one who has the creepy obsession with the lab torches? He's a total pyro, don't you think?"

I nod. One by one I adhere the jewels in place, but my insides churn. Sarabeth blathers on for a minute or two more. "I don't feel so well," I say, cutting her off.

She looks at me. The pain in her face sours my stomach even more. "You think the potato salad at lunch was bad?"

"Yeah, maybe," I say, even though we both know I don't like potato salad.

As I walk to my car, I pray that the tears stay locked up until I'm safely on the road. Purple tints the sky with only a sliver of sunlight left. The road in front of me blurs to a watery haze. The urge to throw up overwhelms me, and I have to pull to the side of the road. I heave, but nothing comes up.

What does Sarabeth think? I haven't given her one reason to doubt that I'm not the person I've always been. But I haven't shared with her who I truly am either.

Is it starting to show? I've kept my true self reined in tight. But maybe not tight enough? I've exposed myself to Bren. And Van of course, because he gets it. With the rest of the world, I was sure I'd been more…discreet.

The lights of the city roll into view, and I turn toward town. Main Street still pulses at the dinner hour. I drive around the Court Square toward home. When I pull into our cul-de-sac, I notice Mother's car is parked in the driveway and not in the garage. *That's weird.*

Then it dawns on me—Billy Arden's truck is probably in the garage for their secret sleepover. *Crap.* I forgot about their little evening and that I'm supposed to be staying at Sarabeth's. As I turn the circle, I pull out my phone to dial Van…Van who has a date with Arthur. I quit dialing.

At the stop sign, I stare at my phone, debating whether or not I should call Bren. Maybe I shouldn't. Sarabeth has already spooked her off today. Plus, calling in desperation would look pathetic. I nibble the tip of my fingernail. What if I stopped by and just said hi? That's harmless, right?

Van said she lives in the Sonoma Creek neighborhood. I zip across Main Street over into the lavish homes by the creek. My plan is to drive around until I spot her BMW...and a Mercedes *and* a Range Rover. Holy Moses, her house is huge.

My nothing-special Civic feels inferior in the spotlight of the streetlamp. Lights are on in the house, but I can't see anyone. Wonder which room is hers?

I'm not sure how long I'm in the street, stalking Bren hopelessly in front of her house. What am I doing here? I don't belong in this Sonoma Creek neighborhood, looking around like a Peeping Tom. I bang my head on the steering wheel, and a light beep follows. *Oh, shoot.* My head snaps up. I'm about to turn the engine back on and bolt when their porch light flicks on. A tall, slim figure peers through the front door. Oh, Kaycee, why do you have to be such a spaz? I palm my face. What am I supposed to say? *Hey, I thought I'd honk out in front of your house and get the attention of the whole neighborhood.* Embarrassed, I get out of my car, and Bren steps out of her house. We meet halfway in her drive. I can smell the yummy chili spices on her from whatever her family is cooking.

"Hey, Kaycee. What are you doing here?" Her face brightens with such happiness, I'm grateful for my idiocy.

"I was at the—the," I say, thumbing over my shoulder, unable to recall the place I just came from. "I—I was talking to Sarabeth and she was saying..." Words get stuck in my throat. I sputter. My stupid self can't seem to come up with a single logical reason for why I'm here. All those cruel things Sarabeth said about Bren flood my brain. The fear of what she may or may not think shuts down my ability to speak. For some freaking reason, tears begin to well up in my eyes. I'm telling that emotional shit to back down and stop its course, but a dam breaks in me, and I can't seem to shut the dang thing down.

"Hey, hey, hey." Bren reels me into her arms before I can vocalize a single vowel. "Shhh." She rubs my back as I sob on my words.

Somehow I manage to pull myself off her and say, "My mom and Billy are doing their thing—whatever that is—so I can't go home. Van has a date with Arthur. And I was supposed to stay with Sarabeth tonight, but she said things—mean things that hurt. I have no place else to go." Crap, I sound desperate and hopelessly wretched. The best plan for me is to roll into a ball and sleep in the tiny backseat of my car until morning.

Bren clasps my chin, forcing me to look at her. "You can stay here." Her eyes penetrate me. "Okay?"

Everything around me stills. The idea of me staying here with her seems surreal. There's no way her parents will allow it. If anyone ever found out, I'd be ruined.

But none of that matters to me right now, because I've never wanted anything so badly in all my life.

"Bren," a soothing voice calls from the house. Her mother stands in the doorway. "Come, bring your friend inside." Cheer brightens her voice.

"There's no judgment here," Bren whispers.

Her voice and touch are smooth as the Pied Piper's. I follow Bren inside.

Chapter 12

My stomach flip flops like I'm driving over a hill too fast, fear mixed with thrill. I want to meet these amazing, worldly parents of Bren's, but I'm not sure what they'll think of a country girl like me.

Splashes of bold color enliven their living room. Spices in the air tempt my taste buds. Bren introduces me to her parents, Analena and Joe. They glance at each other with a knowing look—which does nothing to calm my nerves.

Mrs. Dawson's face lights up. "Oh, Kaycee. We're so happy to finally meet you." Her graceful hand reaches for mine. I smile as I take it. Her skin is incredibly soft.

Bren's father is indeed a handsome man. Tall and striking like his daughter, but he lacks the bronze skin. "Glad to have you. Hope you're hungry."

"I've made shrimp enchiladas verde if you are tempted to eat," Bren's mother says.

The vortex of Bren, her home, and her family spiral around me, and I try to speak intelligently. "Sounds...delicious." I follow them into the dining room.

Candles light the glass table. Full dinner settings mark each place with the elegance of a fine restaurant. Do they eat this way every night? I sit in the chair next to Bren.

"Bren's told us a lot about you." Mrs. Dawson eyes Bren, controlling her smile. There is a connotation to her words I don't miss. I realize they know I'm the *friend*-friend.

And they seem cool with it.

The thought should be settling, but I can't seem to relax.

"Bren was just about to tell us the importance of this float you guys have been working on. What's the prize if you guys win?" her father asks. Mrs. Dawson fills my plate.

"Um, a day off from school before Thanksgiving break," I say.

"Nice." Her father nods. Mr. Dawson wipes his mouth with a colorful striped cloth napkin.

I go into the detail of the theme of the float and how we've interpreted it. Bren explains the importance of the votes and the role of the candy. Her parents laugh at our methods.

"Will there be a homecoming dance for you girls afterward?" Mrs. Dawson asks. I choke on my food.

I believe she means that as in us going together as a couple, but our school would never allow that. They would sooner cancel the dance altogether because if they permitted normal gay couples to attend, it would encourage this type of behavior all the time. That would disrupt their whole belief system that boy plus girl equals the only way to love.

"Bren is a very good dancer," she adds.

I down some water to cool my spicy tongue. "No, no dance for me. And Bren's got the moves all right."

"She gets all her moves from her pops." Her father jabs a confident thumb at himself. Bren and her mother burst out laughing in protest.

"Honey, I love you," Mrs. Dawson leans in to kiss her husband, "but you are the worse dancer I've ever known. You should have seen him the night we met," she says the last part to me.

"It was my macaw mating dance that won her heart."

"He's still in denial. It was more of...what do you say? The funky chicken. Terrible." Mrs. Dawson closes her eyes and shivers as if the memory still haunts her. I laugh.

There's a brief debate over whether she saved him from embarrassing himself or he lured her in. Bren's father was working in Havana with the Cuban government to negotiate health options for their employees when he and Bren's mother met. They retell the story of how they fell in love; her version is much more believable than his.

"Toyota is a big automotive company," I say to Mr. Dawson. "Do you really think you can convince them to move their main factory here?" He cocks his head at me, curious. "I only ask because my mother owns a local business, and if people have to move to Memphis to get jobs, her shop might not make it."

Mr. Dawson nods his head. "I've set the terms of the deal. Made the proper introductions. It's up to Larry Beaudroux and his people to win them over with that southern charm." If the Beaudrouxs have anything, it's southern charm.

"Your mother owns a shop, what does your father do?" Mr. Dawson asks me, taking a bite of dessert.

"Um..." My fingers fumble with the edge of my napkin. I wonder how to say this without sounding like a loser. "I don't really visit him anymore. He lives in Texas with his new family, and they kind of do their own thing." Blank faces stare back at me. Telling people your dad doesn't want anything to do with you is always a real showstopper. I fork the bits of rice on my plate. "These were the best enchiladas ever, Mrs. Dawson. Thank you."

She takes my empty plate. "You're welcome. You'll love the sorbet. The flavors pop in your mouth." She kisses her fingertips.

Bren's parents talk about her being born in Cuba and their visits there. The story of Bren beating up her cousin at her aunt's wedding comes up, and it is way more hilarious when her dad tells it. Humiliation reddens her mother's face, but she laughs. If I ever embarrassed my mother that way, she'd probably disown me if I ever brought it up again.

After dessert, I volunteer us for dish duty. Bren and I clear them into the kitchen. Mrs. Dawson appears in the doorway. "It was a pleasure meeting you, Kaycee. I hope we'll see you more often, no?"

"Yes, ma'am. I'd like that. Nice meeting you both too." I rinse the plates.

Bren kisses her mother's cheek and hugs her father. I'm stunned when her mom says they'll head upstairs for the night to read. The one and only time I have ever had a boy at my house, my mother practically smothered us by sitting between us on the couch.

Bren's parents head for the stairs, and I hear Bren stop them in the hallway. "If it's cool with you, Kaycee is going to sleep over," Bren tells her parents. I go ghostly white and stiffen. There's a brief pause, and I don't have the nerve to turn around and see what's happening. "I'll sleep in the guest room," Bren adds, nonchalant.

"That's fine with us," her dad says. "Might want to clear my papers off the spare bed. Good night, girls." Her parents vanish upstairs.

Bren pops her head back in the kitchen. "Let me go clear my dad's stuff. I'll be back."

I nod with a half-smile on my face. Bren disappears.

Rinse and scrub, I tell my brain. Her parent's approval floors me. I can't even imagine how my mother would handle me having a boy sleep over. Ha, wouldn't happen. Not that she has anything to worry about. I wonder if she'd let Bren sleep over now—which could be dangerous. Bren in my bed...I can't even let myself go there. Oh, wait. If

Bren is sleeping in the guest room...then I'll be sleeping in her bed. Yes, glorious yes.

Water sprinkles my face. "What are you smiling about?" Bren asks, drying her hand off and passing me the dish towel.

"I...was thinking that I don't have a nightshirt or a toothbrush. I sleep over at Sarabeth's so much that I always have stuff over there."

"No problem. Hold up." She goes into a room down the hall. From the small glimpse I get, I see a Chinese lantern hanging in the corner. She returns with a large T-shirt; 10K sponsors dot the back of it. "Try this. Let me see if we have a spare toothbrush." She flips on the bathroom light in the hall. Drawers open and close, and I hear her dig through them. I bring her T-shirt to my nose and inhale deep. It's covered with that Bren-spice I can't identify and the cool breeze smell from the beach. It's pure heaven.

"Here's this—" Bren steps out of the bathroom with a packaged toothbrush in her hand.

My face burns beet red. I pull the shirt away from my nose.

"That's my dad's shirt," Bren says flatly.

My mouth could trap flies with it hanging open like this.

"I'm just kidding." She chuckles.

"You are so mean." I snatch the toothbrush from her and tuck a loose strand of hair behind my ear, hoping the heat in my face dies down soon. "Dora toothbrush. Really, Bren? You've totally shattered my fantasy of you now."

"My mom buys this stuff for my nieces and nephews. I swear."

"Mmm-hmm. I'm sure." Cannot believe I got busted sniffing her shirt.

Bren grabs my free hand, and our fingers interlock. We both stare at our joined hands.

"How's your hand?" I crack open our joined palms to inspect it. She still has my bandage on it.

"It's perfect. Had a good nurse." Her crooked smile broadens mine. "You want to watch a movie or something?" *Or something*, my heart thuds.

My body goes loosey-goosey under her touch, and I do that stupid slow-bounce on my heels thing. "Sure," I say, breathily.

She pivots toward her bedroom, drawing me tight against her back with our clasped hands. I follow close behind her. I'm sure she can feel the thump, thump, thump pounding from my chest.

Vintage movie posters plaster her room. On the bare brick wall, *Casablanca, Attack of the 50 Foot Woman,* and *Dr. No* are framed, the prizes of the bunch. Sunny yellow curtains hang over the windows. Citrus-colored triangles spiral out in a sunburst pattern on her a tribal quilt. Tangerine sheets tuck underneath—her bed is actually made. I set the toothbrush and T-shirt at the foot.

"These photos are amazing." A clothesline of magazine-quality snapshots hangs above her aqua metal desk. In one photo, she's wearing a heavily embroidered tunic in the desert. In another, she's huddled arm in arm with her basketball team.

Bren props herself up against the pile of pillows lining her headboard. "Thanks. My mom has a great eye for photography." She flips on the television to Netflix. One arm tucks behind her head.

Indian style, I sit on the opposite side of the bed, stiff-backed. "Wait a minute, I thought your family didn't own a television."

"Ha. Yeah, well we didn't until about week ago. One of my stipulations for moving here. Basic cable and Netflix only, though." Bren reaches out, hooks her arm around my waist and snuggles me up right next to her. "I promise I won't bite," she says. My body tightens for a moment. Muscle by muscle I allow myself to relax into the pillows, into her. Her fingers softly trace circles on my arm as she searches for a movie.

Her boldness thrills me. Every time she touches me, it's with a sure-ness and confidence I've yet to find in myself. I wonder how many girls she dated to build up that confidence.

"What?" She taps my leg. "You're thinking again. I can tell because you're scowling. Is it about what Sarabeth said?"

I tug at the frayed threads on my cut-offs. "That? Well, she was just being a real jerk tonight. I didn't like some of the stuff she had to say about you, and I don't know what she would think about me being... you know."

"She doesn't know."

"Nope. Does that bother you?" I look into Bren's eyes. "You know I don't live in the same world as you. Your parents are amazing. They seemed almost...giddy I was here to see you. They didn't even put flour on the floor."

"Flour?"

"Yeah." I laugh. "When my mom was a teenager, an ice storm forced her boyfriend to stay the night. My grandmother sprinkled flour on the carpet in the hall so she could see footprints on the floor in case they snuck out of their rooms in the middle of the night."

She laughs. "That's pretty smart. I guess my parents trust me. I've never given them a reason not to. But does it bother me you have to hide the greatest part of you?" We both watch her finger draw on my knee. "I wish it were different, but I've been in this situation before. It's not impossible."

I'd never before thought of my being gay as the best part of me, actually the opposite. I fiddle with her watchband. "So, you've dated other girls before." I hold my breath, daring a peek from the corner of my eyes.

"Yes. Don't tell me you haven't dated before. Chelsea told me how lovesick you were over Dave."

I punch her arm. "Ugh. I abhor Dave." Her body shakes from laughing. "I think Chelsea just told you that because she wanted you for herself."

"Probably. *Chesty* Hannigan is not subtle. She wanted me all right." Bren grins a bit too smugly for me.

"That's it." I stand up like I'm going to leave.

Bren catches my arm and yanks me back, and I collapse onto her bed. "You're not going anywhere." She settles herself closer until our bodies lie parallel, a fist's width apart. "I'm with the one I want, and it's not her." She smiles. Her face is so close, so beautiful. I fight the urge to smooth my fingers over her perfect brow. Out of habit, I glance around the room.

"Nobody's here to see us, Kaycee." Her hand grazes my arm and rests on my hip. Her touch sends tingles across my skin. "You're free to be you. Do what you want." The last part feels more like an offer instead of a suggestion.

What I want is for Bren to press her lips against mine. To see if kissing her is different than kissing the boys I've been with. For once I want to feed the thing inside of me that I've been fighting and let it feast on what it wants.

If the electricity charging inside me is any indication, I will not be disappointed.

But as much as I want this, I'm terrified. Scared I won't live up to her expectations. Scared I won't live up to my own. Scared that once I go there, there will be no turning back to the girl I was before. Too much energy builds between us. I need air. I start to roll myself away from her—

Bren's hand clinches my hip. "Don't run away."

One look into her eyes and I know. "I don't want to run away."

"Then don't." Her gaze drops to my lips.

"I don't know if I'm any good at this." My voice sounds soft and frail. I don't know if I'm talking about kissing or being gay. For the first time, I witness Bren's cool demeanor slip away and her breathing grows heavy. My words are an admission to my willingness to make the next step. It's mine to make, not hers.

"Kiss me, Kaycee." Her whisper-quiet words tickle my insides, imploring me.

I lean forward, erasing the gap between us, and press my mouth to hers. Her lips are just as soft as they were the first time. Gentle pushes from her mouth urge more from me. I concede and open up my mouth to hers. Sorbet flavors tang my tongue. The taste awakens a need in me.

Urgently, like I've been starved for years, I kiss her harder and lose myself in everything that Bren offers. She responds to my need, and then some. Her grip on my hip tightens, and I feel the slight nudge backward. Suddenly it's not enough that I'm kissing her. I don't just want to taste her, I want to feel her, all of her. I let myself tip back from her leaning pressure. The magnetic pull between us brings her body down on mine. The weight of her grounds me, anchors me to my true self.

I spin in the centrifugal force of Bren's merry-go-round. A drunken haze of Bren loosens my entire body, and I'm pliant in her restless hands. They skim up from my hips, over my arms, into my hair, and back down. I can't seem to drink in enough of her either. I grip the nape of her neck and pull her tighter against my mouth. A low moan hums from her mouth to mine—then Bren pulls back.

She wobbles slightly as she leans her body weight on one arm, exhaling heavy breaths. I smile at the sight of her trying to regain her control. She stares down at me. "Thought you said you weren't any good at this."

"Guess I was wrong?" I shrug my shoulders and giggle awkwardly. She smiles and taps a few soft kisses on my mouth. Tenderly she brushes her lips back and forth over mine. The sensation brings a burning from my stomach, and it spreads within me. "Glad you like it," she says over my mouth.

"I do. This is nothing like kissing Dave Bradford," I say before I can stop myself.

Laughter vibrates from Bren's chest. "I hope not." Her head tilts. "You're not thinking of him, are you?"

"Oh gosh, no. No, no, no. Not at all. You don't understand." I notice my fingers are smoothing and stroking the sides of her hair. I stop. "I just mean, this is not disgusting or repulsive—well, of course it's not. I'm saying...I'm actually enjoying this. Like *really* enjoying this." I bury my face in my hands. "Okay, that just sounded pathetic."

"Sounds perfect." She pulls my hands off my face. "You're pretty darn cute when you get flustered." She doles out two or three more kisses.

I sigh. "I've never done this before," I confess. "Not kissing. I've kissed before, but not like this and never with a girl, not for real. I don't know where we go from here." Because there is no going back to the Kaycee I was before.

Bren rolls to her side and props herself on her elbow. She loops my disheveled hair behind my ear, out of my face. A tender kiss dots my lips. "The fact that *we* are going somewhere makes me happy. I get that things are different here than other places, but I don't want my girlfriend to constantly second-guess her actions. I want you to be comfortable. If that means I have to be more reserved under the public eye, then I'll control myself, for now."

The word *girlfriend* echoes in my head.

"Just promise me something," Bren says. "Promise me when it's just you and me, you won't hide."

I stroke her soft hair, and then graze my thumb over each perfect brow. Bren closes her eyes to absorb my touch. "Promise." I kiss her. I'm vaguely aware that her parents are somewhere in the house, trusting us. But the frenzy of Bren's mouth on mine builds again. It's a dizzying high I don't want to come down from.

After a while, Bren draws back. She rests her forehead against mine. "We should…watch a movie," she says. I must have made a whining sound because she follows with, "If you keep kissing me like that, I'm not going to behave." A wildness dances in her eyes, making me nervous and excited all at the same time. She groans an I-don't-want-to-be-good-but-I-should protest and turns toward the TV, tucking me into her shoulder.

I cuddle into the curve of her body. She buries her face in my hair. Warm breaths puff the top of my head when she laughs at the goofy black-and-white comedy we've settled on.

The fact that she's willing to hold my hand while I figure this out melts my heart. I want nothing more than to be the girlfriend she expects, but realistically I'm not sure how to step out into the world as Kaycee, the Lesbian. Her patience makes me want to show her I can do this all the sooner.

I just hope her patience doesn't wear out.

* * *

Bren wakes me some time past midnight. I use the bathroom to change into her long T-shirt and brush my teeth. She sidles in past me to do the same as I exit. She scrunches her nose at my sleepwear. "I should have given you my Camp Chipmunks T-shirt from the fifth grade—way shorter."

"You're such a perv." I shove her in the bathroom and close the door before she can respond.

In her room, I slip under the covers. They're still warm from us laying on them. The smell of spice and fabric softer wafts from the sheets. The idea of me sleeping an entire night on Bren's pillows zips a bolt of energy through me. I thrust my arms and legs out, sprawling over as much of her bed as I can. Giddiness takes me over, and I move my arms and legs open and closed. It's not until I hear the bathroom light click off that I know I'm busted.

"*What* are you doing, crazy Kaycee?" An ear-to-ear grin consumes Bren's face.

I pull her covers over my head so I don't have to actually look at her when I answer. "Snow angel…in your sheets."

Her weight dips the bed, and she yanks the covers off my head. "You are eat up with it. You know that?"

I wallop her head with a pillow. "You don't even know what that means," I say. Too late, she wrestles me for the pillow, but I pummel her with it a few times before she takes it.

"I've heard enough colloquialisms from *y'all*." She pins my arms down and tosses the pillow on the floor. "I think I know when some-one is eat up with it." She's right, I'm totally consumed by everything that is her. She's all I can think about.

We both giggle when I squirm around, trying to get away, but dang it if all those long limbs of hers don't keep me from getting far. She knocks the other pillow off the bed before I can reach it and yanks me back by the ankle.

I stop struggling and snicker at my epic defeat. Bren lightens her hold on my wrists and straddles herself over my legs. I puff the hair out of my face, panting. "Phew. *You*…are the one eat up with it."

Bren's playful smile slips into a solemn tenderness. She leans over into my face. "That, I am." She brushes the sweetest kiss across my lips.

I pray that whatever is eating the both of us up doesn't bite us in the butt later. Because right now I'm falling so hard, I might not ever recover.

Chapter 13

If the Sunshine courthouse is the heart of the city, Sunshine Baptist Church is the liver—a liver ten times the size of its heart. The church where I was baptized sits a stone's throw away from historical court square on Main Street. Pastor Ronnie Olsen has preached at our spirit-filled, God-fearing, and Bible-believing church for the last twenty years. It's one of forty-nine churches in Sunshine, but it's the biggest and the oldest.

This morning I absolved myself of all guilt for staying at Bren's by making sure I was home in time for service. Not Sunday school, though. Mother, none the wiser about where I was the night before, didn't ask me about the sleepover at Sarabeth's, only about decorating the float. The way I figure it, lying is only a sin when it's committed... technically, I have not lied.

As we get out of Mother's car at the church parking lot, Mrs. Perkipsky's voice calls out behind me. "Where is your hosiery, dear Kaycee? With your knees all exposed I suspect your legs are quite cold. I at least hope you have a slip on." Her gray hair helmets her head in a perfect beauty shop tease. Garish coral lipstick stains her lips; tinted cracks seep past the defined lip line. Blush the color of apricot globs on her cheeks.

Nobody chastises her for her ghastly makeup.

Sinful me, I shouldn't have worn my devil-skirt, bearing that oh-so-tempting one inch of flesh above my knees. It wouldn't surprise me if Mrs. Perkipsky requested an undergarments inspection to insure I wore a proper lady's slip underneath. I'd like to inform her that one, it's unseasonably warm for September, and a humid eighty degrees is sure to strike by nine a.m.; and two, at my last check, we were decades past the fifties.

Instead I bite my tongue. "No, ma'am. I'm not too cold. But thank you *so* much for your endearing concern for the welfare of my lingerie." Mother cuts me a look. Quite possibly my exaggerated thanks could be considered a sin.

I'll pray out my sarcasm inside.

Three sections divide the congregation—it's bad enough most churches in Sunshine are racially segregated, but within the church there is an additional separation of status. Mother and I take our usual spot at left center, the humble sinners section. She chats with Ms. Rita while we wait for services to begin. The Sunday school classes file into the sanctuary, and I'm glad I don't see Sarabeth. If I'm lucky, she worked on the float late into the night, and her parents let her sleep in.

But I'm not lucky.

The deacons prop open the front doors to the church. Sunlight radiates into the room from God's holy entrance. Despite the fact that the front steps butt up to Main Street, and the parking lot is behind the church, some people love making that long journey around to the front like it's a red carpet affair. For well-funded parishioners like Mr. Larry Beaudroux, it's all about the grand entrance. He and Mrs. Beaudroux step into God's spotlight in all their pristine glory, and Sarabeth follows behind them. I slink down into the pew and study the church bulletin as if it's the SATs, not that it does any good with my mother waving at them like a flag.

"How are you feeling this morning?" Sarabeth asks as she slips beside me in the pew. She has the gall to have sincerity in her voice.

The potato salad. Right. My incredulous look is enough for her to come off it.

"Okay, so maybe last night," she says as she stares at the church program she rolls and unrolls, "I was a bit harsh. I know Bren is *your* friend. Coming down on her like I did, for whatever reason, isn't cool."

I know the "whatever reason" she's avoiding. I cock my head curtly. "Why is Bren just *my* friend?" This is not the first time this has come up. "I thought everyone was friends with her." Bren seems to know more people at school than I do.

"Come on, Kaycee. It's obvious how much you two...enjoy being friends." Her pause rubs me the wrong way. She quickly amends with, "Maybe I just don't know her well enough. All three of us should hang together. You know, the church has that hayride in a few weeks. Or maybe we can get our toes done or go shopping at that new boutique over in Bristol or something."

Are Bren and I obvious? I've taken every precaution to keep myself in check, but I do get caught up in just being near her. I wonder what Sarabeth would think if she knew I stayed the night at her house. Would she even believe that we slept in separate beds? The smell of Bren's sheets still lingers in my memory. The thought of kissing her again awakens that warm buzz in the center of my stomach.

"So that sounds good to you?" Sarabeth grins at me, hopeful. I'm smiling too, but with thoughts of Bren, not of pedicures and boutiques. Sarabeth drags me to those things often enough. I don't even know if Bren likes that stuff.

"Or something," I say. The organ and piano music key up, sending everyone to their seats. I'm saved from having to define the "or something."

"Okay. Call me later," Sarabeth whispers. She edges her way out of our pew and joins her family center-stage in the front, next to the Goodmans.

Mother nods a silent hello to Mr. Billy Arden at the end of the pew before she sits. "Mrs. Perkipsky said she would help us with the bake sale today." Mother pats my knee, pleased to share her news with me.

Yay me. I'm sure I'll get a lecture on how vulgar my sparkly nail polish is or how the basic fundamentals of makeup include a deep foundation and layers of blush, not just mascara and lip gloss.

The choir begins, and I focus on the gospel of the hymns. There's something spiritual about losing yourself in the rhythm of the songs. Music seems to be the voice of our souls. Our formal choir sings the traditional hymns I prefer. Though I think it might be fun if we had a band like Van's charismatic church sometimes. They sing jazzed up versions of the gospels. Mother says rock 'n' roll in church is sacrilege. I think it's just another way of worshiping God.

After the choir leads us in a few songs, Pastor Ronnie takes the pulpit. "Will you inherit the kingdom of God?" His solemn voice echoes throughout the reverenced sanctuary. He begins with a self-reflective thought, imploring us all to question our actions in life. Calling out the closet drinkers to be honest with themselves. We might not be able to buy beer on Sundays here, but I know a lot of people in this church who stock up on Saturday.

Like most sermons, I start to tune him out.

Ever since I hugged Bren good-bye this morning—we couldn't kiss with her parents watching—every spare second my mind returns to her. Everything about her summons that part of me I thought I had neatly tucked away inside myself long ago. And I love it. When we are together, the need to have constant physical contact overpowers the both of us. She's the more confident initiator, but I'm learning. Her laid-back attitude eats up all my apprehensions and fears. For a short time, only she and I exist.

As much as I didn't want to leave this morning, her family was planning to go to church too. Not to Sunshine Baptist but to St. Mary's Catholic Church, the only Catholic church out of all the churches in Sunshine. I didn't know anyone, until now, who attended there. If I can manage to slip past my mother's radar, I'm going see her again this afternoon. I'll have to gage Mother's mood and hopefully—

"Nor homosexuals," Pastor Ronnie bellows, jarring me from my thoughts.

Suddenly my skin becomes cold and clammy. I tempt at glance at Mother who is thoughtfully listening to the sermon.

"Nor thieves, nor the covetous, nor drunkards..." The pastor pauses to make an accusatory scan of his parishioners. "Nor revilers, nor extortioners will inherit the kingdom of God." He slaps the top of his Bible. "I ask you again my good people. Will you inherit the kingdom God offers us all? Or do your sins keep you from His riches?"

To my left, Mr. Lloyd coughs, and I jump. Ms. Rita glances at me, and my skin flames red. Then she smiles, and I mirror something similar to a smile back. The soft bump of Mother re-crossing her legs causes me to twitch in her direction. Her soured expression refocuses me back toward the pastor. Hellfire and brimstone rise up from the pulpit. It's as if a giant neon sign has pointed an arrow above my head, and everyone in the congregation is glaring at me, knowingly.

The island I lived on for so long is too far off the horizon for me to return to it. Inside I reach out for a life preserver. My eyes flit from Mrs. Perkipsky to my mother and then all the way to the front to Sarabeth. I reach in vain.

I close my eyes and think of Bren. In the darkness I hold on to the thought of her, her warmth, her calm, and her peace with herself. In her ocean, I begin to tread water again.

I remind myself that God loves me. He loves everybody, no matter what. I am in His image, in all ways, I reassure myself. So is every other being in this church. Abominations are incapable of love. Words like "detestable" describe the taste of lima beans or gum stuck to the bottom of your shoe, not one of the Lord's loyal followers. Not me. What's disgusting are the flimsy walls that I caged myself inside of for so long.

By the time I open my eyes, Pastor Ronnie has begun the benediction. For the first time in my life, I cut the strings tying me to the cocoon I can no longer return to. I have evolved. In my heart, I know Pastor Ronnie is wrong in his interpretation of the Bible I clutch.

Suddenly I feel hot and sticky. The urge to step out of this fire raises me to my feet. When Mother smiles up at me, for a brief moment I assume her smile is a sign of her approval of my newfound distaste. But then I realize the pastor has made an altar call. Right now, I'm not in the mood to renew my spiritual commitment. I shave past everyone's knees as I exit the pew. Instead of walking toward the altar, I beeline to the back of the sanctuary and slip out the front doors.

I walk up Main Street. My feet feel light. My steps, assured. I'm almost giddy—until I get mad. Why didn't I ever look at being gay like this before?

The summer afternoon of Charlotte's and my romantic escapades floods my mind, or, more specifically, the evening that followed. At the table that night sat me, Mother, and King James. Corinthians, Leviticus, and Genesis glared back at me while my mother explained to me the error of my ways. For the longest time after that, I wouldn't dare look at Charlotte Wozniak for fear I might turn into a pillar of salt.

Pastor Ronnie is wrong. My mother is wrong. And I'm right pissed off about it. They are the ones who set up the rules in my world, telling me my love for someone would keep me out of heaven. Rules that I persecuted myself over because I thought I was choosing to be this way. I might as well flog myself because of my sandy colored hair or green eyes. I'm not sinning. Sin is a willful and deliberate violation against God. He doesn't punish me for how he made me. No more than he punishes people for wearing a cloth of two different threads.

This tendency that draws me toward Bren, there's no controlling it or taming it for that matter. I've tried and failed in the past. And I don't want to fight it. It's about time I stop punishing myself for something nature intended.

Sweat beads on my forehead. Blisters burn my strappy sandaled feet. I stand in front of a storefront window, confused. A large painted red heart blares at me. All the colors of the rainbow burst out of it and ripple across the window. The only part of the glass widow that isn't painted is the small area around the Hot Flix's lettering.

So this is the big craft project Mrs. Betty was working on. I wonder what inspired her sudden openness to express her pride. The backlash she'll get for this will be hellish.

An older couple in their church clothes passes with no more than a casual smile at the window before they go into the diner next door. Who am I kidding? We're talking Sunshine, Tennessee, here. I doubt anyone around here even knows what this rainbow symbolizes, or, more specifically, that it represents acceptance of this family's gay son.

Why couldn't my mother paint rainbows instead of instilling the fear of God in me? To take something as valuable as my faith and use it against me is appalling. It's not just about being gay…I'm not good enough for her. I'm tired of trying to be the perfect daughter. Why does my wardrobe have to be just so, or my hair neat and straight, or my toes painted in a single, acceptable color? Fear and worry about my mother finding out I'm gay fades away because I believe she already knows, but she's knee-deep in denial. So was I.

"Shall I commission my mom to make a mini version for you?" Van asks. His keys jingle as he unlocks Hot Flix's front door. "Or would you prefer to stand out front all day for a look-see?" He laughs as he holds the door open for me.

In that moment, I need to know. The one thing that has consumed and controlled me my entire life stands before me and demands to be validated or dismissed. "Are we going to burn in hell, Van?" My feet are cemented to the sidewalk, waiting, needing his answer.

The smile on his face flattens. Van tilts his head, curious. His eyes scan my clothing and stop on the Bible I'm barely hanging on to. "Absolutely not," he says with such conviction I believe him.

There is just enough authority in his voice to get my blood circulating again, and I walk past him into the store.

"Well," Van amends, taking a second look at my church clothes after he flips over the open sign. "You might burn for wearing that horrid navy floral skirt. Where the heck did you buy that thing? The Goodwill?"

I chuckle. "Mother made me wear it." I sink into the sofa. The video store has an eerie dead feeling without the lights on, the flat screen playing, or the fresh smell of popcorn in the air.

"Is your mother legally blind or what? Oh, wait—" Van flips the lights on. "The only time you wear the clothes your mother buys is when you're feeling guilty. What have you done, young lady?" He raises his brow with a devilish grin on his face.

My cell phone beeps from the pocket of my ugly devil-skirt. It's a text from Mother.

Where are you? Are you feeling okay?

"Speaking of the legally blind..." I open my phone to text her back. I really don't want to look at her right now, much less endure an afternoon of belittling from Mrs. Perkipsky while selling baked goods. "I stayed over at Bren's house last night." A hundred-watt smile beams from my face.

The blank stare from Van is priceless. "You slept with Long and Tall?"

My phone beeps again, but this time it's Bren. "Speaking of Long and Tall..."

Mom is attempting to make fried catfish and hush puppies?!? Please tell me hush puppies have nothing to do with dogs. Save me?

While I'm texting Mother back, I answer Van. "And no, I did not sleep with her, innocently or otherwise. She respects her parents—who know I'm not just a BFF—so she slept in the guest room. That's just the kind of honorable person she is. Sickening, right?"

Feel fantastic. Headed over to Bren's for lunch. Will be home late, I text mother.

"Bren's a downright saint. I hope it's not infectious." Van pours the kernels into the popper.

"I know."

I text Bren back, You've never had hush puppies?!? You haven't lived until you've eaten hush puppies! On my way.

"I've gotta go, Van. And I need to borrow the Nova. Bren invited me over for lunch."

"You cannot drop a bomb about staying the night with her and then take off with my only set of wheels." But he reaches into his pocket for his keys.

"You said it yourself—this skirt is awful, and if I go back to the church to get our car, Mother will make me stay and help with the bake sale. I'll leave the keys under the floor mat, and your mom can drop you by my house later to pick it up." I reach my hand out, but he holds his keys for ransom. I offer him a little holdover. "Her parents are amazing. Her T-shirts smell like ocean and spice. She's the best kisser I've ever had the pleasure of making out with."

Van dangles the keys over my palm. "Did she sneak back in the room after her parents went to bed?" His eyebrows wiggle.

"No." I take the keys. "But she confessed she was 'eat up' with me. I promise I'll call you tonight and tell you every gory detail," I holler behind me as I leave.

The Nova's engine rumbles a deep purr. I get another text from Mother. I think you just need to eat at home. I have lots of leftover spaghetti I don't want to go to waste.

I text her back. Why don't you call Mr. Billy Arden? I'm sure he won't mind having spaghetti with you again. I add a little smiley face.

From here on out, Kaycee Jean McCoy is going to follow her heart. Others will just have to deal.

Chapter 14

My life consists of eat, sleep, and Bren. Every morning Bren picks me up for school. Sarabeth was less than happy about not carpooling with me anymore. For lunch, Bren and I no longer sit with the rest of the group in the cafeteria. We take our lunch backstage in the Drama classroom. On afternoons when I don't have to work at Mother's boutique, we veg at Bren's house. Most of my dinners are eaten with her family.

The last couple of weeks have put my mother in a foul mood. The way I see it, as long as my chores are done, grades are good, and my duties at the shop aren't neglected, Mother has no reason to complain. Besides, I have not said one word to Mother about publicly dating Mr. Billy, despite the rumors I hear at church about a possible affair prior to his divorce.

Waiting on the couch while mother cooks a romantic dinner for Mr. Billy, I get another text from Sarabeth. It's the fourth time I've blown her off for a night with Bren. A part of me misses hanging out with Sarabeth and catching up in the car ride before school. I want to spend time with her, but I also don't want to have to explain my sudden Bren fixation.

Hayride next Friday night. Don't say no, pleeeeease. You should invite Bren :D

I cringe at the fact that she has to beg and then bait me with an invitation for Bren to get me to consider hanging with her. I've seen the classic ditch-your-friends-for-the-new-relationship move, and I hope it doesn't look that obvious. We've been best friends since preschool. We haven't missed a church hayride since we were eleven. Of course the last two years I didn't see much of her on those hayrides because she and Andrew were occupying one of the dark corners of the wagon where all the couples make out. Third wheels tend to squeak a little less if they group together in the center. Not sure where Bren and I fit in that picture.

Sure. Count us in, I text back.

The doorbell rings. "My ride is here, Mother. I'll be home by midnight," I call into the kitchen, then open the front door. Bren wears a vintage Sex Pistols tee under a soft gray collared shirt, unbuttoned. Dark-washed couture jeans—that she did not buy within a hundred mile radius of our fashion dead zone—hug her long legs.

My eyes stop at her feet. Kelly green Chucks pop below her cuffed jeans. "Please do not tell me Van is doing your shoe shopping now."

"They're awesome. Look." She twists her foot around. On the outside reads "Long and Tall" in a custom rainbow stitch.

"You're ruined now. Next thing you know, you'll be critiquing Johnny D movies."

"We did analyze *Ed Wood* at lunch today."

"That's it. Give me your phone." I dive for her back pocket. "You're banned from seeing Van. I forbid it." Her long arms keep me at bay. We both squirm and laugh as I try to wrestle her phone from her.

"You two girls going out…alone tonight?" Mother's voice is stiff.

Out of instinct or self-preservation, I step away from Bren, signifying a more than appropriate distance for friends. Spending 24/7 with Bren is one thing, declaring it more than a friendship to my mother is another. I'm not there yet.

"Mother, this is Bren. My gir—good friend from school." My hands slip off my pocketless leggings, looking for shelter. Instead I twiddle a thread at the end of my shirt and bob on my heels.

"Hello, Ms. McCoy," Bren says. Mother's bitter smile keeps Bren from crossing the threshold to shake her hand.

Mother scans my attire. The wide-rimmed neck of my plum shirt hangs off my shoulder, and the urge to pull it back up overwhelms me. I tug it up tight to my neck.

"Um, actually we are picking up Van," Bren says, and smiles at me. "I think he said we were going to Lawrence? They have a fall carnival or something."

"Oh yeah. They're having an Okra Festival." I grab my phone off the entry table, mildly aware that the Bible has been turned to Leviticus. "Later, Mother." I skedaddle on out, and conscious of the front door being solid glass, I make no move to touch Bren. I'm relieved Bren doesn't open my door for me when we get in the car.

Bren waits until the end of my street before she grabs my hand and kisses my knuckles. "Missed you," she whispers against them.

"Missed you too." I lean over for my kiss. At the stop sign, she takes her free hand off the wheel, clasps it behind my neck, and pulls me in. Soft and easy lips push against mine, tickling the flutter in my stomach. The dizzy-spin feeling takes over my head again. Our lips separate with a quiet smack. Her hand lingers on my neck, her thumb strokes lightly against my pulse. The way she stares at my lips, it seems like she's debating another kiss.

"It's already past seven." I smile. "Van is going to make us pay if we're any later." I give Bren one more peck for good measure.

A few turns later, we pull into Van's drive. He's already halfway out the door. "Midnight," Van calls back to his mom. Mrs. Betty waves enthusiastically from the door. I wave back.

"Your momma is so sweet," I say to Van through Bren's open window.

"She's a peach. Let's go."

Bren slides out of the car to let Van into the backseat. He's sporting a new fedora and pristine white Converse high-tops. "Captain Jack" is airbrushed along the side.

"Okra Festival," I say. "Really, Van? If my memory serves me correctly they stopped allowing rides. It's just dunk tanks and cheesy carnival games run by toothless hobos. Maybe we should—"

Van pops his head between the seats. "Sorry to disappoint, but we are not going to the Okra Festival. We're going dancing."

"Dancing," Bren and I say at the same time. She is all Chipper Chipmunk. I snarl.

"I'm not going to Sonny Dee's." It's a bright and cheery teen club where anyone aged thirteen to nineteen can go. They don't even dim the lights. Mostly the pre-acne crowd goes over there, or the super holy. Sometimes they rock out to Christian techno. Ugh.

"No, sweetie." Van rests his hand on my shoulder. Bren backs out of the driveway. "Okra Festival is what I told goody-two-shoes Bren because we know she cannot tell a lie."

"That's not true," Bren protests.

"Pa-lease," Van says. "You couldn't even ditch sixth period on Friday, even when Mrs. Bellefleur gave you permission to take the Community Swap books back to the public library with Kaycee."

"It's true, babe. You're infected with honesty. It's an honorable trait but sucks when deceiving the parentals." I pat Bren's hand, teasingly. She shakes her head at our patronizing and smiles.

"Tonight, ladies, we're going to man up. We're headed over to Memphis…to Breakers. Turn left up here Bren, toward the interstate."

"We cannot go to Breakers." My nerves knot in my stomach. My hands turn clammy. Technically it's not a gay bar, but quite a few eccentric people go there and some gay people. I've heard they have three dance floors with a maze of seating areas full of dark corners. "You have to be eighteen to get in." I remind Van.

Van digs into his pocket for something. "Since you're the only jail-bait in the car…" He frees an ID from his wallet. "You will be Mindy Lovelace tonight, who is actually nineteen."

"Your skuzzy cousin from Hillville?" I snatch the license from him. "I look nothing like that heifer." I check out her picture. She has the same nondescript hair color as mine, but with a defined curl. Freckles dot her face, and braces tack her teeth. "I don't have braces *and* she'll be twenty next month. I cannot pass for almost twenty." I give the ID to Bren to check out.

"Yikes," she says.

"I'm not dressed for dancing." I say this even though I know I'm looking awfully cute in my galaxy print leggings, black wedge high-tops, and deep purple shirt with the neck so large it hangs off my shoulder.

Bren pecks a kiss on my exposed shoulder. "I'm liking it."

"Traitor."

"Kaycee, relax. They don't care about the people under 21. It's the drinking age IDs they scrutinize. Trust me, we're going to get in that place, and then we're going to dance our asses off." Van snaps and wiggles in his seat.

Bren squeezes my hand. "We'll let you go first. If they don't let the jailbait in, we'll leave."

"Exactly," says Van.

"Stop calling me jailbait, you dorks." I roll my eyes at the two of them, smiling.

Van parks his face center stage between us. "Dancing is way better than fried pickles at Lawrence's county fair. Don't you think, Bren?"

"Way." Bren kisses my knuckles again.

* * *

After an hour of Van spazzing out over Bren's satellite radio and pumping the speakers with his "Booty Shakers" playlist, I'm actually a little stoked to dance now too. We drive by the front of Breakers, doing a slow roll in Bren's black-on-black BMW. The long line to get in extends all the way to the corner. It's a grab-bag mix of giddy teens and fresh, young twenty-somethings. Various flavors of people of all different orientations pepper the crowd. And we're not talking chocolate, vanilla, and strawberry. More like Cotton Candy, Bubble Gum, and Rainbow Sherbet. There are all types of bizarrely dressed people. A few skanked-up girls smile at Bren as we pass in her BMW.

"I might have to knock some teeth out," I mumble, scanning the line.

"Simmer down, hot rod," Van says. Bren squeezes my hand.

"Oooo, Van, did you see that guy in the cowboy hat?" I nudge him. "He looked a little sweet on those guys he was talking to. You're way hotter than them."

"Mmm-hmm. But Arthur's meeting me here so Van is going to be a good boy," he says.

"Arthur, Arthur? Yay! I can't wait to meet him." The thought of meeting someone Van is attracted to piques my curiosity. I've never even considered what type of guy he'd be interested in or what he'd look like.

Bren pulls into the lot behind the building, parking her car in a lonely space at the very back. The nerves in my stomach have commenced their own dance party. As if waiting in this long line is not nerve-racking enough, Bren's hand is on the small of my back, which is quickly becoming a sweaty puddle. I know she's keeping it there to try to calm my nerves, but I wonder if others notice. There is a group of rebels-against-their-parents hetero couples in line, punked-out with bright-colored hair, face piercings, and edgy low-waist clothing. They lock lips like there's a kissing contest happening while we wait in line. There are a few tatted up girls who might be twins of Charlotte Wozniak with their sleeveless plaid button-ups, Dickie shorts, and chain wallets. There are guys in line standing shoulder to shoulder, way closer than two corn-fed boys from Sunshine would be.

Suddenly, I feel at home.

The bouncer hands me back my "Mindy" ID with a bored expression and waves me on in. Bren pays the twenty bucks per person for the two of us without flinching.

We emerge from the dark entry tunnel into a pulsing room of electronic beats and lights. Black lights give everything white in the club a phosphorus glow. Obscure graffiti images wrap around the curved bar and cover the walls. Apparel stickers cover the dance floor. Besides the patrons who cross it to reach the bar, the dance floor is empty.

"Arthur." Van lights up like a Christmas tree.

A studious guy with designer rimmed glasses, disheveled spikes atop his head, and Abercrombie chic clothes shyly nods to Van. As Van hugs him in greeting, I'm a mix of paranoia and excitement, happy to be here but hopeful that we don't run into anyone we know. Introductions are made. Arthur's voice lacks any kind of accent, southern or otherwise.

"So are you from Tennessee?" Bren notices too.

"Yes. From Lawrence." Arthur says in his crisp pronunciation.

"But you don't have an accent." I blurt out.

"Okay, we're keeping this real. Let's not embarrass Arthur with interrogations." Van laughs, nervous, and I give him a what-did-I-say look. "What do you want to drink?" he asks Arthur, not us. "Cherry Pepper?" Arthur nods, and it makes my heart go pitter-patter that Van knows his soda of choice.

"I'll go with. What do you want, Bren?" I realize I have no clue what she drinks besides water and Gatorade.

"No, babe. I'll get—" She moves to stand.

"Please, the cover was highway robbery to get us in here. I can handle a soda."

"Diet."

I make a disgusted face at Van. "Did she just say *diet*?" I ask it with as much love as I might have for a pair of sweaty socks. "I don't know if I can associate with her anymore." Van and I both shun her with our laughter as we walk off toward the bar.

"Arthur is eat 'em up cute," I comment to Van once we've moved away.

"I know. He's so controlled and methodical and articulate. And he says he doesn't have an accent because of all his musical training. He doesn't like to tell people he loves opera. It makes me gooey."

I stop dead in my tracks. "Did you just say 'gooey?'" There's a moment of doubt in Van's face that I wish I could snap a pic of. "Van, that is so freaking awesome." I hug him. He relaxes. We both look back toward our significant others. "They look like they're getting along." I lean up against the bar, contemplating what Bren and Arthur are all chatty about.

"They're actually laughing." Van feigns seriousness. "Look at the way Bren's gesturing. She better not be telling him about my Depp-loving side. Embarrassing."

But I'm not looking at them. I'm staring at my happy, lovesick

Van. The regret that I feel—and should have felt a long time ago—grounds me to the floor. "Why'd we hide this part of us?" I ask.

Van's posture softens, and he gives me his I-love-you-like-my-own smile.

"Us of all people," I say. "We're from the same mold. We share the same fears and religious guilt for who we are, but *we* never shared this between us. Why?"

He clasps his hands over mine. "Maybe it's because I never shared and you never admitted. Together we just sat in a bucket of silence."

"The echo was painful."

Van squeezes my hands and nods. "But our bucket runneth over now. And there isn't any going back." His sentiment is my motto. I smile. "And if you don't hurry and order our drinks, Arthur and Bren will fall in love, and you and I will be screwed."

I take the cash from Van. He goes back to the not-quite-wed couple, and I order our sodas.

"Nice tan you've got." A snaky finger grazes my bare shoulder. I slink out from under the touch. It's the guy with the cowboy hat that we saw outside. He stares me down.

Reflexively, I tuck my hair behind my ear, which signals to him I'm flirting, but I'm only reacting to my jolted nerves. "You have yourself a good time, you hear?" I say, turning my back to him, shutting off the conversation. I pay the bartender for the drinks, steadily ignoring the eyes piercing my back. I work to balance four drinks between my hands.

Cowboy Hat stands and scoots in closer. He's a smidge shorter than me. "Why don't you dance with me? Show me what you've got." Pungent beer breath assaults me, but I notice he doesn't have an over-twenty-one wristband.

My first impression, from when we drove by, was of his cute

dimples and stocky build. Up close, he's a stump—thick and low to the ground. He's hanging on to the desperate end of "not quite twenty-one," looking like he's been rode hard and put up wet.

I struggle to breathe and put on my best "I'm friendly but not interested" hat. "You know, I'm just here with some friends, trying to keep it laid back. I'm not big on dancing." I hold my breath.

"I've got it." Bren's assertive but smooth tone punches between us as she grabs two of the drinks. She smiles down at me, feigning ignorance of the waste of life behind her.

We walk back to Arthur and Van who have claimed a bar table in the middle, no stools. By now, bodies are streaming into the club more fluidly, and the dance floor is beginning to crowd. The DJ calls all the "single ladies" to the dance floor, playing the infamous song. Van drags Arthur out on the floor. They bust into a frighteningly accurate version of the video, minus the leotards and high heels. Bren and I burst out laughing. The thought of dancing with Bren makes me nervous. Old habits die hard, and I scan the room. Not that I actually expect to see anyone from Sunshine here among the deliciously bent.

The beat changes to a remix hip-hop song. Like bees on a honeycomb, bodies swarm to the dance floor and spill over into the seating areas.

I tip up on my toes into Bren's face, lips so close I'd kiss them if we were anywhere but here. "Want to dance?" I ask. She eases a hand onto my lower back and with a smooth stroll, she guides me to the dance floor.

The thickening crowd swallows us up. In the dark, bodies start to blend. One big melting pot sways to the beat of the music. In all the push and pull of people around us, it's hard to tell who's who and what's what. Some girls grind with girls, a show for their boyfriends. A few guy couples swing their hips together. No one gawks or points in horror at them, so I let my nerves calm down. Cowboy Hat squirms between two girls, thrusting with his Wranglers, only to get shoved to the side by the both of them.

Bren laughs at the spectacle and shakes her head. She slips me a hooded smile, luring me closer to her. I slide my arms around her neck and let my body speak my desires. The action drops her hands to my swaying hips, and she mirrors the motion.

She lowers herself around me and scoops me in closer, never missing a beat. Her lips are hot on my ear. "You're driving me crazy." Her words set off a frenzy in my body, lighting it on fire. It makes me wiggle against her more.

Thirst and exhaustion eventually win out, and we go back to our table that has long since been claimed by someone else.

"Let's go to the back," Arthur calls over the crowd. He guides us through a hallway that opens into a small lounge area.

My eyes adjust to the dimmer lighting. Blood red furnishings haunt the shadows, and faux candles flicker an eerie castle glow. The bartender—who I'm sure is wearing powder on his face and eyeliner— slaps four waters on the counter, per Arthur's request. We gulp them down without pausing for a breath.

"Hello. Get a room," Van says, nodding toward a groping couple in a dark corner. They come up for air and depart from the love seat, and we leap at the chance to sit. My legs drape across Bren's lap as we squeeze together in an oversized chair, while Van and Arthur take the small sofa.

Bren wraps one arm behind me and curls the other over my legs, tugging me more fully onto her lap. "I think he's found his equal," she says. She's totally right. "And I couldn't be happier with mine."

My eyes meet hers. I've never been so smitten with someone. The cool ease and certainty she emits is like the sugary scent of honeysuckle that lures the butterflies. I can't drink up enough of it. The dim light catches the glossy wet of her lips, calling me. The heat of her body underneath mine urges me forward. It's a quick, easy kiss, but it fuels a burning deep in my belly. A wildfire spreads to the rest of my body and tingles.

"Y'all want to dance some—" Van's voice drops off as he realizes what he's interrupted.

I pull away from Bren's lips, grateful that the lack of proper lighting hides my blush. "Yes, let's go dance." I jump off her lap, eager— even though that's the last thing I want to do right now.

They rise to their feet. Movement in the far corner catches my eye. The outline of a cowboy hat looms in the dark. It leans forward slightly, so the floor lights illuminate his face, creepy like a flashlight under the chin. His leering gaze causes me to shiver. He takes a swig of his beer, then makes an exaggerated show of snaking his tongue across his lips, licking the foam off. It flips my stomach sour. I'm not sure how long he has been watching us.

"You ready?" Bren tugs at my hand. Arthur and Van have already taken off through the side tunnel to the other dance floor.

"Yeah. Sure." I chipper my voice and find my smile. Bren cranes her neck to see around me, but I pull her through the archway, tight on Van's heels. *Please let the shadows gobble Cowboy Hat up again before she gets a peek.*

We dance some more. My eyes continue to scan the perimeter. Like the predator I suspect Cowboy Hat is, he slinks along the wall, working his way around for a better position to watch us.

"Let's dance in there." I point to the adjacent room with another more crowded dance floor and a DJ. I lead the party train over to the other room and bury us in the middle of a thriving mob on the dance floor. My sights are locked on the passageway we just traversed, expecting a black Stetson to meander through. Two songs later, I start to relax when no one remotely like Cowboy Hat follows behind.

Bren snaps her fingers above her head, snaking her hips from side to side. I let myself loosen up and mentally smack myself for letting paranoia eat me up. Cowboy Hat has probably rustled up a set of girls and is riding the pony with them right now.

"Top this, baby," Van yells at Bren, and he busts into his best dance routine. Arms flail and hips thrust as he does something between the Hustle and the Cabbage Patch. It's awful but hilarious. I have to back up to keep from getting knocked out by a flying fist. I'm laughing so hard, tears well up in my eyes. Bren's trying to contain herself, but she can't help but laugh too. Van waves his arm in her direction, as if he's passing the moves over. She accepts and pop-and-locks her own version, putting Van's absurd jive to shame.

At first I think the push from behind me is coming from another onlooker bumping into me—until the guy's arms lock around my waist and press me hard against his pumping pelvis. The tip of a black hat juts into my periphery. The musk of body odor offends my senses, and stubble scratches my cheek. I wriggle and writhe, trying to escape Cowboy Hat's grasp.

"That's it, sugar. Get on it." He grunts in my ear, and his sour beer breath nauseates my stomach.

"Let go." I try to pry his arms off me. In the middle of the struggle, he's managed to pull me away from the action happening on the dance floor, and I can barely see the top of Bren's head over the crowd.

"Don't worry about her. She don't have the equipment to give you a proper good time." He quickly replaces his hands the moment I pry one loose.

I search the faces bobbing around me, hoping to snag somebody's attention for help. No one seems to notice the bear hug this guy has on me or the panic in my eyes. My pulse breaks into double time. The best I can do is swivel in his arms and face him. More of that stench of beer slaps me in the face when I do.

"That's right, work on him," he says, pushing his boy-parts into my thigh. "You won't be the first carpet muncher I've had to set straight."

The fight in me throws up a fist. I clip the bottom of his chin. The chomp of his teeth snap his mouth shut. His hat flips off his head.

He steps back, holding his mouth. "You made me bite my tongue, you bitch." *Now* people turn their attention to us. He bends to pick up his hat.

Bren's lean build steps into the newfound space between Cowboy Hat and me. "Keep your *fucking* hands off her," Bren barks. I have never heard her cuss, much less imagined the f-word flying out of her mouth. Her arm blindly reaches back for me, and I latch on to it for dear life. As bold as her words may have been, her body shakes like a leaf. Granted she's a towering oak and he's a stump, but she's still a girl. Surely she's not going to fight him. I'm vaguely aware of Van and Arthur flanking my sides, huddling more than protecting.

Where the heck are the bouncers?

Cowboy Hat wipes the blood and spittle off his lip with an angry swipe. "Seems like the both of you need a little of *this* to straighten you right up." He grabs his groin and gives it a good shake. All eyes scrutinize Bren and me, as if they are just now putting two and two together. The music pulses around us, but no one is dancing.

"Excuse me?" I pop off, shoving past Bren. I stand face to face with the POS. Now that I'm out here, I'm not sure what I planned to say. Old survival instincts kick in and my mouth just dumps the first thought that comes to mind. "Are you hitting on my boyfriend?" I gesture to Bren.

Holy shit, I cannot believe I just said that. Bren's athletic build and short hair buy me some doubt but not much.

Cowboy Hat scrutinizes her for a quick second, shaking off his uncertainty. He looks like he's about to say something that will set everyone straight on just exactly who and what we are, but I cut him off before he can speak.

"Hey, just keep your Justin Bieber obsessions to yourself. Okay?" I thread my arm through Bren's and march us right past him, holding my breath the whole time.

What the hell was I thinking? I glance over to see a jaw-dropped Van and a stoic Bren. Oh man, this is not good.

Outside, as fresh as the night air might be, it's not enough to fill my suffocating lungs. My heart gallops the Kentucky Derby.

"Holy crap, Kaycee." Van wraps a congratulatory hug around me and jostles me with his enthusiasm. "You just called your girlfriend Justin Bieber." His body shakes with laughter.

Nervous laughter tumbles out of me. I squeeze Bren's hand. She forces a smile on her face but refuses to look me in the eye.

"You shocked the crap out of that redneck," Arthur says.

"I was sure she was going to rope you and me in there, and call us her bitches," Van says to Arthur. They both laugh, replaying the scene—especially what I said about Bren. They razz her for having a boyish smile, telling her she should drop basketball and try a career in pop music.

Adrenaline rushes through my body, making my hands shake. I watch Bren politely laugh, but she's not happy. My feet move forward, headed toward the parking lot, but I'm numb all the way to my toes. I'm not sure what came over me. Yeah, I hated the guy for his cruel words and hateful slurs, but honestly, I said those things because I didn't want to be called out for being a lesbian.

The reality of what I just did sinks in, and I know I've totally screwed up. I'm sick to my stomach knowing how bad I must have embarrassed her. Denied her.

We walk Arthur to his jeep, say our good-byes and nice-to-meet-you's. Bren and I leave them alone to say their own private good-bye. I lean against the hood of her car, happy the back of the lot is devoid of streetlights. She settles next to me, but not cuddle close like she normally is.

"I'm sorry," I say. "I didn't mean…it just came out of me."

Bren sighs and looks up at the stars. I can tell the way she bites her lips, she's chewing on her words. Her silence tortures me.

"Dang it. I've totally effed this up, haven't I? See, I told you I sucked at this." I use my shirt to blot under my eyes.

"Don't go and do that." Her arms wrap around me, and I bury my face in her chest. "This is not the end of the world. I just—please stop crying. You're killing me." She briskly rubs my back. "Hey." Bren tips my chin up and witnesses a tear drop. "No one's hurt. We're fine." She releases a resigned sigh.

"It could have gotten real ugly, Bren." I lay my head against her chest again. "And I chickened out and called you my boyfriend. I didn't even have the balls to defend what I am." Tears leak from my eyes like they're spigots.

"Please, babe. No more tears." Bren eases me off her, gripping my shoulders. Her stern brow pinches tight. "I just…I want to make sure you know what I am—I'm your girlfriend. I can't pretend to be some-thing else. I don't want to be something else. And I need to know you're not pretending I'm anything but your girlfriend. Okay?"

"Boys are disgusting," I say and get a small smile from her. "You are like smokin' hot. God, your hair, it's so freaking sexy." This gets me a bigger smile. "I swear, I know exactly what you are. I've thought *a lot* about what you are, trust me. Okay that sounded perverted. You know what I mean. Tonight, I was scared. That's all."

"I get it. You said what was necessary to keep you safe. That's all

I want. For you to be safe." She pulls me back in. Her arms squeeze around my head. "I don't know what I'd do if something happened to you. But I'm glad to know you can handle yourself, even if it means getting creative. Did you seriously clock him in the chin?"

I laugh against her chest. "Yes."

"Good girl." Her hand makes circles on my back. "I don't think you have any idea how much you mean to me, Kaycee."

The sound of my name from her lips makes my insides purr. I look up at her. The streetlamps from the back of the club barely light her face. I want to ask her just how much I mean to her.

She cups my cheeks. "You're so sweet and beautiful," she says, as if she's read my thoughts. My heart pounds in my throat. "You have an amazing spirit for life. I love how you see nature as cupid, dropping hints of heart shapes everywhere. You have this cute habit of bouncing on your heels when you're excited and rocking back and forth when you're nervous. You've got the sexiest little twang I've ever heard. I could listen to you talk for hours with that little accent of yours. I love how you draw out my name." She closes her eyes as if recalling the memory. She opens her eyes again and swallows. "There's nothing about you I don't love."

My heart skips a beat. Her last words echo in my head, tattooing themselves to my memory. It's how I feel and then some. That raging need that I've quieted for so many years has taken on a voice of its own. It screams, "Feed me." It's not enough to have her arms around me. I want to be closer, nearer, to crawl inside her skin and be one with her. Love her.

I don't want to go home and say our good-byes at the door, only to hold my breath until the next time I get to see her. This night—or the part where I'm here in her arms—I don't want it to end. Not yet.

"Sleep over?" The words whisper out of my lips. I'm not sure she's even heard me. Or worse, I'm worried she will deny me. She has so much trust with her parents; I can't imagine she'd ever break that confidence. The fact that I've asked her makes me regret the position I have put her in.

The silence kills me. I can see the wheels turning in Bren's head—how she's trying to figure out how to tell me *no* without crushing me. Just when I'm about to tell her I take it back and exclaim that it's a stupid idea…she bends and kisses me.

Her lips are firm and wet and just as hungry as mine. I feel her hand move down my side and stop dangerously low on my hip. Her thumb caresses the crook where my leg joins, and she squeezes. Like an invitation, I push my body up against hers, wanting more. She grips tighter in approval.

I'm not sure if she's agreeing to sleep over or distracting me. I don't care.

Bren pulls away, leaving me hanging in the air, openmouthed. She raises her thumb and gingerly grazes it back and forth over my lips. "My, my, what a sweet thing," she says.

Instantly, my body stands to attention.

"Of course I'll stay. How can I say no to you?" The knowingness and wickedness in her eyes reminds me she's been firmly in her shoes for some time. I've only recently put on my shoes, much less broken them in.

I haven't really played out the particulars for when we get to my house, or what I will say to my mother. She'll be asleep when we get home. In the morning, she'll probably freak and then—*Do not think about Mother right now*. What will Bren wear? What will I wear? Where in the heck will we sleep?

Bren's mouth is hot on mine again. Our tongues circle and prod, and it's all I can do to inhale her in. All the tedious details seem to fade away. My hands slide themselves into the sides of her open shirt, pulling her against me. Her hand creeps lower to more responsive places, and she presses herself right up against—

Bang! Bang! Bang! Van pounds the roof of the BMW, scaring the wits out of me. Bren doesn't even flinch.

Van comes around to our side. "Let's hit it, kids. Pumpkin time is in forty-five, and we've got an hour drive. Are you ready?"

"Yeah, Kaycee. Are you ready?" Bren grins. Her brows pop up twice, full of suggestion. My stomach flip-flops, a mix of anticipation and something that might resemble doubt, but I won't know for sure unless we decide to—yeah, not going there.

Chapter 15

What I'm *not* going to do is panic…or chicken out. I creep up the stairs to my mother's room and take in a deep breath. The attic air is stagnant. The low-ceiling loft takes up the entire space, but it spans the width of our house, making it the largest of the bedrooms. Red digits on her clock peep at me through the crack in her door, well past midnight.

I face the numbers away from her bed, just in case she wakes up enough to think about checking the time. "Mother." I nudge her.

"Hmmm," she says in a sleepy haze.

"I'm home."

She grunts an uh-huh back to me and snuggles into her pillow more.

"I'm having a friend sleep over. Is that cool?" I cross my fingers, hoping she's too out of it to put two and two together.

"What?" she asks, lifting her head off the pillow, bleary-eyed.

It takes me a second to gather my courage to ask again. "I said I'm having a friend sleep over. Is that cool?"

"Okay, honey. Lock the front door." She rolls over into her covers.

As I creep back down the stairs, I am very well aware of the fact that she has no idea what she's agreed to. Asleep or not, I will maintain my defense in the morning that she said it was okay.

Back in my room, Bren leans over my Civil War scrap metal collection, sifting through the findings. Her legs look ridiculously long—and off-the-charts sexy—in the gym shorts I gave her to sleep in.

"What? No snow angel in my sheets? I'm so offended," I say. It gets a chuckle out of her. I join her next to the box.

"These are awesome." She holds up a half-eroded uniform button. "Did you collect them all?"

"Mostly." I admire the button myself. "Some of them my nana gave me after my grandpa passed away."

"Sorry to hear it."

"It's okay. It was a long time ago, back when I was in eighth grade. We used to hit different farms near all the big Civil War battle grounds and search for metal with his detector. We'd come up with barbed wire and old soda cans, but every now and then we'd hit a treasure trove. The really good stuff we donated to the Shiloh museum." I pass her back the button. She nestles it among the other trinkets and gently closes the lid.

Every molecule in my body hums with awareness from her closeness. This is a two-bedroom house, no guest room. The not-as-big-as-you-think-it-is queen bed looms behind us. Bren will be sleeping inches away from me...in my bed. I clear my throat and grab a nightshirt and shorts. "I'm...just gonna change." I stumble as I back out of my room.

After I change in the hall bathroom, I brush my teeth twice, rinse with mouthwash, and tousle my declassified hair. It does nothing to change the wavy wildness of it.

In the mirror I look myself dead in the eyes.

"It's a sleepover. This means nothing," I say quietly to myself.

Or it can mean everything.

"Shut up. You only do what you want to do. Take it slow."

Or jump right in feet-first. That's fine too.

"Shut. Up."

"Kaycee?" Bren calls from the other side of the door.

Great, now she hears me talking to myself. I pull the door open. "Yeah," I say, trying to hush the voices in my head.

"Do you have an extra toothbrush?"

"Yep." I open the smaller cubby drawer and hand her one of the many dental office samples we have stocked. "It's adult size. Sorry, no Dora." I pucker my lips.

"Funny." She takes the brush as I slither past her.

In my room, I stare at my bed. Not ready to cozy up under the covers just yet, I lean against my dresser as if it's a casual, comfortable space on which to lounge. The edge of the furniture digs into my tailbone. I shift to the foot of my bed, sit on one corner, then move to the other. I'm not even sure which side of the bed I should take. I usually just hog the middle.

All my furniture crowds the tiny space. Walls shrink in around me. The collar of my T-shirt chokes my neck. Air refuses to fill my lungs.

"You okay?"

I leap to my feet, startled by Bren's voice. "I was just…trying to…" My hands go for my nonexistent back pockets—palms slip off my shorts, and I bounce on my heels. I rub my hands over my thighs and shift into a very relaxed pose of arms locked tightly across my chest.

"Yep. All good," I say.

A soft, knowing smile curls up the edges of Bren's mouth. Heat rips across my cheeks, tinting my face. She watches me bob up and down. Remembering what she said at the club, I force myself to still. It's like trying to stop an earthquake.

Bren pulls back the covers on the right side of the bed, and eases in with grace as if this is her bed, not mine. Long arms tuck behind her head, her large watch *chinks* loudly on her wrist. She removes the bulky piece of jewelry and lays it on the nightstand, returning her arms to the relaxed position. Her pearly whites gleam like a tiger's grin.

This is *nothing* like having Sarabeth stay the night.

I swallow. The lump in my throat gets stuck like a pill. How do I act when Sarabeth is here? Be casual…and don't just stand at the foot of the bed, bouncing on your heels and gawking at her like she's an apple pie. I stroll over to the other side of the bed. Bren's eyes trail me, and I trip on the nothing on the floor. A nervous chuckle escapes me—it sounds more like the grunting of an ape.

Once I'm under the covers, Bren faces me, leaning on her elbow. There's a heaviness to her eyes that makes my insides explode. Needs my body has never known awaken. The thrill of fear and excitement creeps around my neck and forces me to shiver.

"We don't have to do anything." Bren stretches a hand out and smoothes the wild waves of my hair behind my ear.

The thought of doing nothing is not what I had in mind either. A little sigh slips out of me.

"Or we can just…play it by ear." Her brown eyes gaze upon me, turning my skin hot.

"Yeah." I nod. Let's go with that.

Bren scoots closer, and I feel her legs touch mine, zinging electricity up the length of my body. She slips her hand under the covers and pulls me closer for a kiss. The scorching heat of her hand on my hip is a stark contrast to the coolness of the sheets. Our mouths melt into each other. Our tongues find a pleasing rhythm. I ease back, pulling her over me.

150

Every touch, every movement, every deep kiss thickens the air with want. Just when I think I can't breathe, her mouth trickles off mine. She goes to work kissing my neck, burning my skin with the touch of her mouth. The puff of her warm breath tingles my insides. She kisses my ear, drowning me in a haze of ocean and spice. Bren slides her hand to rest on the hollow of my belly, just under the edge of my shirt. My body purrs at the feel of her skin on such a sensitive area. Bren moans a reply against my neck. The tips of her fingers glide over my rib cage until her thumb grazes the bottom of my breast.

I freeze.

Her mouth returns to mine. I'm not sure if she's distracting me or if the closeness of where her hand rests is igniting her own building desire. Soft lips are replaced by an urgent, starving mouth. My mind begins to dissect what is first base versus third. How far is going too far with her? I am a virgin. I never wanted to have sex with a boy, for obvious reasons, but I'm not sure how far I'm willing to go here with Bren either. Technically, she is my first girlfriend. And at what point in what we're doing does it mean I'm no longer a virgin?

Her thumb lightly strokes back and forth, and the touch is oh so light, but glorious nonetheless. It's not that my body doesn't want this. No doubt it's the first time my body actually knows what it wants. It's nothing like the time Greg Nettle asked to touch my boob our freshman year, and after a good squeeze, he laughed all goofy and said, "Squishy."

Seriously, I'm thinking of the time Greg Nettle groped my boob while I'm macking down with Bren? God, help me. *Oh no. Don't think of God.* Don't need to think of Him while all this is happening.

Too late.

The flames that consume me feel a little more like the fires of hell. Whatever Bren has been kindling starts to fizzle and smolder out. I don't mean for the shutdown to occur, but this train is barreling down the track fast, and I'm not ready for the ride. The scenery is going by a bit too fast and it's blurring for me.

As if sensing my distance, Bren pulls away with a gasp. "Everything…okay?" she pants. Her leg rubs up against mine, soothing, wanting.

"I—" I'm not sure what to say. The last thing I want her to think is that I'm some kind of tease. When I invited her here, my mind was there, but now that we are actually here, well, I don't want to go there yet. Just because I've decided to accept myself being a lesbian, and I've opened up myself to her, doesn't mean I'm ready to give up everything.

Not that I won't ever explore this path again, but here, now, in the small space of my bed, it's just too real. I want to be in love. Be loved back…for a while, and not just in the thirty seconds after I think she's telling me she loves me in the parking lot of a nightclub.

Heck, I might even be in love with her, but if I have to guess and calculate whether or not I am in love, then I surely don't need to be chugging full steam ahead.

"I'm not ready." It comes out in a rush. I feel stupid for saying it out loud. Maybe it was only going to be a touchy-feely session. Maybe I was the only one whose mind was veering down that path of getting naked and doing everything.

Bren shakes her head and looks away from me.

"Don't hate me. I just…I mean, we've never talked about…you know—" I stall.

"Hate you? This is all my fault. I'm sorry." Bren runs her fingers through her hair and breathes an exasperated breath.

"Sorry?" I'm totally confused as to why she feels the need to apologize. Especially after I grinded against her on the dance floor, practically jumped her in the parking lot, and then invited her to stay the night. "I'm the one who should apologize."

She laughs at that. I'm not sure why it's so funny, but I muster up something like a laugh too.

She caresses a thumb over my lips, biting her own. "I shouldn't have pushed myself on you. I shouldn't have been so…aggressive, especially if you've never done something like this before."

My mouth feels cotton dry. "You've…done this before?" I blurt out before my brain can stop it. And we both know I'm not talking about kissing.

"Um." She shifts her glance away from me. "There have been girls."

The plural does not escape my notice. I feel like a total loser. I cover my face. Questions like *How many? Did you love them?* and *Did you like being with them more than me?* fly through my head.

Bren pulls my hands off my face. "Hey. Look at me. I'm crazy about you." She laces her fingers with mine. "More than crazy." Her eyes drink me in, saying what her lips don't.

A long space of silence fills the air, and I wait for her to say more. To say *it*.

After she chews on her lip a bit, she finally says, "How about you set the pace, and I will follow. If it happens, it happens."

"If it doesn't?" I scrunch up my face.

"Then—" Bren takes a breath. Her eyes focus on our clasped hands. "We'll take up bingo."

"Bingo." I laugh. "That's your solution?"

"Yep. Bingo." Bren's laughing at her own ridiculous suggestion. "I hear it's all the rage at the Sunshine Nursing Home." She settles back on the pillows and pulls me to her.

"Okay, bingo it is." I bury my face in her neck, grateful there's no pressure. Even more grateful that if I do decide to do this, it will be with someone like her.

* * *

The familiar creek of floorboards above my head penetrates my subconscious. I know this has a meaning, but the fog of sleep keeps it at bay. Where I am, I want to stay forever. It's peaceful and warm. It's not until I hear the shuffling steps of Mother's slipper feet in the kitchen that my eyes bolt open. I'm wrapped up in Bren's arms, snuggled in the crook of her neck. Our hands are laced together in a sweaty tangle.

"Oh, crap." I shove myself away from Bren as the handle on my door clicks open.

"Kaycee, time to get up. We are not going to be late for church—"

Awkwardness thickens the air and freezes my mother in the doorway. Bren and I are safely on opposite sides of the bed, but the hand-in-the-cookie-jar look of guilt is all over my face. Mother stumbles over her words about getting ready for church and closes the door in a rush.

"Oh shit," I say.

"I should go." Bren gets up to leave.

"Oh my God, I'm so sorry. *So* sorry." I say while scrambling around to get dressed, like I'm the one who needs to get out of here. Bren is all calm, cool, and collected like a cucumber. I pull my shirt over my head and turn around. There's a brief pause where I realize we've just changed clothes in the same room.

Bren breaks the moment, saying, "You're going to be okay, right?"

"Yeah. I think it's fine. We're cool." We are *so* not cool, but that's my bad, and I don't want it to scare Bren away. Dang it, I'm fairly certain my mother didn't see anything, but there was this total moment of what-the-heck-is-going-on-here look on her face. Maybe that was just her look of surprise because she forgot that in her deepest moment of sleep, she said yes to the sleepover. Something I will most definitely remind her of.

"Call me later, babe." Bren pulls me to her and pecks a quick kiss on my forehead. Our hug is just as clipped.

We manage to make it to the front door without a Mother sighting. As soon as I close the glass door and turn around, Mother's standing there, gripping her coffee mug something fierce. I'm all deer-in-the-headlights frozen still.

"You know my rules in this house. I expect you to ask for permission before you invite just anybody into my home."

I can't remember when the last time I actually had to *ask* for permission for Sarabeth to come over was, but now's not a good time to point that out. "Yes, ma'am. That's why I asked you last night when I got home. And you said it was fine." I weasel past her through the kitchen toward my bedroom. Out of the corner of my eye as I pass her, I can see the memory of me waking her up last night registering.

Mother follows me, tight on my heels. "How good of a friend is this Bren girl anyway? I really don't know her family all that well. I'm not sure I like you being buddy-buddy with her all of a sudden. Have you thought about how this might make Sarabeth feel?"

I swing around in my doorway so fast, it catches Mother off guard. "It's not 'all of a sudden.' And Sarabeth and I are still BFFs. No worries there." Even though I really don't know where we stand after the other night. I give Mother my brightest smile. She cracks her lips as if she's about to add something. "I've got to get ready for church. We don't want to be late." I shut the door in her face.

For the longest moment, I rest my forehead against the wooden door. Oh my God. Oh my God. Oh my God. What the *heck* have you gotten yourself into, Kaycee?

The memory of Bren's body next to mine flashes into my thoughts and makes me all warm and giggly. It's useless to fight it. I've gone and done it. I've fallen in love, and there ain't no going back.

155

Chapter 16

A blanket and a boyfriend—or girlfriend if that's the case—are the only two things you need on a hayride. I don't know what I was thinking when I agreed to come on this.

Orange wispy clouds slide thinly across the sky as the day ends. Bren and I wait in the church parking lot along with the entire youth group. Brother Mark, our youth pastor—who bounces around like a Jack Russell terrier—divides the youth into two groups: older and younger. Two parent chaperones round up the younger, rowdier bunch of kids. Hay fights ensue before the tractor even starts.

Mrs. Kitty, Brother Mark's new wife, clips across the parking lot in jeans and heels, ready to be our sole chaperone. God help her. She's all of five feet, maybe five-four with heels, and sweet as kittens. The newlywed couple saddle up on the tiny tractor seat, "trusting" us older, more responsible youth to conduct ourselves in a Godly manner.

Yeah, right.

"So we just ride around on this trailer of hay?" Bren asks. Her voice is full of puzzlement.

"Yep."

"I don't get it."

I smile. "Bren, honey, there's nothing to get. It's a just a good ole southern tradition. Just sit back, relax, and enjoy what autumn has to offer." I point over to a hundred-year-old oak tree full of orange and red leaves.

"Hey, guys." Chuck links arms with Bren and me as we climb onto the hay trailer. "No chaperones tonight," He whispers. He waggles his brows.

Sarabeth overhears. Her eyes swing back and forth between Bren and me as if she half expects us to confess something. Or it could just be my paranoia running loose again.

"Should be fun," I say with a shaky laugh. Twelve kids from high school ride in the trailer. All of them pair off into obvious couples except Bren and me. Even Chuck the Buck brought Kimi, a girl from the Methodist Church.

The churn of the tractor engine sputters and pops to life. I grab the railing as the tractor jerks forward, starting the long ride out to the pastor's farm where a Bible study, weenie roast, and s'mores await.

Hay bales line the wood-slat walls of the long trailer. Loose straw covers the floor. Standing on my tiptoes, my chin rests on top of the railing, and I can see houses creeping by. Bolls of cotton dot the roadside. The evening wind blows over my face. Bren stands next to me, her hair flapping and her mouth open wide with a huge smile.

"Once we get on the highway," I yell over the tractor's chugging engine, "you better close your trap, or you'll be picking bugs out of your teeth."

Bren clamps her mouth shut and leans back inside the trailer real quick like.

"Don't worry, I think I could overlook a few bugs," I say, bumping shoulders with her. I suppress the urge to smooth her windblown hair.

From behind, I catch Sarabeth observing us. After a moment she walks over. "You don't mind if I snag her for a sec, do you?" she asks Bren, as if she needs permission to borrow me.

"Not at all." Bren gives me a quick glance, checking to see if I'm okay talking with Sarabeth alone. I reassure her with a smile, even though inside I'm a bundle of nerves. Bren helps some of the other girls untangle and straighten the wire hangers for roasting.

Sarabeth and I should talk. Avoiding my best friend because I'm worried about what she knows or suspects isn't the answer.

"I'm glad you brought Bren. I can see you're *close* with her." There's a tightness to her words. I can't tell if it's jealousy or restraint. "It feels like forever since we've carpooled to school. You're, like, MIA at lunch, and we never catch up after school either."

"Yeah, I know." There's a whole lot of guilt eating me up for how distant I've been. I'm dying to have my BFF around and to tell her every giddy detail about Bren and me, but I'm not sure how she'd respond. Moments like now, I want to believe she loves me enough to accept me for me.

"Who am I supposed to subject my fashion prowess on if I don't have you around to torture? I tried with the M&M twins, but—ugh—they're beyond help," she says, nudging my knee.

I return the nudge. "I miss you too." I know exactly what she means. I miss her scatterbrained excitement, even at the cost of a wardrobe assassination. I didn't mean to get caught up with Bren like this, but I can't seem to get enough of her, no matter how much time I spend with her.

Bren looks up from bending hangers and smiles. I return her smile.

Sarabeth watches our exchange and frowns. "I'm just not sure if I've been replaced…or what." The "or what" lingers heavy in the air.

A long silent moment passes, as if I'm supposed to clarify one way or the other.

When I don't offer anything, she says, "I know it's not easy for you to talk to your momma about stuff. And you know I'm your best friend; you can tell me anything." She seems to hold her breath.

This is my moment. It feels like it's her way of telling me she's accepting me for what I am, that I can talk with her about it openly. That I can tell her I'm gay, and that Bren's my girlfriend. I could start small—tell her how close I feel toward Bren—and ease my way into the full-blown truth.

Here's my opportunity to take a chance with someone I trust and love, and risk…

Everything.

But I'm too chicken to admit anything. "Yeah. I know," is all I say.

Her mouth presses into a tight line. "The last thing I'd want is to lose you as a friend. I don't have to worry about that, do I?" Her brow pops up in question.

"All's good here." I attempt a smile and leave it at that.

* * *

At the pastor's farm, a white fence surrounds the property. The long driveway leads to a quaint farmhouse next to a well-used barn. Huge round bundles of hay stipple the open field. Crickets chirp in staccato with the bellowed calls of bullfrogs.

A circle forms around the bonfire; the younger kids are drawn to it like bugs to a porch light. The Bible study is short and sweet. No hellfires nip at my heels tonight. After hotdogs are eaten and marshmallows are burned, the chaperones allow the younger kids to play. Mason jars are passed out to the little ones to catch the lightning bugs. A few others play spotlight tag.

As the night grows darker and the chaperones less attentive, couples slip away into the dark. Bren and I are the only older kids still hanging around the bonfire. The temptation is too strong to resist.

I motion with a nod of my head for Bren to follow me. She silently does, her lips fighting the urge to smile. I can't help but feel like I'm luring her to my evil lair. Female giggles peal from the hay trailer as we walk past. Someone else taking advantage of the dark.

Just beyond the glow of the barn's floodlight, darkness drinks us in. Bren's warm hand glides over mine, and she pulls me along as she sees the giant hay bale I'm headed for. The second we are out of sight, her lips find mine with only the slightest bit of fumbling. She's warm and unhurried, taking her time with the kiss. I tip up on my toes, seeking more of her mouth, wanting to drag her down on me.

Tonight, being conscious of that appropriate distance for friends has been draining. About the only place I can relax and be Bren's girlfriend is at her house. Being here with her, under the stars with a fat country moon to hypnotize us, I can't imagine any other place I'd like to be.

"Spotlight on—" Sarabeth's voice cuts off. A ray of light centers on us.

A cold shot stops my heart, and I shove Bren away from me. The push is so quick, it's like a punch. Bren's broken expression pains me.

It's too late; Sarabeth has already gotten an eyeful. The flashlight tips lower in Sarabeth's hand. Her jaw hangs open. The numb expression on her face—it's as if she's seen a ghost.

"Sarabeth, we were just—" What? What can I say that would make her believe anything other than what she just saw?

"How could you?" Sarabeth's voice is small, incredulous. Her face contorts as if she's about to be sick.

Andrew rushes up behind Sarabeth and shines the flashlight on us too. "Who'd you catch—Oh…are y'all playing too?" he asks with a lopsided grin.

My heartbeat thuds in my throat, cutting off my oxygen, my words, my life. The pit of my stomach drops. I look to Bren, half expecting for her to brilliantly explain this all away, but she stands there, stoic. Pissed.

Sarabeth gawks in shock. I should say something. Explain myself.

Offer up an apology. Something. I ease closer to Sarabeth, and she begins to back away, as if I might infect her.

Andrew aims his flashlight at each one of us. "What kind of sick shit is going on over here?"

Sarabeth jerks her head toward Andrew and opens her mouth to speak.

"Don't—" I blurt out to her, my eyes pleading. "Please," I beg, for what, I'm not sure. Forgiveness. Understanding. Silence.

She just shakes her head in frustration and storms off. The way Andrew glares at me, I'm thinking he's pretty clued in on what's happening. Disgust radiates off him like a heater. Bren refuses to look me in the eye.

"Sarabeth, wait." I chase after her. But her angry steps have taken her almost to the barn. "Sarabeth, please. Talk to me." I have to jog to catch up with her. "Sarabeth." I bark a harsh whisper, trying to stop her before she joins the rest of the youth group by the campfire. When she doesn't slow or respond, I grab her by the elbow. "Please, talk to me. Let me explain."

She whips around, tearing free from my grasp. "Explain what?" Venom and spite lace her voice.

Her anger pushes me back a step.

"What are you thinking?" Sarabeth checks over her shoulder to see who's in earshot. Even though we are far enough away from the group not to be heard, she pushes me more behind the barn to keep us out of sight. She plants her hands on her hips. She lowers her voice. "How could you do this to me?"

"Do this to *you*?" I can't seem to grasp how on earth I could be causing her harm.

"I defended you, Kaycee. Everybody kept speculating these last couple of weeks, but I told them they were wrong. I put it out there several times for you to open up to me, but no, not one peep. I'm your best friend for God's sake, if anyone should know it should be me! Now you've made me look like an idiot. An idiot for believing I knew who you were better than them, while *everybody* else knew what you were."

I'm dumbfounded into silence.

"Bet you opened up to your buddy Van, didn't you?" she asks, the last words with a grave note of conviction. Betrayal sours her face. I want to make it all go away, to disappear, and yet I can't seem to find the words to speak.

"Was our friendship all a lie?" her voice cracks.

Every since we were little, we dreamed and schemed about our future. Houses built next door to each other. Daughters who were best friends just like us, inseparable. Except the farm I dream of doesn't exist in Sunshine, where people still think being gay is a "lifestyle." The children I want might not ever be accepted in this small-minded town. I've always dreamed of the happily ever after, but there has never been a man at the end of the aisle waiting for me. How was I supposed to tell her that?

"No. I just…it was never supposed to be like this. I never knew how to tell…" I stop. I want to reassure her it's me. It'll always be me in this skin no matter what I am. The words feel small, unimportant. Years of tradition and moral rules have been bred into the both of us. Nothing I can say or do can melt those years away. Even I can't let go of the fear of admitting what I am. Here and now, it stares me in the face and threatens to take away my best friend.

Sarabeth shakes her head. "No. No." Her head keeps shaking. "You can't do this. Not here. Not like this. I won't let you. This is a church hayride. Your mother, do you know what this is going to do to her?"

My heart skips a beat. "Please don't tell her, Sarabeth. She can't know. Not now. Not ever."

"You can't keep something like this from her. What if you get hurt? Or hurt yourself? People can be brutally cruel. Gay suicides are all over the news. Have you considered how this will affect your mother? Imagine her shame. The embarrassment. You're not thinking this through."

I surge forward and clasp Sarabeth's hands between mine. "Oh God. Please don't say anything. I swear it won't ever happen again. I…I promise. You can't tell my mother. I'll stay out of harm's way, and you won't need to say a word. Please tell me you won't gossip about this with anybody."

"Wow." She yanks away from my grasp. "I can't believe you'd think I—you know what? This isn't on me if it's out in the world. You should have thought about that before you decided to make out with a girl in front of God and everybody."

"I don't know what came over me. Bren was just there. It was nothing. She's nothing." I hate myself for saying it. For letting my fear of exposure overtake me. But I can't seem to stop myself. "It was nothing but me experimenting. I swear." I try to step closer to her, but she only backs away as if I'm diseased. Her lips pinch together, but her eyes scan over me, as if she's considering the validity of my words.

Sarabeth huffs. "Even now you're lying to me. And here I thought I knew my best friend." Sarabeth glances past my shoulder and scowls.

I know Bren's standing there without even looking, though I'm not sure how long it's been. I'm terrified to turn around and face her.

"You know what? Fine, might as well go ahead and label me an anti-gay bigot just like the majority of the people in this town. Because obviously, you think I'm too close-minded to be anything else," Sarabeth says, glancing at Bren one last time. Then she marches off to join the others.

Slowly I pivot around to face Bren. There's a sickening look of shock mixed with sadness on her face. Andrew walks up behind her. He glares at her, then at me as he passes, not saying a word. I'm not sure what Bren said to him. I peek back over my shoulder and wait until he's around the barn before I speak.

I'm horrified at what has come out of my mouth. Angry at myself for being a chicken. I'd do anything, *anything* to take it all back. Every single word. "Bren, I'm so—"

She raises her hand to silence me. She stares off to the side as if she can't stand the sight of me. "Nothing?" Her eyes are filled with so much hurt. "It was more than nothing to me. I thought it was for you too."

"I'm sorry, Bren. But I just, I didn't want..." I can't meet her eyes. Those eyes that had so much sparkle before now look upon me with so much hate. I shrink down to nothing. I feel lower than the scum on the bottom of my shoes.

"You know what, Kaycee? You were the last person I'd ever think to use me. I thought you were different. I thought you were better than that. Better than them. But really, you're just a coward." She spins around and stalks off.

I wrap my arms around myself and shiver. Silent tears stream down my face. I just want to curl into a ball and die. I hate that I let myself say those words. Even more, I hate myself. I can only imagine what Bren thinks of me. In one night, I have lost two of the most important people in my life. By morning, I will have probably lost my mother.

What have I done?

I should have never brought Bren.

I should have never come here tonight.

I should have never allowed myself to take it this far.

Chapter 17

"Are you going to puke in my car?" Van glances at me from the driver's seat, skeptical.

I feel sick but not from a virus. I sit up a little straighter. "No. I'm not sick. I'm just…nothing. Okay."

"Are you going to tell me what you and Bren fought about?" He keeps his eyes on the road.

"No." At the mention of her name I glance at my phone. No messages. No "I miss you" heart pics on Instagram. Nothing. Just like the hundred other times I checked the dang thing today. Not a single word since last night. "And no, for the fiftieth time, I don't want to talk about it."

"Suit yourself."

From my periphery I see him sneaking glances at me. Maybe I should tell him what happened, but the way I figure it, if I don't talk about it, then maybe it'll go away. Then I can wake up from this nightmare.

Sarabeth never outed me to my mother, or I wouldn't be going to a movie with Van tonight. It was supposed to be a double date. I didn't tell Van until he picked me up that Bren wasn't coming. Based on my cheery persona, it took him all of two seconds to determine she and I had had a fight. I debated whether or not I should stay home, but being in the same vicinity as Mother and Billy was borderline revolting.

"You know if you just called her—"

"Vander," I warn. I wanted to call her instead of texting her, but I couldn't find my voice or the words. I dismissed her like she was last week's trash. How do I even begin to apologize for something like that?

"I'm just saying. I don't know what happened, but I'm sure this can be worked out."

Doubtful. I think it's too late for that. It's too late for a lot of things.

I fiddle with the strands of my frayed jean shorts and stare out the window. Houses blur past. Van talks about the finished float, updates me on the latest Chelsea Hannigan gossip, and goes on about some Johnny Depp project. He doesn't get more than an uh-huh or oh from me. I don't have the will to muster up a full sentence.

When Van mentions we are going to the movie theater over in Lawrence, I'm grateful it's not in Mason, where we have a big chance of running into somebody from school. Nobody would drive an extra fifteen minutes to Lawrence's small rundown theater with Mason so close. I don't know if Sarabeth will gossip about me, and I have no idea what Andrew will say either. It's best to avoid everybody for as long as I can. Permanently, if possible.

* * *

At the Plaza, Vander hands me my ticket, and I have no clue what movie we're going to see. The theater is a hole in the wall compared to the multiplex over in Mason. Threadbare carpet covers the floor, large stains cover the pattern. Only two movies show at a time and there's no stadium seating. The third theater was gutted years ago with a huge opening cut into the cinder block as a doorway. They turned it into an arcade room. There has to be some kind of fire code against lining up a couple hundred-pound machines on an inclined floor like that.

Arthur bounces over when he sees us enter, adorable as always. His squeal of delight snags the attention of a few teenage couples, locals I'm sure. They observe us a bit longer than I feel comfortable with.

We share a couple clipped hugs, then Arthur asks, "Where's Bren?"

"Sick," Van says. I'm grateful for the little white lie. It's easier than having to explain something that I'm trying to will out of existence. Without skipping a beat, they break into a conversation, excluding me. I'm more than happy to be pushed to the side so I don't have to make small talk.

On the screen, buildings explode, cars chase, and guns kill. I peek at my phone several times, afraid I didn't feel it vibrate. No messages. Bren must have believed what I said to Sarabeth. She has to think I am a horrible monster to lead her on so. If she would just call me, then I could explain I said those things out of self-preservation and fear. I meant none of them.

But that isn't the point, is it? Whether I meant them or not, by saying those things I denied what I am. What she is. I've only fooled myself into thinking I've changed.

"Hey, try not to look so morose, will ya?" Van whispers to me after the movie.

"Sorry." I numbly follow them into the arcade.

Blinks and chinks echo in the room. The angle of the floor unbalances me with its fun house feeling. We pass a couple kissing in the corner. My first thought is I will probably never kiss Bren again. Obviously I stare too long because the lip-locked couple's friend, a guy with buzz cut hair and a cigarette tucked behind his ear, watches us walk to the back of the room. Even after we pass him, he makes a show of turning around and leaning up against a pinball machine to continue the stare-down.

Instead of tossing a few quarters down a machine, I sit cross-legged on a boxy wooden bench while Van and Arthur play a bowling video game.

"So, Bren's sick?" Arthur asks between one of his turns.

"Huh?" The mention of her name pulls me out of the fog. I munch on some popcorn I don't remember us buying.

"You look like you might be coming down with it too. What did you say she had?" Arthur takes an obvious step back, teasing.

"Just her sinuses." Van throws over his shoulder. "Nothing contagious." He waves off Arthur's concerns with the flip of a hand. Van gives me a get-your-shit-together glare.

"No, I'm not sick. I'm fine." *Fine as a popsicle in the desert.* I hop off my perch as if that proves I'm not sick. "Long night, that's all."

"He-llooo." A colorful voice calls from the other side of the room. The way Arthur jerks his head to attention, it's obvious he recognizes it.

That's not the only thing that's obvious.

The guy's pink polo with its turned-up collar, paired with his overly big wave from way across the room makes him look like a dancing flamingo. The sway in the guy's walk screams gay. I tuck into my shell and try to disappear. How can he just walk in here so openly gay? Doesn't he notice the questioning looks from the brooding Buzz Cut in the corner?

Another not-so-flamboyant friend trails behind.

Arthur snaps his head toward Van. "I didn't invite him here. I swear," he mumbles before the boys make it to us.

"Arthur," the flamingo boy says. There's a show of stiff hugs. "Who are your friends?" He eyes Van and me like pieces of candy— more Van than me.

Arthur introduces us all to Carlos—pink, loud, and proud—and John, soft and invisible. They're both from Culver, a neighboring town to Lawrence. They've known Arthur for a while. The way Van stands is so stiff it makes me wonder if there is history between Arthur and Carlos.

"Omigosh, I kill at bowling." Carlos scoots Van to the side and takes over the controls. He makes fun of Van's score, then spin-slaps the rolling ball with arrogance and nails a spare.

My protective instincts kick in, and I want to dropkick this pissant. But I don't have to take a step. It's Arthur who's all Johnny on the Spot. "I think it's cute he's letting me win." *Aww.* Arthur winks at Van. Carlos shrugs off the dismissal. John, who has not said two words, seems a bit shutdown. Van takes his turn again, with Arthur giving him pointers.

"You dating one of these bozos?" A heavily twanged voice mumbles over my shoulder. Stale cigarette smoke follows his words. The hair on my neck stands on end.

The boys are engaged in a bowlerama. But I know if I needed to claim Van's arm as my boyfriend, he'd follow suit and ad-lib if need be. Slowly, I incline my head to confirm it's Buzz Cut haunting my shoulder. "Um. We're all *just friends*." I hope the "just friends" covers any suspicions.

He makes a sucking noise as if he's clearing food from his teeth and gives me a satisfied cat grin. He pulls up a stool right next to me as if I've invited him closer.

"Um, who invited the trailer park?" Carlos murmurs, but I'm sure the guy hears.

"You got something to say, pansy?" Buzz Cut gets up off his stool. He bumps my shoulder in the process. Everybody but Carlos cowers back from this guy's obvious distaste. The fear grows inside of me. All I want to do is get out of here.

"I just call 'em like I see 'em." Carlos preens.

Van steps in, using his body to separate the two boys. "He's just talking shit. Just ignore him. No harm."

I widen my eyes at Van, hoping he gets that I'm asking him what the heck he thinks he's doing.

"You know what I don't like?" The guy cocks his head as if he's analyzing the lot of us—"People like *you* who think they own this fucking town."

At this point, the few people who are in the arcade crowd behind Buzz Cut. It's an army compared to the five gays. Where are the theater employees? And not the sixteen-year-old concessions stand boy who wouldn't be able to fight his way out of a wet paper bag.

"What I want to know," Buzz Cut looks to his cronies for backup, "is why faggots like you think they can prey on innocent little sweethearts like her." He tugs at the hem of my T-shirt, pulling me to his side, as if I'm some kind of victim in this massive homosexual scene. I shrink closer to the pinball machine.

"Don't touch her." Van steps forward—all big brother—and everything blurs.

Buzz Cut reaches to shove Van, and I strike forward to stave off the coming fight. When my hand lands on Buzz Cut's shoulder, it sets off a spring-loaded reflex, and his elbow flies back, accidently bashing me in the lip.

The impact is so fierce, my head snaps back. I flail my arms to catch myself, but the angle of the concrete floor throws me off balance. My body twists, tangling my feet together, and I fall, smacking the edge of a pinball machine with my face. Pinpoints of light burst in the black.

Even though I feel the weight of my body thud against the floor, the only pain my brain zeros in on is the pulsing at my eye socket and jaw.

My lids open and close with slow, heavy blinks. Blood tinges my taste buds, metallic and flat. Through my blurred vision, I watch the scuffle. The scene seems to double and split. I think it's Van who struggles to get past Buzz Cut, but I can't focus enough to tell for sure.

Loud Spanish curses fill the air. "Faggot," "your kind," and "wetback" retaliate back. I tell my body to roll over and get up, but it won't listen.

A deep, full-bodied voice thunders into the room and silences the bickering. I manage to lift my head, but it's Arthur who lifts me to my feet. I wobble a bit, and he pulls me against him.

"You're okay, Kaycee. Just lean on me." Arthur's smile is so soft, kind. Van is going head to head with Buzz Cut.

A potbellied man with a balding head jabs his finger in the air toward Van and Carlos. John is nowhere in sight. "You and your troublesome friends need to git your asses out of my theater. This ain't no homosexual social club. You take your gay crap to California where all them other liberal hippies live. Law or no law, you'll never be equal in my book. And you ought to be ashamed," the owner says, stabbing his finger over to me. "You all disgust me. It ain't normal, I tell ya. You gay people are destroying marriage and family values across the country. We don't tolerate that around here. Now git out before I call the sheriff."

Van says nothing and grabs the other side of me, and together we scurry out of there. I glance back over my shoulder. Carlos humphs. He kicks his chin up as high as he can and prances right though the hateful glares of the rednecks. He pauses just in the doorway as if he's about to mouth off one last thing—

"Carlos. Let's go," Van hollers back just as we push though the front door. He doesn't wait to see if Carlos obeys, but he does.

Outside in the parking lot, I pull away from my escorts. "I can walk." I ease off Arthur's shoulder and test my legs the last few feet to the car. "Am I bleeding?"

Both the boys look at me with grim faces. "No," Van says. "Well, a little from your lip, but that's all."

"Then why does it feel like the right side of my face has been through a few rounds?" I sit against Van's car. The cool metal kisses the back of my exposed legs. I'm half tempted to put my face on the car to sooth the swelling.

"You're going to have a shiner," Arthur says, grimacing. He presses his cold soda against my face. The pressure stings, but the coolness feels great. "There's a good sized bump too."

"Lovely." I glance back over my shoulder. "We need to leave before they do call the cops."

Across the lot, Carlos watches us a moment before he and John get in his Chrysler LeBaron.

"I'm sorry about Carlos. His mouth gets the best of him some-times." Arthur shrugs.

"You don't say," Van says, unenthusiastic.

"Look, I hope this doesn't make problems for us. He's just—"

"A pompous jerk who doesn't know when to keep his mouth shut," Van finishes for him. He tightens his fists. I can tell he's itching in his skin. Van hurriedly opens my door and helps me get in. "My best friend has a fat lip and a black eye, and it's that little shit's fault." Van points in the direction of Carlos's car—which is screeching its tires, racing out of the parking lot.

I sigh, exasperated. "Look, guys, Carlos mouthed off. I got a stray elbow to the face. The black eye was an unpleasant result, an accident. Van, don't let that Miami POS come between you and Arthur. Let's just get gone before those guys decide to come out here and make their point a little clearer. Say your good-byes and let's go."

Arthur looks like a wounded bird. It's obvious he's flogging himself good for something out of his control. "Okay." He tosses a low wave. "Later, guys." Moping, he gets in his car and leaves.

I can see the strain in Van's face. We take off right behind him.

*　*　*

Silence carries us for most of the drive home. I flip down the visor to check my mug in the mirror. There's a nice bump on my cheekbone. Light purplish-pink shades under my eye and around the outer edge. I hope it's just redness from being a fresh hit and will not turn into a bruise, but the throbbing says otherwise. My bottom lip bulges out into a ridiculous pout. A bloody crack splits the middle.

"Do you think we need to take you to the hospital? Get it checked out?" Van asks as I push the visor closed.

"No. I'll be fine. I didn't lose consciousness or throw up." Saw stars, but who wouldn't? Mixed emotions transform Van's face. I hate that he's blaming Arthur, or worse, himself, for some douche bag's actions. Heck, even the guy who did it didn't mean to put an elbow to my face—not that he apologized about it either. He probably figures it serves me right for running with the like. Wonder what he'd do to me if he knew I *was* the like. Maybe teach me a lesson like Cowboy Hat promised.

None of this would have happened if Bren was here. It hurts my heart just to think her name. She's so much smoother in these situations, diffusing things with her Bren-magic before anything even unfolds. I wish I could call her. See her. Let her long arms curl me in and just hold me.

I lean my head against the glass and close my eyes. From my memory, I recall her cool ocean scent. Let the waves of her calm me like the tide. A small tear trickles down my face and over my mouth. I lick my lips, tasting the salt and cracking open the cut. All I want to do is go home and crawl under my covers and *never* wake up again. This weight on my shoulders is too much to bear despite the good Lord's promise to never give us more than we can carry. Maybe this is his way of punishing me for being what I am. These little events are signs from God, telling me I've gone down the wrong path. In my head I hear the preacher booming his damnation. I wonder if it *is* me who has the scripture all wrong, interpreting it for my needs.

Van's hand on mine snaps me back to reality. "Maybe you should call her."

"No." I wipe the tears off my face. "Don't say anything to her. Don't tell her about tonight. No one has to know."

Because once again, just like I did last night and like I've done for all these years of denial, I think if I ignore it, it doesn't exist. That's what I have to do to survive this town.

Chapter 18

The alarm buzzes its irritating burr, pulling me from the peace of my subconscious. As I slowly waken, the cold hard truth and feeling of dread eases back in like a nightmare. The loss of Bren, the knowledge Sarabeth has, and the shame of my bruised face punches me in the gut.

"Honey, if you're still not feeling well, maybe you should stay home from school today." Mother comes into my room to turn off my alarm. The infinite silence makes all the other crap in my life pound louder.

Or maybe that's my face throbbing.

I keep the pillow over my head, for fear the makeup hiding my bruise has worn off. "I'm better. I've got a huge test today I don't want to miss." Which is a lie, but I hope the fear of failing squelches her nurturing instincts. Because, really, what kid wouldn't take the opportunity to miss school? Oh yeah, that would be me—the total loser who needs to see Bren even though the thought of facing my peers is horrifying. I just need to get a glimpse of her, if only from afar.

That's not pathetic in the slightest.

Faking sick did get me out of church yesterday, and it bought me an entire day curled up under the covers in the fetal position. Van tried to coax me out with his six hundred texts. Guess my I'm-fine-don't-worry text wasn't convincing enough. But I can't live the rest of my life hiding under the pillows. My plan, if I can survive a week of cover-up and foundation, is to make it past the worst part of this hideous bruise and move on to the next chapter of my life, living as a hermit or a nun. I haven't decided.

School will probably be safe to attend, as long as Sarabeth keeps quiet. The way I figure it, if Sarabeth hasn't ratted me out to my mom so far, then maybe she won't at all. And if she didn't tell my mother, then maybe she won't tell anyone. I have to believe that our years of friendship count for something.

Even though she's angry and feels like I've betrayed her.

I hear Mother shuffling around my room, picking up clothes and straightening things. Something she never does, so my guilt for faking sick yesterday lingers a bit heavier.

"Well, if you really feel like you have to go…" I can feel her staring down on me. She wants me to come out of hiding so she can see for herself that I'm well, but I can't let her see my face. I'm sure my botched makeup application has worn off on my pillowcase.

I clamp the pillows around my head and do a flip-roll to the other side of my bed, away from her. With my back to her, I pop out of bed and head straight to the bathroom. "See, I feel great," I say, a little too chipper.

In the mirror I see most of the concealer *has* worn off. The bluing bruise that darkened my skin yesterday has turned into a nasty purple-black nightmare. Concealer is not going to cut it today. At least the bump has gone down, mostly. The thickness of my lip is only slight, and the tiny bruise just underneath is nothing compared to the monstrosity around the outer edge of my eye. I open up the drawer of Merle Norman makeup products Mother always hassles me to wear.

✳ ✳ ✳

As I pull into the school parking lot, I scan it for Bren's BMW. I don't see it. She'd rather run the risk of tardiness than be forced to see me. Head down and tail tucked, I make my way into school. A group of kids watches me as I walk by. I can't tell if they're just observing me or gossiping about me.

Great. Paranoia strikes, and I'm not five seconds on campus.

I head straight for the bathroom to check my makeup one more time. A circus clown with a face full of foundation and blush stares back at me in the mirror. I scrunch and fluff my hair over the right side of my face. A single eyeball peers out through the veil of hair like some kind of mopey Goth girl.

A toilet flushes in the stall behind me, and I jump. The thrumming of my heart pulses at a ridiculous pace. I hold my breath, as if I expect the devil himself to appear. A slim girl I don't know steps out. She gives me a polite smile as she washes her hands in the sink. I breathe a sigh of relief. *Relax, Kaycee.*

Eventually, I will have to face Bren and Sarabeth—separately I hope.

After third period, I race over to the library to see if I can catch Bren coming out of study hall. I'm like a Peeping-freaking-Tom, skulking from behind one of the library shelves, hoping to catch a glimpse. After the last student leaves and no Bren, my heart aches. She's definitely avoiding me. Probably got a hall pass from Mr. Wallace to miss class for the gym, knowing I might try to find her. *Dang it.*

"Kaycee?"

I just about jump out of my skin at the sound of Mrs. Bellefleur's voice.

"Are you okay?"

"Um, I was just…" I talk with my head half turned away from her so she can't see my bad side, as if it's the most natural thing in the world to hold my head at this awkward angle. "Looking for Bren."

"Oh." Her brow deepens. There's a grave tone in her voice. "She wasn't here." She shakes her head. "I think she—"

"Later, Mrs. Bellefleur."

Down the hall past the librarian, I spy Sarabeth coming out of class, and I know I'm not ready to deal with her yet. I pivot on my heels and take off.

In lab, I hunker down in my seat and concentrate on the Bunsen burner in front of me. It takes all my energy to focus on the experiment. Burning down the school because I can't keep it together is not a good idea. But it's eating me up that I haven't even seen Bren yet. Usually I can spot her halfway down the hall from her height alone. The fact that she's going to such lengths to avoid me is really beginning to sting.

Two girls at the front of the class giggle, looking at me. One of them reminds me of a weasel—pointy nose and small chin. A sweet, woody scent singes the air. Behind me Pyro Boy sets fire to his pencil. The two girls exchange glances and then whisper some more. Are they talking about me or Fire Boy?

"Stare much?" Pyro glares. I swivel back around. Weasel Girl laughs and blatantly cups her hand over her friend's ear while scouring me with her eyes.

I am in a living hell.

Throughout the next class, I decide I will hunt Bren down and force her to listen to my apology with the promise to never bother her again. It's for the best, for both of us. We only have until next May to suffer through school together, then both of us will be off to college; me at community college and Bren hundreds of miles away at some big-time college, playing basketball.

There was never a future for us anyway.

"Can I help you, Kaycee?" asks the drama teacher.

"Nope, just looking for a friend." I scurry out of the theater, disheartened. Not that I actually expected to find Bren behind the stage, eating her lunch, but I hoped. I check the lunchroom, gymnasium, and the unofficial smoking section by the bus drop-off and pick-up side of the school.

What the heck? I'm beginning to think she ditched school altogether. That's when I realize, I need to check the parking lot and make sure her car is here. My feet pick up the pace as I walk to the other side of the school. Does Bren think Sarabeth will talk? She doesn't know Sarabeth like I do. Sarabeth reacted, but she's not the vindictive type, and she would never run her mouth. I know this.

I. Know. This.

Here I am running all over school, waiting for the chance to apologize in person, and if Bren's not here—Bren wouldn't do that to me, would she? Leave me to deal with the gossip, the whispers, and the judgments? Just abandon me?

Glass windows line the office wall just before the front door. I smile at Mrs. Young, the secretary, as I walk by. Off campus eating is not allowed. If she tries to stop me, I'll tell her I'm getting my English book out of the car. My phone beeps. A quick glance and I see it's Van again. I ignore him and keep heading to the parking lot. The front metal doors swing open. From the drop-off circle drive, I can see most of the parking lot, especially the last row where her car is usually parked. My heart drops. Just to be sure, I walk the rows of cars. My knees feel a little weak as I shuffle back inside. Maybe it's because I haven't eaten breakfast or lunch, but suddenly I feel like throwing up. Tears threaten. I clench my teeth.

Mrs. Young, no longer at her desk, tarries in the hallway, waiting for me.

"I was just—" I realize I don't have a book in my hands to claim for an excuse. "I thought I left my English book in my car. Guess it's at home." I try to creep past her.

She lays a soft hand on my shoulder and stops me. "Are you okay, sweetie?"

My lip trembles, but I'm able to pull my mouth into a smile. "Yes, ma'am. I'm fine."

"You know if you need to talk to the guidance counselor, she's always available."

Guidance counselor? Panic ices my veins. Instinctively I pull my bangs over the right side of my face and hide behind them. "Um, okay...I'm good." I duck my head and rush double-time to the bathroom to check my makeup. Normally I don't wear this much. I didn't even think to bring it with me to school to reapply.

The bathroom door slams against the concrete wall as I burst through. Some girl at the sink startles. I don't even try to make apologies. From the glimpse I get of myself in the mirror, I think my makeup looks to be intact. I dart into the handicapped stall to hide until she finishes.

Lunch must be near-over because a few more girls come and go, then a few more. I'll wait until after the bell if I have to. I shouldn't be here. I could skip. Go home and tell Mother that after my "test" I couldn't hold on any longer.

Yeah, because I really do feel like I'm about to fall apart.

Through the crack, I watch the last girl exit. The volume of voices from the nearby cafeteria increases as she opens the door. A burst of giggles explodes into the bathroom.

"She looks ridiculous," says a girl shuffling in.

I'd know that condescending voice anywhere. It's Chelsea Hannigan. I peek through the stall-crack and catch a glimpse of Chelsea, Misty, and two other girls. One of them is Weasel Girl from my lab class.

"All that makeup. What do you think happened to her?" asks Misty.

"I know what happened to her. One of the guys from the football team told me she got caught making out with that Bren Dawson chick," says Chelsea.

Oh my god, people know. A clammy sweat breaks out all over my body. I huddle at the back of the stall against the cold slab wall. It doesn't do much to sooth my churning stomach.

"Kaycee is a lesbian?" somebody asks.

"You have biology with her, Lindsey. How did you not know?" Chelsea accuses. "You can't go around Sunshine, flaunting your gayness on a church hayride and shoving your immorality in people's faces and expect them to take it. It looks like somebody tried to teach her a lesson."

"That's horrible. I can't believe people would attack her," says Misty. "I mean, no matter what she is, you can't hurt people like that."

"Are you a lesbo or something too?" Chelsea asks Misty. "Serves her right for going around and dyking out with that Bren girl. Next thing you know, they'll be ruining our homecoming dance with a gay couple's petition or some crap. They're popular; it *could* happen."

"Oh no. We can't go to homecoming with a pack of lesbians forced in our faces. They just can't come in here and treat us like this. It ain't right," says Weasel Girl.

"Didn't you go out with *that* Bren girl once, Chelsea?" asks Misty.

"I didn't go out with her like *that*," Chelsea says. "I thought we were just going to play basketball after school as *friends*, and she practically attacked me." More of the gasping.

That lying little skank.

"Let me borrow your lip gloss, Lindsey." It's silent for a moment, until Chelsea speaks again. "Maybe I should go to the guidance counselor and tell her what happened." She presses and puckers her lips in the mirror. "You know, I'm a victim here." She snivels.

Through the slight opening, I can see one of the girls rubbing Chelsea's arm tenderly. They crowd around her all supportive. Bren would *never* do that to anyone. It takes everything I have in me not to rip open this stall door and beat Chelsea to a bloody pulp.

My phone beeps with a text message. All three girls snap their heads in my direction. Chelsea spies me through the crack. "How pathetic."

My skin goes cold, and I can't hold the bile in my stomach any longer. I crouch over the toilet and let everything go. Between my gagging, I hear them whispering to each other.

"Is that her?"

"I think she heard us."

"Who gives a shit?"

"Should we get the nurse?"

Next period bell rings, pushing them out of the bathroom.

"She's probably bulimic," are the last words I hear before the door shuts behind them.

Lies. How could Chelsea—who I'm pretty sure is bisexual— say those horrible things? About me. About Bren. Bren has never, could never.

A string of spit hangs from my mouth. I dry heave and cough. I scrunch down next to the toilet and rest my head on my knees. As the queasy subsides, my anger catches hold and starts to boil over. Another beep from my phone. In the cramped space, I manage to dig it out of my pocket. There are three texts from Van.

Where r u?

Been looking 4u all day. Word is out.

The most recent one: R u in the bathroom?

Beep. I know you're in there.

Beep. If you don't come out I'm coming in.

Beep. I mean it.

The bathroom door creaks open. "Kaycee?" Van's voice echoes from the doorway. From the lack of sound outside, I gather most students have hustled to their next class.

"Go away." I tear an angry strip of toilet paper off to blow my nose. I use another to wipe my mouth. Makeup smears onto the tissue. What's the point of hiding under all this muck if people know what lies underneath?

I flush the toilet and jump to my feet, bursting out of the stall. Van hovers in the doorway, half in and half out, with his foot propping it open.

"Well…I guess the cat's out of the bag." He gives me a lopsided smile, shrugging his shoulders.

I scowl at him. "Is this funny to you?" I ask, then turn to the mirror. Red puffy eyes take in the disaster that is my face. Tear tracks streak down my cheeks, revealing my bruised cheek.

"Geesh. No sense freaking out. Everything is going to be okay."

"Really, Van? Does this look okay?" With a bitter wave of my hand I air a gesture to the black and blue around my eye. The late bell rings, but I don't care. I look around for more than toilet paper. Coarse paper towels with rancid school soap will have to do. I soak a wad of brown paper and scrub.

"Don't yell at me. I wasn't the one who got caught making out on a church hayride. It's out now. Just own it."

"Own it? Why of course, why didn't I think of that? Easy for you to say with perfect parents who love you no matter what." I return to the task of removing this god-awful mask. "News flash. Not everybody gets to be special like *Vander*. My mother isn't going to paint some stupid rainbow to support me. No, I'll probably be on lockdown until I graduate. That is, if she doesn't send me away to my shit-for-nothing father." I should've never let myself be free. With each dab and flash of pain, I tell myself never again.

"Sitting in this bathroom crying isn't going to make things better. At least I'm not the one who's ashamed, confirming to all these bigots they're right to judge me," Van says in a harsh whisper.

"Let me ask you something. What makes you such an expert at being out in the open?"

He crosses his arms over his chest. "I never said I was an expert. But at least I don't hide," he says weakly.

"Bullshit!" My voice booms and echoes off the bathroom walls. I couldn't care less about keeping my volume down. "You do hide. You've never tried to date anybody from Sunshine. And we both know there are other gays who go to this school. No, you sneak over to Lawrence or Midland and hang with your secret gay crew there. So don't stand there and act like you don't hide being gay."

"Keep your voice down." He steps farther into the bathroom, letting the door shut quietly behind him. "You have no idea the kinds of things I've had to deal with at this school for being gay," he says through gritted teeth.

"You're right. I have no idea what you've been through because you've never freaking talked to me about it. All you do is hide in plain sight. You stay safely within the imaginary lines *they* draw for you. As long as you don't flaunt your gayness around here, they leave you alone. It's like instituting your own personal 'don't ask, don't tell' policy. It doesn't get more hypocritical than that." I chuck the soiled towels into the sink with a fleshy thwarp. "Did you ever think you could have paved the road for others? For me?"

"What the hell would it have mattered if I'd paved a road anyway? You wouldn't have taken it. You know what, why don't you go back to making out with guys? You're better at that. Less freaking drama."

"Screw you and your drama," I spit. I brush past him, yanking open the door. Just before I exit, I turn back to him. "You think you're safe because all the attention is on me. Next time they need a gay target, you'll be it." I stalk off and let the door clap shut behind me.

At least fifteen people stand outside the bathroom, staring in silence and awe. They all get a gander at my face too. Chelsea's lips curl up into a smooth pursed smile of satisfaction. Shock and disgust ooze from the rest of the audience who overheard everything. You know what? I don't feel one ounce of guilt for confirming to the world that Van is gay. No sense in me going through this hell alone.

Sarabeth shoves through the crowd and rushes up to me, her eyes wildly scanning my face. "Omigod, Kaycee. What the hell happened to you?"

"Oh, now you're concerned for me? What the hell happened to you Friday night, huh?" Everybody's getting an earful, and I don't care. I lean into her face, so my words are clear and cut her like they did me. "What word did you use Friday night? Oh yeah, 'embarrassment.' Well don't fret yourself over an *embarrassment* like me."

"What's happening out here?" Mrs. Young stands with her hands on her hips, eyeing the students who lingered past the bell. It scatters them like roaches in the light. I follow suit, but instead of going to class, I leave school.

I drive straight for the interstate, wanting to put as much distance between me and all those judging eyes as possible. My phone lights up with text messages. But I have nothing to say to anyone so I switch it to vibrate.

Before the end of the day, everyone at school will know. The thought sours my stomach so badly, I have to pull over at the truck stop to throw up again. Tears and spit mix on the ground, and I use the back of my hand to wipe my mouth. I roll down my window to get some fresh air on my clammy face.

My phone vibrates every three seconds, rattling the change at the bottom of the cup holder. Half the text messages are from Sarabeth, wanting to know where I am and if I'm okay, pleading with me to just text her back that I'm all right. Nothing from Van. Freaking figures. There's even a text from Dave Bradford, apologizing for making me turn gay. He's such an effing idiot. I toss my phone back into the cup holder. Gravel spits a cloud of dust behind me as I speed out of the truck stop and back onto the freeway.

Each vibrating jiggle of the coins feels like a shake to my shoulders, reminding me of the gravity of what's happening to my life. The shit storm that is about to come. What if the teachers are looking for me? What happens when they find out? What happens when my mother finds out? Oh my God, the whole world is going to know, and there's nothing I can do to stop this spark of information from burning up my entire life.

Snippets of Chelsea's and Sarabeth's and everybody else's hateful words nip at my thoughts until I can no longer drown them out with the radio. And that goddamn vibrating is driving me insane.

I snatch the phone out of the cup holder. "Leave me the fuck alone!" I scream at it. Before I can stop myself, I fling it out the window. In the side mirror, I see myself grinning wildly as I watch it smash into the ground, bouncing several times. Pieces fly off with each hit until it skids to a stop. The wheels of an eighteen-wheeler grind it to bits.

I sit back, relaxing in the silence and calm. I exhale a satisfied breath.

The only thing on my mind now, is how far I can get from Sunshine.

Chapter 19

One hundred and sixty miles south of Sunshine in Grenada, Mississippi, is as far as I can get. My dreams of escape rest on little more than a quarter tank of gas and six bucks. I'm at the point of no return.

Sitting in the Sonic drive-in, my head rests on the steering wheel. I have to decide if I'm going to grab a Frito Chili Pie to shut up my grumbling stomach and then live a life of prostitution in this one-horse town, or buy more gas that will take me back to Sunshine.

"Sunshine…ha." I laugh to myself. The name of the town is an oxymoron. There is *nothing* sunny about going home. I don't want to go back. Back to the hate and loathing…the loneliness.

Nothing waits for me there but an empty pathetic life as an outcast. I don't want to be one of Charlotte Wozniak's bitches.

I stare at the six dollars and change in my console. Now I'm seriously regretting the fact that I threw my phone out the window. It was so satisfying to see it skid down the interstate.

Not so satisfying now.

But I didn't want to talk to Sarabeth. Van sure as heck wasn't calling. I couldn't care less what any of them had to say now. And Bren,

I've given up on ever hearing back from her again. Not even so much as an email from her.

A tapping on my window lifts my head. "Hon, do you need anything?" A girl with a blue and red shirt waits with an empty food tray propped between her arm and hip.

"I'm still trying to decide what to order," I say, even though I know I've been here for an hour now.

Horror bugs her eyes out. "Are you okay?"

The freaking black eye from hell just keeps becoming an issue. "Yes. I swear. I had a run in with a pinball machine days ago. I'm good." She narrows her eyes at me, trying to decide what to make of my answer. After a moment, she goes inside, choosing to overlook me.

Wrong. Inside she has a word with her manager. He tips back on his heels, jutting his chin out to get a look-see.

"Ugh." Why can't everyone just leave me alone. I start the Civic, back out of the space, and leave.

* * *

Six bucks in the tank and a grumbling stomach later, I'm back on the highway, returning from whence I came. It feels suspiciously like defeat. Since I doubt Grenada, Mississippi, would be a successful option for my prostitution ring, I have no other choice but to go home. The only other option I have lies in Texas with a perfect family of four, where a daughter from a life long-forgotten does not fit into their world.

Especially a gay daughter.

It's a small glimmer of hope that, on the drive back home, I'll be able to fabricate a solid enough lie to explain my bruised face to my mother. And that by some tiny miracle, she'll buy it. If I can keep it together until I graduate high school, I'll get a job in Lawrence. Eventually I'll save up enough to leave, forever.

This is my plan. This is what I have to believe in to justify why I'm going back to where I don't want to be. Ten months of keeping my head low and blending in to the background. I can do it.

A few hours later, the "Sunshine, Tennessee. A good place to be," sign mocks me as I drive past the city limits. Dread and unease squeezes my heart when I turn onto our cul-de-sac. An older sedan is parked in the driveway with a "Jesus is my co-pilot" bumper sticker. The car looks familiar to me, but right now I can't quite place who owns it. I park in the street out front.

It's past six o'clock. I don't recall Mother mentioning that we were having company over for dinner. Even though my feet say "Don't do it," I tread up the steps and hold my breath as I open the door.

"Brother Mark?"

Our youth pastor sits on the sofa and smiles at me, earnestly.

"I didn't realize you were coming to dinner," I say. I drop my keys on the entrance table. He holds a glass of iced tea in one hand and his Bible in the other. I glance around the room for more surprises. The clack, clack, clack of heels taps across the kitchen floor and Brother Mark's wife, Mrs. Kitty, steps out. Her red nail-polished fingers cover her gaping mouth.

My black eye! I tug and scrunch my jungle of hair over it. Mother rushes out of the kitchen right behind Mrs. Kitty, almost knocking her over. The phone is pressed tight to her ear.

Has she been crying? I know I didn't tell her where I was going, but it's only dinnertime. It's not like I've been gone that long. *Shit.* I bet the school called her and told her I skipped. She probably tried to call my cell, couldn't get a hold of me, and panicked.

Mother gasps too. "Oh God. It's bad. It's bad," she says to the person on the other end and darts back into the kitchen. Her voice breaks into sobs. "Okay. See you in a few," are her last cracked words before she says good-bye, and the phone beeps off.

Brother Mark rises to his feet, and his wife huddles against him. Mother returns with a tissue in her hands, wiping her face.

I'm frozen in the doorway, unable to step inside my own home out of sheer fear. "My cell phone broke," I say, barely able to find my voice. But not being able to get a hold of me isn't their issue. Something more than a worried mother is going on here. Awkward silence holds us all in standoff positions. The only sounds are the soft sniffles of my mother and the monstrous thundering of my heart.

Brother Mark puffs his chest out and takes a deep breath. "Let's start this off with a prayer." He rests his Bible against his heart and bows his head. Mrs. Kitty nods to me, as if encouraging me to bow my head too. It's the look of pity she gives me that frightens me most. Like I've just been told someone I love has died, and now I'm the fragile flower who needs to be carefully tended to or I might wither away.

I bow my head and tell myself we are praying for the meal we are about to receive.

"Dear Heavenly Father. Tonight, give us the strength—"

The click-rattle of the front door opening clips his words. "Oh, thank God you're okay." Sarabeth steps in with a hand over her heart. She hugs me, but I stand there stiff as a statue.

"What's going on?" I ask Sarabeth, nobody else.

"Honey, why don't you just sit? So we call all talk," says Mrs. Kitty.

I stare down at Sarabeth. She shrinks back. "What. Is. Going. On?" I demand from her.

Her bottom lip quivers, and she starts shaking her head. "I was scared. When I saw what they did to your face and then you disappeared...well I thought maybe you'd done like that boy over near Mason. I wasn't sure if you had hurt yourself. I had to tell your mom."

Every cell in my body goes numb. The icy threat of anyone finding out I'm a lesbian—most especially my mother—is now out in the open. It's no longer my secret. My heartbeat thrums so loudly my blood pressure blocks my eardrums. The entire room begins to spin. Sarabeth is talking to me, spilling apologies, crying, and begging for me to listen to them. I'm vaguely aware of Mrs. Kitty guiding me to the sofa. Even from there, the room doesn't stop moving.

Mrs. Kitty sits on one side, Sarabeth on the other. Brother Mark uses our sturdy oak coffee table as a chair. On instinct, I want to tell him coffee tables are not for sitting, or at least Mother should say something. Sarabeth holds my hand between hers. Her lips move, but I don't know what she's saying. The words sound rote and rehearsed. Red splotches stain her pale face. Perfect blond hair bounces when she talks. She only lets go of my hand to wipe her tears. I can feel the wetness against my skin as she re-clasps my hand.

Mother stands just inside the room by the kitchen door. A frail, thin smile trembles on her lips. Why doesn't she come closer?

"And then you'll be fixed and everything will go back to normal," Sarabeth says. I turn back to her. "Won't that be perfect?" She smiles, but it doesn't reach her eyes.

"You want me to go to a gay camp?" My brain picked up more of the conversation than I realized. I don't know if I could survive a death sentence like that. Surely Mother wouldn't send me away, like a trip to the repairman is going to make it all better. My chest tightens.

"It's more of an evangelical homeschool. Straight Path With God is a wonderful program," says Brother Mark. "The good Lord didn't intend for you to get all mixed up." He smiles, like a father would to his daughter, or so I imagine. "It's held year-round up near Frankfurt. You can attend for as long as it takes. Probably best to stay until you graduate. Don't worry about your schoolwork, they teach the same curriculum there that they do here, but you'll be homeschooled. The family you will stay with is real nice. You'll spend your days in scripture and your evenings in prayer." He beams as if he's just handed me the greatest gift of my life.

"They have an opening starting at the beginning of November." Mrs. Kitty tucks a springy hair behind my ear. "You'll be able to come back for Thanksgiving. You can even take some of your pretty things from home to keep you company."

I'm shocked that in the span of a few hours, my entire future has been planned out for me. It happened so quickly...but it couldn't have been planned so quickly. This really shouldn't be a surprise. Mother has not been as naive as I thought. In the back of her mind, she must have always had a plan that if this gay thing ever reared its ugly head, she'd squish it quick. But when I turn to my mother, she seems trapped by the doorway, nibbling on her thumbnail.

"I don't want to go away. Don't make me go," I plead. The small flower that was growing inside of me begins to wither and die.

Mother bursts into tears and refuses to look at me.

"Look at me, Mother. Tell me you honestly believe this is the right thing for me."

She stays silent.

Brother Mark and his wife break into their spiel about how this is what's best for me, for everyone. A good session with God can straighten me out.

"Sometimes outside influences sneak into our small town. Demons come in all forms," Brother Mark explains. "And young folk like yourself get wild ideas about things." Young folk? He can't be more than twenty-five himself, but he's talking like he's fifty. "Next thing you know, the whole town is run amuck. Like a plague carried by the rats." He opens his Bible. "But we can root it out." He winks.

"Root it out!" Mrs. Kitty shakes an amen-fist in the air.

"Let's pray." He starts up with rebuking the devil, praying for a cleansing. His wife repeats some key phrases Brother Mark speaks. I look over at Sarabeth with her head bowed. She senses me glaring at her; I know she does.

"Why did you do it?" My voice is barely a whisper. "How could you?" She turns her bowed head away from me and squeezes her eyes shut, tightening her hold on my hand. I rip it from her grasp. I look to Mother. Her eyes dart anywhere but on me. She runs a nervous hand over her hair, bites her bottom lip. I know she can feel the heat from my stare.

"Why, Mother?" I blurt out at her, not caring about the prayer. "You can't really believe I'm filled with some demon. You can't believe this crap."

Brother Mark and Mrs. Kitty's prayers strengthen as if my outburst is proof of the demon inside me.

"They know what they are doing," says Mother. "It's for the best... it's for the best," she mumbles to herself as if she's the one who needs convincing.

I stand, shove past Mrs. Kitty's legs, and walk over to Mother. It only interrupts the prayer and Bible reading for a moment, then they are at it again. Brother Mark's words pound at my back as I face my mother. Her arms cross tight over her chest.

The plan, I tell myself. Ten months and I'll be eighteen and graduated, and I can go anywhere, do anything. That's all I need—just to buy myself some time.

Ten months.

"What if I tell you I was experimenting?" I ask in a low voice. A flicker of hope flashes in Mother's eyes. She wants to believe the lie. I can see it. "What if I tell you I got all caught up in how...different the new girl was," I say, picking my words carefully. Encouraged now that she's listening to me, I go on. "She's so popular, athletic, and different." It stabs my heart to think of Bren. I clench my teeth to bite back the tears. "Her family is different too. Cultured from all those places. I mean, who doesn't dream of traveling to foreign countries and speaking a different language? I just wanted to be like that. To be like her. You know."

She gives me a tiny nod, and I continue. "But it didn't quite work out that way. Did it?" Mother shakes her head. "I promise you, as long as you let me stay here, I will never make that mistake again."

The prayers have stopped and everyone listens to me, holding their breath.

"I've seen the error of my ways. I don't want to hurt you or anyone else ever again. I'll go to school, work, and church. Nowhere else. You won't have to worry or wonder about me. Okay, Mother?" Silent tears stream down my face. "I'll be the best daughter you always dreamed of. Just please, please don't send me away." I swipe my cheeks clear, but the flood just keeps on coming.

Mother's chin dimples. She fingers her lips lightly, barely holding back the break of a dam. "It'll be okay," she whispers and opens her arms to me. "You have some time before you go. And you'll be safe there. Sending you there will be a good thing. You'll see," she says.

Her unyielding decision causes me to break down into a fit of hysterics in her arms. Mother interprets my tears as submission, but I'm grieving for the part of me they just killed.

The consoling only lasts a moment before Mother rights herself. The soothing swirl of her hand becomes an awkward pat. I remember the audience behind me that we must compose ourselves for. Manners and formality square my mother's shoulders. She clears her throat and goes over to Brother Mark and his wife. Quietly she thanks them for stopping by. Brother Mark says something to the effect of the Lord works quickly, and I will probably be well and back at home in no time, as if I have some kind of sickness.

As Mother walks them to the car, Sarabeth approaches me like a homeless dog, starving for scraps but wary on the approach.

I'm numb. I want to be mad at Sarabeth. Hate her. But I feel nothing; for her, for Mother, for myself. The only person I feel for…I can't reach. Like a piece of paper, I fold up those emotions for Bren into a tight square and push them down into the recesses of myself. Deep, so the darkness takes them, and I can no longer see them. Feel them.

"We'll figure it out, okay?" Sarabeth steps forward as if to hug me, but I slap her hand back. She recoils as if she's just been burned.

"Get out." I let all my seething hate push her away. Tears streaming down, she bolts out the door. It smacks against the wall with a loud clap before closing.

We'll figure it out, okay? The familiar words echo in my head. It's the same promise Bren gave me that rainy day that feels so long ago. It's another thought I neatly fold and tuck away.

I just don't know if I can survive ten months of brainwashing. What if they succeed? What if they strip me down to nothing but a shell? I'd be a zombie, going through the motions of the living but dead inside. I'm not sure I can stick around here long enough to find out.

I have one month to come up with a plan B before they ship me off. One month.

Chapter 20

"Honey, you don't have to go. Why don't you call in sick to school for the rest of the week?" Mother stands over me, wringing her hands.

I pick at the piece of raisin toast on my plate and consider her offer. The thought of lying in my bed under the covers—for the rest of my life even—sounds like bliss. If I truly thought she was concerned about my mental sanity and not about the embarrassment I was causing her with the horrid bruise on my face, I might have taken her up on the offer.

The damage is done. My secret is out. No amount of hiding will change that fact. Sure, my mother wants to believe I was "experimenting," but if she truly did, she wouldn't be sending me away to bury the truth. The big fat ugly truth of what I really am…gay. Sin. Shame. Call it what you will, but delaying the inevitable of facing my peers at school will not change that fact. With only a month left of normal, I don't want to waste it at home. Besides, it's the only place I'll get to see Bren, even if it's from afar. And since Mother password-locked the home laptop, it might be my only access to a computer.

"No, I'll go. It's better if I keep to my routine." The new numbness I've adopted will get me through. I leave my uneaten toast on the table and get ready. I dab on just enough concealer to lighten the black eye so at least I won't have to hear the shocked gasps along with the whispers.

Mother stops me at the front door before I leave for school. "I was thinking, you should take a few days off from working at the shop. You know, until you're feeling better."

She smiles that unreadable smile, but I know her intentions. Having to explain the black eye to her customers is humiliation at its finest. Even if we could create a little white lie, they'd learn the truth eventually once the gossip made the rounds.

"If that's what you want." My voice is barely a whisper. I let the door clap shut behind me.

* * *

I keep my head down and blend into the background as much as I can. It's an easy job since everyone at school is playing the Let's Ignore Kaycee game. At lunch I crunch on an apple outside in the unofficial smoking section by the bus drop-off. Where there is no chance of my friends ever venturing.

Again, Bren is not at school.

The only glimpse of Van I get is when he completely ignores me as we pass in the hall of my Social Media class. Before Mr. Peterson can make it back from the teacher's lounge, I hop on the computer and go around the school's firewall to check my email. Nobody loves me except spam. And worse, I can't even stalk Bren on social media because all her accounts are gone, probably because she's blocked me. To be cut off completely helps the darkness inside of me grow.

After the final bell, I dash out of computer class and hurry to my car. I want to be off campus as quickly as possible. But I can't bear to go home either. It would be nice if I could go to work to keep my mind off of how much I'm missing Bren or to keep it from wondering what awful things people are saying about me. But Mother has banned me from the boutique, and by November she'll have me banned from the house.

If my mother wants me gone, then I'll make her wishes come true. I'll give her what she wants right now. I get in my car and drive toward the interstate.

After a two-minute interview with Betsy the waitress, I take a job bussing tables and washing dishes at the truck stop—it's a suck job with crappy hours and sketchy clientele, but there is plenty of work. Enough work to keep me busy and gone so my mother will never have to see me.

And I won't ever have to see her either.

For the next week, I bus tables past midnight, half-ass my homework on breaks, and do the minimal amount of chores to keep Mother from complaining. I eat a hearty dinner of saltines and iced tea before I crash into my bed and pray for sleep.

* * *

"Did you hear?" a girl asks.

I snap my head up from foraging in my backpack. Panic kick-starts my heart. Three sinks down from me, a girl washes her hands in the sink. It's been so long since someone at school has spoken to me, I'm stunned speechless. Until I see—in the reflection of the bathroom mirror—her friend emerging from the bathroom stall.

"Andrew and Sarabeth are homecoming king and queen. Pretty perfect, huh? I hear the seniors' float is freaking amazing. Do you think the freshman even have a chance?" The girl and her friend have a small discussion about homecoming, mums, and what they're going to wear. To them, I am as noticeable as the cinder block walls.

As their idle chat continues, I apply my lip balm. A gaunt face stares back at me. My black eye has faded to a gorgeous shade of rotting green and yellowish-brown. Not even worth the effort to cover anymore.

I wait in the bathroom until the last possible minute, before grabbing my books from my locker for my next class. As I leave the bathroom, a brief thought to congratulate Sarabeth passes through my mind, but why? She has done a good job of avoiding me, especially with Andrew shielding her from my presence whenever our paths cross. I haven't seen Van around them either. I guess they've shunned him too. But he doesn't seem to be as isolated as I am because I've noticed he spends a lot of his time with the art students, when he's not avoiding me. My popularity seems to have sunk to the depths of Charlotte Wozniak.

"You all right there, McCoy?"

I peer past my locker door and see Chuck standing at the end of the hall, alone.

I wipe the tear off my face I didn't realize had escaped. I'm half-confused why he's talking to me and half-shocked he even cares. I give him the slightest nod. He stands there starring at me, like he's not convinced and won't move until I assure him better, which confuses me even more. The bell rings, snapping him out of his thoughts.

"Good," he says with a small smile before going to his class.

* * *

By Friday, I stand in front of Mrs. Bellefleur, waiting for her to get off the phone. I glance around the library, hoping to catch a glimpse of Bren, but I know she's not here. She hasn't been to school since the Friday before the hayride. When no one is speaking to you, it's hard to find out what's going on. The only rumor I've heard is that they are in Boston, visiting her grandmother, and I overheard that from one of the teachers. Something about the rumor didn't feel right. It wasn't so much what the teacher said, but how she said it, with worry and dismay in her voice. I hope her grandmother isn't sick or something.

The phone clunks in the cradle as Mrs. Bellefleur sets it down. "How have you been, honey?" She gives me a heartbreaking look over the top of the coffee cup she sips from, waiting for me to answer.

I want to crash into the chair in front of her desk and spill my soul to her. Tell her that I'm barely hanging on. That I miss my friends so bad it's physically starting to hurt. The pressure on my chest is unbearable.

But I don't say any of those things. I muster up the best smile I can, which Mrs. Bellefleur sees right through but doesn't call me out on. "I'm fine." It's my staple response to anyone who asks.

She sets her coffee cup down, and her fingers drum the side. She sizes me up, as if contemplating what she should say to me next.

I rock from one foot to the other under her scrutiny. I admire the contents of her shelves, the papers on the desk, the stack of book boxes along the wall, and look at anything except her eyes. My hands find their home in my back pockets, and my heels jog me up and down. The long silence toys with my nerves, and I fight the urge to bolt.

Mrs. Bellefleur sighs in resignation. "There's only a short stack of books to shelve this week. Guess the parade floats have occupied the students' time."

It hurts to hear about the parade and know that I'm not a part of it.

"That was Jackie from the public library on the phone. She has a couple of books for us." Mrs. Bellefleur nods to the stack of books on the bottom of the cart. "Those need to be returned to her. Just bring the books they have back to school with you on Monday. Don't hassle with coming back today."

"Yes, ma'am." I grab the cart to wheel it out.

"And Kaycee…" Mrs. Bellefleur stands.

I stop in my tracks but refuse to meet her eyes, so I stare at the floor.

"If you ever need to talk, I'm always here."

The invitation tempts me, but I cough to clear the frog in my throat. "Yeah, sure. Thanks, Mrs. Bellefleur."

I tempt a glance at her as she picks up her coffee cup. It's not her usual Forks, Washington, black mug. It's white with an arch of a rainbow. In surprise, my eyes lift from the cup to her, but she's already busy at her computer.

Not sure what to think or say, I swivel out of the room, pulling the cart with me.

Stuffing the books on the shelf, I think about the cup. It's probably just a rainbow, not a *rainbow* rainbow. I can't imagine anyone in this God-fearing town knowingly showing their support.

Except Van's mom.

Thinking of the painted heart and rainbow makes me miss him.

All the horrible words I yelled at him come flooding back at once. Of all people, he should have been the one I leaned on, not pushed away. Maybe if I just talked to him, explained myself then maybe he'd—

"Come on, Lindsey. You have to go with us," Chelsea's voice pleads.

Through the reference section, I spy Chelsea sitting in the make-out corner of the library with someone. The sharp chemical smell of fingernail polish burns my nose. She glosses on a coat. Gently I slide a book out of place to see who she's sitting with. It's that weasel girl from my lab class, Lindsey.

"You will love Breakers. It's so fun."

"Well, I don't know," Weasel whines.

"What are you, a wet blanket? Why would you say no to fun?" There so much indignation in her voice, I can't imagine how Chelsea maintains friends. "I'm telling you, my buddy Carlos and I go over there all the time. It's the shit." She goes back to her nails. "He's got this vintage convertible that's the tits too." Lindsey gasps.

Ugh. Figures she's friends with someone like Carlos.

"Relax, Lindsey. It's an expression. Geesh." She blows on her nails. "So you coming or what?"

My hate for Chelsea blooms a little more. That skank tries to pretend she's not gay or at least bisexual, and here she is recruiting for Breakers. I have half a mind to jump out from behind the shelf and scream to Weasel Girl, "She's gay. They're gay. Everybody's gay!" I'm sure Chelsea would feign shock and swear she had no idea Breakers was a known place for gays. It wouldn't do any good to out her. She would keep hiding like a coward.

I slip the book back into the shelf with a sickening realization. Here I am, wanting to throttle Chelsea for not owning the fact that she's bisexual. And yet I haven't owned up to being a lesbian.

The whole world knows I'm a lesbian, but I'm still hiding. I drop my face into my hands and rub my temples. I have no idea how to fix this mess. I wish I could talk to Van. He'd know what to do.

Automatically, I reach into my back pocket for my phone, only to find it empty. The image of my phone skip-skip-skidding down the highway to its death flashes in my mind. Until I earn enough money to buy another one, I'm stuck with using the home phone only.

No problem. After I'm finished putting away the books, I'll zip over to the public library and wait for Van at Hot Flix. That's what I'll do. Face to face, not some phone text apology. It will take begging and groveling and probably a few torturous weekends of Johnny Depp-worshiping marathons, but I will do what I have to to make it up to him.

I make quick work of the remaining books I have to shelve. Just before I leave, I dip into Mrs. Bellefleur's office. "Um, I'm going to take off now. If there's anything I missed, I'll finish it up next week." I start to exit, then pause, unable to walk away quite yet.

"Forget something, honey?" asks Mrs. Bellefleur. Her question is innocent, her voice expectant. As if she's waiting for something, something that's long overdue. That's Mrs. B for you. She knows what's what long before you do. It's like her secret librarian superpower.

I poke my head back in. A quick glance at her rainbow mug builds my confidence. I step into her office and plop down in the empty wooden swivel chair across from her desk. My feet push off the flattened gray carpet, turning me from side to side. For a long moment I don't say anything, just stare at the massive chaos crowding her desk, and she watches me patiently.

"I've known you a long time, Mrs. B."

Mrs. Bellefleur gives a solemn nod and settles back into her equally uncomfortable wooden swivel chair, with her fingers clasped over her stomach. She's not old enough to be one of those sweet grandmother types, but she's too old to be my mother. Besides her endearing grumpy husband and three tabby cats, I know nothing about her family. Maybe she's an aunt or sister or the black sheep for all I know. What she is, is someone I've always felt at home around. Someone I can be myself with.

The words thicken on my tongue. My nerves jitter my knees up and down. A long breath exhales out of me, a release of all the anxious energy I've been storing up for years. "I just figured two people who have known each other for this long should be honest with one another. I don't really feel comfortable around too many people when it comes to...certain aspects of myself."

Mrs. Bellefleur doesn't say anything. Casually she picks up her coffee and takes a long, slow sip. She raises a single brow, encouraging me to continue.

"I guess all I wanted to say was...you probably should know that... I'm a lesbian." I choke on the last word. Not from embarrassment or fear but from the sheer joy of freedom in having just told somebody. Someone who I'm fairly confident won't tear me down for it.

Fried nerves jolt me out of my seat before she can respond, but I don't get halfway out of my chair before Mrs. Bellefleur snags me by my wrist—the woman has lightning-quick reflexes. She makes her way around her desk and pulls me into a smothering hug.

"Thank you, Kaycee," Mrs. Bellefleur whispers into my hair.

I don't understand why she's thanking me. It's not like I did anything for her. For some reason her thanks brings on more emotion, as if my body understands why before I do. The battle for fighting off the tears becomes harder. I try to pull away from her. She squeezes tighter.

"Thank you, sweetie, for trusting me." She gives me a hearty pat on the back before releasing me.

I do an awkward spin-away move and scurry for the door. "Yeah, sure thing." Then I stop and lean back in. "Nice mug, Mrs. B."

She grins huge and winks.

There's an actual smile on my face when I walk away, the first one in a while. The chance that Van might talk to me and that I will have one friend to reach out to while I'm in exile makes my future a little less hellish.

A little something flutters inside of me: life.

* * *

"Where do you want these, Ms. Jackie? The returns cart or the drop-off bin?" I stand at the public library's front counter with the stack of books, waiting for her to finish binding the latest periodicals with plastic covers. The familiar scent of paper and lemon Pledge greets me.

Ms. Jackie's salt and pepper hair sags from the heavy bun in the back. At least two pencils poke out of her hive like misplaced chopsticks. She makes quick work of the magazines and turns around to face me. Leathered cracks crinkle around her eyes when she smiles. "Oh good. Just put them there. There's a couple for you." She hands me three books and pulls a set of keys from her drawer. "Let me check the drive-thru drop box to make sure we don't have any more."

"Yes, ma'am." As Ms. Jackie heads out the front door, I check out the latest arrivals on the YA rack next to the front desk. The first book I pick up is a summer romance. No thanks. The next is a sad cancer story. I'm not even going there. Why don't they have a good ole zombie apocalypse story to cheer me up? A were-creature book is the closest thing to non-depressing I can find. As I read the back, I'm hoping the prom queen gets eaten.

"I heard they moved back to Boston," a woman's voice says at the main counter. A couple of books thunk into the library bin. I stop reading the back cover and listen.

"Good. He can take that wetback wife with him too," a second woman says. The hard edge of her voice is unmistakable. It's Mrs. Goodman, Andrew's mother. The rack I stand behind barely hides me. As long as I keep still, maybe they won't notice I'm here.

"I'm sick and tired of being attacked because I believe in upholding family values. Serves them right to be run off for raising that girl to be a lesbian. Next thing you know, she'd have had every kid in town confused, thinking it's okay to be a homosexual." Both ladies uh-huh in agreement. Heat flares all over my body. I have a death grip on the hardback I'm holding.

"That'll teach them. They can't come to Sunshine and corrupt our children," Mrs. Goodman says. "We don't need foreigners "fixing" things around here, no way. We're better off without them. I'm glad Larry fired that man. The factory can go to hell. We've got farming."

"Amen. I hear that daughter of theirs attacked that Hannigan girl. And these are the gay rights those liberal activists are fighting for. I just don't know how much more we're going to have to endure."

The tiny bit of the lunch I consumed earlier rolls in my stomach. Fear and anger mix in my blood, icing me frozen. How could it be okay, in any world, to run somebody out of town? Bren's father has been fired, and the factory is going to close. Do these ladies have any idea what this does for my family? For lots of small-business families here in Sunshine? I just don't understand how these women can be so selfish, so small minded.

"Got one more for you, Kaycee," Ms. Jackie says behind me. I startle. A quick glance to my right, and I see Mrs. Goodman has taken notice of me.

My eyes hit the floor. "Thanks, Ms. Jackie," I say in a whisper, as if that might make me smaller, more invisible somehow. I grab the book, give her the worst excuse for a smile, and head for the door. As I pass Mrs. Goodman, I keep my eyes on the carpet and pray she doesn't say anything to me.

Just as I push through the door, I hear Mrs. Goodman speak loud and clear. "Only way to protect our kids is to run every last one of them out of town."

* * *

The keys jangle in my hand so bad, it takes me several tries before I am able to unlock my car. The second I'm behind the wheel, I turn over the engine, throw the car in reverse, and get the hell out of there.

Panic builds in my body, and I can't seem to find enough oxygen. Holy crap, Mrs. Goodman knows. She knows! It's unmistakable—that comment was aimed at me. I'm sure of it. It's one thing to know the kids at school gossip about me and know I'm gay, but it never dawned on me they would tell their parents or even talk to their parents about this stuff.

And now Bren is gone, for good. My body seems to shrivel up a little more at the thought. A part of me feared that was why she hadn't been at school, and now I know. They up and left, moved back to Boston. Over what happened at the hayride? That seems a bit extreme. But then again, if Chelsea is telling people Bren attacked her…oh my God, who lies like that?

Haters, that's who. How can Sarabeth stomach being Andrew's girlfriend with a mother like that?

Maybe they left because her father got fired. It's ridiculous to think that he would get fired over something his daughter did. That would have to be illegal or something. Didn't Larry Beaudroux think about how his actions could hurt this town? Or maybe he was too worried about his upcoming election for Mayor and reputation to give a damn.

I park down the hill from Hot Flix, aware that I drove here but don't remember the drive from there to here. The giant Wildcat painted on the brick wall glares at me. I imagine that if it were alive, it would hate me too.

In an instant, my fear and aguish flip a switch inside of me. I slap my steering wheel as hard as I can. "I hate that woman!" How dare Mrs. Goodman say such awful things? And she's going to heaven and I'm not? Mrs. Goodman and her stupid friend act like they're the ones being violated. The problem is they're convinced people can be turned gay, like we're vampires or something. It's the most ignorant thing I've ever heard.

For God's sake, I've tried to let the heterosexual rub off on me. It didn't work. These are the people that I hide my true self for? I'm allowing the most hateful, judgmental people control my life. People I don't even like or care about. I get out, slamming the car door behind me, and I march up the hill to Hot Flix.

Once Van accepts my apology, I'm going to fill him in on the crap I just heard. Then I hope he can enlighten me on the real scoop as to why Bren's family left.

"Well, don't you look mad as a hornet?" Mr. Bobby's voice stops me. I lift my head to address the old man. I smile when I see Ms. Doris sipping a cup of coffee across the little bistro table from him.

"Hello, Ms. Carver. What a pleasant surprise seeing you here," I say.

"Just happened by, that's all." She takes a delicate sip of her coffee, all business as usual. Her salt and pepper hair is beauty shop perfect. Her Sunday-nice church dress on a Friday says more than "happened by."

"Isn't that lucky Mr. Bobby just *happened* to be here? What a coincidence. Well, y'all enjoy your Friday." I cock my head to Mr. Bobby. The old man grins from ear to ear.

With that I grab the handle on Hot Flix's door and stop. Slightly off-center to the heart Mrs. Betty painted on the glass is an indentation. A rock or a brick was thrown at it but not hard enough to finish the job. Cracks run through the glass, splitting the heart and breaking it in half. A few fractures spread out further, slicing up parts of the rainbow, distorting the colorful arcs.

The weight of my words stills my breath. Even though I wasn't the one who threw the brick, I am the one to blame. If I had never said anything about Van being gay that day in the bathroom, this would have never happened.

I stare at the door and will myself to step forward. The chances of Van forgiving me now are slim to none. Now, more than ever, I need to make my apologies. I grab the door handle and pull—

The locked door jars me forward. Did they have to close down shop because of the window? My face smooshes against the glass, and I cup my hands around my eyes to see in.

Lights are on. *Edward Scissorhands* plays on the big screen. Fresh popcorn overflows out of the popper bin. But nobody is manning the counter.

My fist pounds on the glass door. "Van, are you in there?" With no answer I pound a little louder. "Van, it's me, Kaycee. Let me in."

Something moves in the back. Van must have seen me coming while I was chatting with Mr. Bobby and locked the door. Oh man, he hates me that much.

"Come on, Van. It's three in the afternoon. You're not closed."

One of the black curtains waves and the rubbery white toes of a pair of sneakers peek out at the bottom.

"I see you hiding in the porn closet."

Feet shuffle and the curtain shimmies.

"Please, Van. I want to tell you I'm sorry. I was wrong."

A lady passes me on the sidewalk and looks at me like I'm a psycho.

"I said some really mean things to him, and he locked me out," I tell her. Oh yeah, because that doesn't sound crazy in the slightest. Once the woman is some distance away, I turn my attention back to the door.

"I'm not going away until you open this door. You have to go home sometime."

No response.

"Okay. You're making me do it. I don't want to, but you leave me no choice." I take a quick glance around to see who's in the near vicinity. I flash a quick smile to Mr. Bobby and clear my throat. "I'm gay, and I'm proud," I say in my normal tone against the glass door.

Nothing.

I take a deep breath and I say it again, a little louder. "I'm gay, and I'm proud." It's a mix of terror and freedom all in the same. I slip a glance to Mr. Bobby who grins back at me.

A small part of the curtain peels back, and I see an eyeball peeping out at me.

I inhale a lungful of air and scream it. "I'm gay, and I'm proud."

Van jumps out from behind the curtain and races to the door. He can't get the darned thing unlocked quickly enough. "Shush." He drags me in by the elbow and scans the street for witnesses before joining me inside. "Be quiet before you scare all the heterosexuals away." He crosses his arms over his chest and glares at me, chewing the inside of his jaw.

Here goes nothing. "I was wrong. Way wrong. I should have never said all those awful things."

Van opens his mouth to say something, but I cut him off.

"You were right. I was being a hypocrite too. I denied who I was to myself and tried to cover it up with boyfriends. At least you didn't do that. I panicked after the hayride. I had my head up my ass and flipped out. I was angry for the lies Chelsea spread about Bren. I was angry because Sarabeth picked Andrew's side. I was angry at you because you have parents who love you no matter what. That's just not fair. Annnnd I'm stalling, because what I really want to say is that…" I exhale. "I'm sorry. I'm sorry I spilled the beans on you. All those things I blurted out, those private things about you and being gay…" I swallow. "They were not mine to speak aloud."

I look over at the broken window. "Not only have I caused you pain, but I've caused your family pain as well. I don't ever expect you to forgive me, but I just wanted you to know that I feel horrible about what has happened between us. I never imagined our friendship would end this way. I couldn't let you go the rest of your life without knowing how truly sorry I am."

Hold breath.

Van stares at me, lips pinched. His eyes begin to squint as if he's so freaking mad, he could shoot laser beams out of them and slice me in half. "You're an idiot. You know that?"

Okay, not what I expected, but I deserve it. "Yes. Yes I am."

"You're not an idiot because of the crap you said." His arms unfurl. "You want to know why you're an idiot?"

I hesitate a moment, not sure if this is a trick question or if he really expects me to ask him why.

"You're an idiot because you think we could have one fight and I'd end our friendship. If you'd bothered to return a call or a text, or to even talk to me, you would have known that I wasn't able to go more than few days angry. Heck, you've been a ghost at school."

My phone. Oh crap, my phone. "I chucked my phone out the window on my way to Mississippi," I confess. He had me on the invisibility act I was pulling at school.

"Mississippi?"

"After that day in the bathroom, the weekend prior, and everything else that's happened, I needed to drive. And I didn't want to talk to anyone."

His shoulders drop. "You do know those things have an off button."

"I know. It's just…my head was exploding, my heart was breaking, and I needed to kill something. It seemed like a good idea at the time." I give him a crooked smile.

"Get over here." He opens his arms to me and pulls me in with a great squeeze. "I'm sorry too. I shouldn't have pushed you so hard to come out. This last week has been hell. I don't function well without my Kaycee fix, you know?"

I nod my head against his chest. I've missed my Van so much.

He grabs my shoulders and pushes me off him, looking me in the eyes. "Are you eating? You feel all boney."

"Yes. I'm eating." Not very much though; my stomach can't handle much.

"As far as telling the school I'm gay, you didn't say anything everyone didn't already know." He flings his arm out. "For Christ's sake, my own mother drew a bull's-eye on the storefront window. You can't get any more gay pride than that."

I swipe the tears from under my eyes and chuckle. "Yeah, but most people around here don't even realize what that means." Even cracked and broken, the window is a beautiful thing. "Your mom does have a flair for over-the-top."

"Yeah, she does. Now sit down on my couch and let me shrink all your problems."

I accept the invite and plop down on the sofa. The smell of popcorn, infused in its fibers, welcomes me back home. Van goes behind the counter and perches on the barstool, entering in the new inventory.

To clear up the rumors, I tell him what actually happened on the hayride and what Sarabeth said to me. Instead of feeling indifferent toward her, anger reignites the fresh wound of betrayal. The gay intervention that followed, and now the fact that I'm going to be shipped off to a brainwashing rehabilitation, surprises the crap out of Van.

"What? You don't actually think she's going to send you away, do you?" he asks.

"Maybe, I don't know. It almost felt like she was being pressured into making the decision. I keep thinking I can change her mind but I'm not sure how." I sit up. "You know, Van, maybe I'm wrong, but I don't think she hates me because I'm gay."

He nods.

"I think Mother has always known. For her, I think she struggles with the years of biblical teachings and her love for me. Like if she accepts one, she has to give up the other."

"She doesn't," Van says matter-of-factly. "Your mother's not a monster. You should talk to her. Tell her who you really are." He holds a hand up to stop me from interrupting. "Or you'll end up hating her over something you never gave her the opportunity to process."

He's right. Deep down, Mother knows what I am. I'm sure we could pretend between each other that it doesn't exist. I could move away. Slowly but surely distancing myself from her until eventually we are no longer connected. I don't want that. Neither does she. I truly believe in my heart that she would rather have me in her life than out, no matter how difficult it would be.

"I heard Bren and her family moved back to Boston." The thought of not seeing her ever again scores another wound to my chest.

I inform Van of the awful gossip I overheard Mrs. Goodman and her friend discussing at the library. He relays back what he knows—that Bren's father had brokered a deal with a new factory but final negotiation hadn't been made before they fled town.

"Fled? What happened?"

"Bren's family was run out of town. That Saturday night you and I had the run-in at the movies, Bren's Instagram account started to fill up with comments. It was small stuff to start. People saying things like 'Gays are ruining our society' and 'Sinners burn in hell.' After her accounts were deleted, someone started a "Save Sunshine's Religious Liberties" account. People started reposting its anti-gay propaganda and cruel jokes. I think the final straw was when they posted a photoshopped picture of a Boston Celtics basketball with a gun pointed at it, saying 'Do the right thing.'"

"Oh my God, Van. Are you serious?" Goose bumps prickle across my flesh. I haven't logged into my accounts in forever. Who knows what they said on mine. "Who would do that? How could anybody even have known so quickly?" Sarabeth wouldn't be a part of something like that. It had to be someone she told. Maybe Andrew? Could he be capable of something so awful? That is, if he had half a brain to know how to even use Photoshop.

I think about me trying to text Bren that weekend and not getting a response back. It's because of what her family was going through. Of course they left Sunshine. They had to protect their daughter, themselves.

I bury my face in my hands. "She hates me, Van. I know she does. I've totally screwed up with Bren, with this town. I'm a total loser. From here on out, my life is going to be hell, and there's nothing I can do to change it."

"Stop being dramatic." I feel the weight of the sofa dip as he sits next to me. "Drama Queen doesn't suit you. Your life isn't going to be hell forever. They've already forgotten about you with homecoming next week."

"Homecoming," I groan and lift my head. "Aren't you sad that we're not going to be a part of it?" He gives a what-can-we-do shrug. "It's going to be the single most amazing event of our senior year, and we aren't going to get to leave our mark on it for all future Wildcats to marvel and awe." I stop and stare at Van as I chew the inside of my cheek.

His brow scrunches. "What? Why are you looking at me like that?"

I sit bolt upright, my face smoothing into a smile. Screw this town and all their bullshit. If I'm going to be booted out, I'm going out with a bang.

"Kaycee Jean McCoy, what's percolating in that little brain of yours?"

I cock my head to the side, Cheshire grin to boot. Fear and anticipation knot my stomach. What I'm considering could mean some serious retaliation, but I can't let what they did to Bren go unanswered. I can't let them think we will stand for that kind of treatment. People like Mr. Bobby fought for equality in the sixties; it's my turn to stand up now. Most importantly, this town needs to wake up and join the twenty-first century. And I have just the idea to get their attention with a little gay pride. "Who says we can't leave our mark?"

"This does not bode well. We're not going to do anything…illegal, are we?"

I'm fully aware that he has just signed on as an accomplice to whatever it is I'm scheming.

"It's only illegal if we get caught."

Van's eyes twinkle.

Chapter 21

I check the messages on the home phone again, hoping there's one from Bren. Nothing. I called Bren earlier in the week with one long rambling message of apology. Not that I really expected her to call me back, but I had hoped.

I also clued Van in on my master plan, knowing the only way it was going to go down without a hitch was if he swore to absolute secrecy. What we're doing tonight is what I wish someone would have done for me. Like Mr. Bobby did a long time ago.

He stood up for an injustice. When he did, he gave others the strength to stand alongside him. It didn't matter that he wasn't black. What mattered was people accepting others for who they were and letting them live equally. For others like me who live in shame or fear, I want to be their strength, their hope.

My last instructions to Van were to dress in black, meet me at the Walmart parking lot at nine thirty on Thursday night, and bring a flashlight. I'd take care of the rest. I throw on my dark jeans, a black sweater, and my black canvas Toms. The sweater is baggier than I remember, but it'll do.

"Where are you going?" Mother asks.

I jump like I've been caught with my hand in the cookie jar. She stands in my bedroom doorway with a dish towel in her hand, staring at me. No anger in her voice or judgment in her eyes, but something hard in her face. Concern.

"I uh…I know I'm grounded and can only go to school, work, and church, but…it's just this one thing I wanted to do tonight. That's all. Last-minute homecoming stuff." Not a lie. I had no intention of sneaking out, unless she said no. I cross my fingers she doesn't ask me who I'm going out with. I know she's heard the rumors by now that Bren's family is gone, so she doesn't have to worry about *that*. But telling her I'm going on a secret mission with Van is also maybe not such a good idea.

"Do you have a minute before you go?"

The lack of the third degree shocks me. I hesitate to answer because I'm not sure if I'm walking into a trap or what. "Yeah…I guess." I walk toward my door, but Mother surprises me when she comes into my room.

"Talks" are usually held at the kitchen table. On instinct, I scan my room for stray clothing, unmade bed, or any other untidy infraction she might catch me on. My room looks utterly unlived in since I spend so much of my time at the truck stop and school. Betsy had no problem giving me the night off either.

She takes a seat on the end of my bed and pats the space next to her.

Yep. It's a trap. I'm sure of it. Mother in my room at all, much less sitting on my bed—I can count on one hand how many times this has happened. Once when she told me I had to get my tonsils taken out, once when my grandfather passed away, and once when she told me my father left us. Only big events around here prompt my mother to have come-to-Jesus meetings. The only living grandparent I have is Nana, who was the epitome of health the last time we drove up to

Nashville to visit her. Man, that was this past summer. I hope things didn't go south for some reason. Old people are like that—healthy one day, dead the next.

Regarding her like a grizzly bear, I make a big circle and sit on the far side of her. As if distance will somehow soften the blow.

"This sweater looks too big for you." She reaches to touch the black wool, but her hand doesn't go the distance. "I don't think you've been eating enough."

My mother is not in here to discuss my eating habits, which have been for shit lately.

Maybe between the gossip about me and Bren's father getting fired, my mother has already started to see a drop in sales. I knew all of this would affect us, but it doesn't make sense that it could have financially affected us so fast.

"You know, I could make you a bologna sandwich before you go, maybe some chips too." Mother moves as if to stand, but I snag her by the elbow. I have to know what she's doing.

"I ate dinner already. I'm good. What's going on? Is this about the shop? Are you worried about the factory closing?"

"Oh no. Not worried about that, yet. There's nothing like a half-off sale to get people spending again." She tries to pass off a shaky smile, but I can see underneath she's scared. "I heard the Japanese people are still considering us for one of their factory locations, but Larry Beaudroux doesn't know the first thing about negotiations with foreigners. There's just no way of knowing what's going to happen." She breathes a deep sigh and sits back down. The bed sags heavily from the burden she brings with her. Her hands wring the dish towel into a choke hold.

Then I know. This little chat is about sending me away. Somehow, she's found a way to get rid of me sooner. The hairs on my neck stand on end. Life begins to seep out of me like water down a drain. The resigned gurgle is almost audible.

Mother speaks but doesn't look at me. "When I was in junior high, they found this black boy's body next to the dumpster behind Big Star grocery. He had been beaten so bad, his own parents couldn't identify him."

My heart drops to the floor. Mother *never* speaks about her past or of unpleasant incidents. It's tacky and vulgar to do so. I keep as still as a statue. Scared that if I move, I'll spook her and won't get to hear what she has to say.

She stares at the rag in her hand. "I don't remember his name, but he rode my bus—a senior I think. You could tell he was different. Too flamboyant for the likes of folks around here. I do remember he had two little sisters and a little baby brother. His mother used to clean our church, but for some reason after that, they fired her." Mother keeps her eyes pointed downward. A teardrop hits her dish towel. A fat dot spreads on the absorbent cloth. She takes a breath. "One of the siblings died that year from pneumonia, maybe the baby. I don't remember. I've always thought about that boy and wondered what horrible thing he must have done to get himself killed like that." She pauses.

I'm not sure if she's finished or if she has more to say. I memorize how the wrinkled lines of her khakis match her hands. The slump of her shoulders—they're wilted over, not tight and back like they should be. A trail of moisture glosses over her powdered cheek. It's a rare moment to witness my mother weak, vulnerable. Right here and now she's sharing a piece of her soul with me. And I wish it were like a piece of brass from my military collection—something I could hold and savor forever.

"It took me a long time," she breaks the silence, "many a year of growing up before I realized he had done nothing wrong." She looks up at me, glassy eyes on the verge of spilling over. "They killed him because he was gay. That's all. The killed him because the good Lord didn't make him like the other boys. He was different and that scared them, so they killed him. When they fired his mother for no good reason, they killed that baby too."

My vision blurs, and I'm sobbing hard before I can stop myself.

Mother grabs my hands. "I'm just scared they're going to kill you, because you're…different." She uses the dish towel to wipe the tears from my face. "But I've come to realize these last few weeks, that if I force you to be something you're not, I'm going to be the one who kills you, not them. I may not understand or agree, and I can't say I'll ever get used to the idea, but I'm willing to give it a try. I know no matter what you are, you will always be my baby girl. And I love you."

I collapse into her arms and heave uncontrollable sobs. She squeezes me tight, and I can feel her body taking in ragged breaths. Shame on me for thinking she could never love me as her gay daughter. It brings on tears of guilt. It never dawned on me that Mother's rejection was born out of fear for my safety—her way of protecting me from the hate of others or from harming myself. I always assumed she detested that part of me.

I'm not sure how long I stay there, wrapped in her cradling arms. And she doesn't push me away to resume her stuffy persona when I've reached what could be considered a sufficient amount of blubbering. She holds me until the tears dry and my breathing is even again.

I sit up and use the dish towel to blot the wet stain on Mother's blouse.

"Don't worry about that." She stops me. "This thing needs to go to the dry cleaners anyway."

We sniffle at the same time, making us both giggle a little.

"I'm sorry, Mother." I'm not sure why I'm apologizing—maybe for not being the down-the-aisle kind of daughter or maybe never trusting her to keep loving me, no matter what.

"Well." She tries to tuck my wild waves behind my ear, but they're too stubborn. "I'm sorry I never gave you a safe place to turn when you needed one." She smiles down at me. "And I just think a place like Straight Path With God will keep you safe."

I've already made up my mind that I'm not going, and there's nothing she can do about it. I shake my head no with more confidence than I ever have in my whole life. So it really doesn't surprise me when the words come out of my mouth calm and strong. "No. I'm not going. I understand what you're trying to do, but I won't be safe. It'll make me miserable. And if you make me go, I'll fight you tooth and nail. I'll petition the court for emancipation, or I'll run away if I have to, but I will not go to that place. You can't make me."

Her lip quivers, and she stares at me. "I know. I'm terrified of what the world will do to you. I'm terrified of what you'll do to yourself if I force you. I'm terrified of what will happen if I do nothing. I don't know what to do anymore. The idea of sending you off never settled with me. I think a part of me hoped your behavior was something you were doing to be trendy, or maybe it was teen rebellion or something. But it's a part of you, right? Always has been. I can't pretend any longer that I didn't suspect all along. There's only so much I can do to protect you. But all I've ever wanted was to protect you and keep you safe. That's all any mother wants for her child." She reaches over and squeezes my hand.

"Thank you, Mother." My tears have choked my words to a whisper. I realize that now I'm out in the open, there will be consequences that will befall upon her as well. She'll lose business, friends, and maybe even her boyfriend. "You think this will mess up your chances of ever getting married to Mr. Billy?"

She straightens her spine. "Well, that won't be a problem, because I told him to take off. I don't need an asshole like him in my life."

My eyes bug out. My mother just said "asshole."

When did she kick Mr. Billy to the curb? I've been so lost in my own fog, I never even noticed. As much as I want to ask what happened between them, I don't want to push Mother over the edge. And I have a sneaking feeling it has something to do with me.

She stands and smoothes her slacks. "You said you had homecoming stuff to do?"

"Uh huh," I say. There's a brief, uncomfortable moment as we both resume our normal tone, as if what we just discussed was only a hiccup in our lives. I check my alarm clock. It's almost nine thirty. "I shouldn't be back too late." Though I have no clue how long it will take Van and me to do this.

"I look forward to watching the parade tomorrow. I hope y'all win," she says. And just like that, Mother is composed and complacent, and I am the ever-obeying daughter.

Until tomorrow, that is.

Chapter 22

The Walmart parking lot on a Thursday night in the middle of October is not where covert military people converge. But in a small town like Sunshine, it's that or Big Star grocery. Van gets out of his car. He's dressed in commando black—turtleneck, military fatigues, and beanie. He slings a duffle bag onto his shoulder, and the contents inside clank. His heavy swagger over to my car tells me he's been watching way too many black ops movies this week. He tosses something dark to me, and I catch it. "Wear this. You don't want to be recognized," he says in a flat, deep tone. I choke down a giggle from his tough-guy voice.

What he tossed me is not a beanie cap, but a full-on ski mask, eye holes only. "Seriously? You're scaring me, Van. I don't think driving through town with a robber's mask on my face is going to go over well with the cops." I shove the thing into my console as we get into my car.

I start to drive out of the parking lot and Van asks, "You know we're going to get some serious backlash for this, right?"

I look at him with a mock cold stare, my face the epitome of stone. "Sometimes it takes a slap in the face to wake people up. Sunshine is about to get bitch-slapped." I waggle my eyebrows.

Twenty minutes later we creep down the old Sunshine highway, lights off, about a half a mile from Andrew's farmhouse. I pull over into one of the entrances that lead out into a cotton field. It curves behind a grove of trees, blocking my nothing-special Civic from the view of the road. It's one of the Goodman's fields I'm sure. I'm wishing I had a case of toilet paper with me, but as much as I'd like to vandalize Mrs. Goodman's house, that is not the mission tonight.

"Van, are you ready? We can do this," I whisper, even though it's pointless to do so when the only house within miles is the Goodman's. Knowing what we are about to do, the need to be stealthy overwhelms me. Both of us get out of the car and shut our doors with soft clips.

The musky smell of dirt from the field thickens in my nostrils. Cricket chirps ricochet all around. Glowing lights from the fireflies twinkle along the tops of the growing cotton. Off in the distance, the yelp of a coyote floats on the night air. The country, with all its peaceful but untamed nature, chills me until I shiver.

"You got your flashlight?" asks Van.

I pull out my penlight and click it on.

"That's the worst excuse for a flashlight I've ever seen." Van retrieves a handheld spotlight and clunks it onto the trunk of my car with a damaging thunk. "Now that's a flashlight."

"What else you got in there?" I lean over to look in his bag.

"Nothing much. Road flares, smoke bombs, tape recorder…just the usual spy stuff."

I aim the penlight on his face. "You watch *way* too many movies."

"Hey, a good spy always comes prepared."

"I think that's the Boy Scout motto."

"Shut up. Whatever. You'll thank me later."

Headlights down the road yank our attention that way. I dive into the ditch next to my car. Briars and sticks jab my legs. "Get over here, Van. They're going to see you."

I jerk my arm for him to come down with me. He completely ignores my military hand signals. Instead, he walks straight up to the edge of the road like a bonehead, points that big spotlight toward the vehicle, and flicks the thing on and off.

"Vander! What the heck is your problem?"

The diesel engine chugs as it approaches. The big white Chevy Dually slows to a stop right in front of him. Van steps up to the passenger window as it rolls down. If that is Mr. Goodman, this whole mission is canned. I squat lower, in the hopes of disappearing in the brush.

"Is that Kaycee cowering in the ditch?"

I stand to attention at the sound of her voice. Sarabeth stares at me like I've lost my ever-lovin' mind.

"What are you doing in the ditch?"

Van laughs. Sarabeth shakes her head as she pulls the truck over and parks it beside my car.

"Ha ha," I say and slap away the hand Van offers me. "I've probably got poison ivy all over me now. Thanks, Vander." I scrabble up the side of the ditch.

Once up top, I sweep away the debris on my pants and sweater. I cut my eyes to Van when Sarabeth walks over. "What is *she* doing here?" I'm well aware *she* can hear me, but I don't care.

"We can't steal the float with a Civic, now can we? Sarabeth offered her dad's truck."

"You swore to secrecy. Traitor," I say. "And I didn't say anything about stealing the float. I said we'd make a few changes. That's it."

Van clamps his hands down on his hips. "Seriously? You expected us to redecorate with a bag full of streamers and colorful balloons?

First of all, Sarabeth has more supplies left over from decorating committees than you have Civil War scrap. And technically, it's not stealing since we are all seniors and have part ownership. We're just relocating and redecorating."

"Under the cover of night in black ops clothing...yeah, that's not stealing at all. I said we were going to adjust a few things on the float. Change some of the colors. Not take the whole darn thing."

"How do you expect us to make any changes in the comforts of Andrew's shed? And did you really think we could redecorate and have Andrew *not* rip the stuff off tomorrow morning?" he asks. I say nothing. "Exactly. Besides, Sarabeth has a key, so that will keep us from violating any breaking and entering laws."

She jangles the keys in her hand.

Van's eyes travel between the two of us. He whips out a spiral note-book from his duffle bag. "I, uh, I need to make a plan and check Sarabeth's supplies to see what we have to work with." He scurries over to her truck and buries his nose in the boxes she brought. Not obvious at all.

Sarabeth watches Van walk away before she speaks. "I'm sorry, Kaycee. I really am."

Arms tight over my chest, I stand there, refusing to say a word.

"I was scared of what they'd do to you. Of what they did to you. I just thought your mother should know before something really bad happened to you."

"It wasn't your place to tell her."

"You're right. It wasn't. I had no idea Brother Mark would take it so far. He was wrong—you are not broken."

I'm shocked that she admitted to being wrong, and I'm relieved she doesn't think I need to be "fixed." "It doesn't matter, because I'm not going."

"Your mother changed her mind? Oh, thank God. And honestly—"

"No, she didn't say she wasn't sending me. But I'm not going. And she knows she can't force me."

Sarabeth drops her head down and makes circles in the dirt with her foot. "Well, that's good, because I feel like this was all my fault. Maybe if I hadn't been so jealous of you and Van—"

"Jealous?"

"Yeah. Can you blame me? You two have something in common I am never going to understand. I was hurt you didn't trust me enough to tell me. That you didn't tell me because you thought I was just another homophobe or gay basher or whatever you call those mean people. Maybe you were right not to trust me. Not because I like those mean people, but because...I had my own selfish doubts."

"Doubts about what?"

"Well, I thought if you were gay, it would mean we could no longer be friends. I thought if you finally admitted you were gay, then somehow, I'd lose you. That I wouldn't be able to be your friend because you'd hit on me or something, and then everybody would think I was gay too."

"God, no. I'm not attracted to you, Sarabeth. Never. Just like you're not attracted to Van. It doesn't work like that."

"I know. All these years we've been best friends, it's always been just friendship. Nothing else. And then I finally find out you're gay and what do I do? I flip out because Van wins BFF of the Year, and I didn't. It's stupid. And I said some pretty horrible things to you that night, and it cost me my best friend because of it. I don't know if you can forgive me for abandoning you when you needed me most, but I'm here now." She shrugs.

The apology sounds so familiar. It's the same thing I said to Van. A lifetime of friendship and one mistake wipes it all away? I don't think so. If Van was able to forgive me, then I can forgive Sarabeth.

"Well, I should have trusted you, told you what I was instead of spending all my time being something I'm not. It wasn't really fair to you either."

"So, does this mean we're good?" She sways back and forth, waiting for me to answer.

"Yeah. We're good." I give her a long overdue hug. "Though I can't say Andrew is going to be happy with you in the morning."

"Well, yeah...about him. Nobody calls my BFF a dyke and gets away with it. I told that closed-minded country hick to kiss my lily white—"

"You did not!" Van gasps.

"Eavesdrop whore," I say, turning to Van. "What the heck is on your face?" Rainbow stripes cover his cheeks.

"War paint." He nods his head all serious like. "It's camouflage."

"What, you planning on hiding in a rainbow?" Sarabeth asks. "Don't even think about putting that stuff on my face." Sarabeth pushes his rainbow-colored fingers away.

Van just shrugs and smears his purple-, blue-, and green-coated fingers on my face. "Nice, Van. Thanks." He dips his fingers into the cheap plastic face paints and globs the second half of the rainbow on my other cheek.

"Are we done with the clown makeup?" Sarabeth asks Van as he cleans his hand on a cloth. "Good. What's the plan?"

"Operation Rainbow is fairly simple—"

"Whoa, whoa, whoa. Operation Rainbow?" Sarabeth asks. "Seriously. I'm not feeling the whole unicorn love here tonight. Can't we call it like Operation Gays Kick Ass or Operation Hetero Takedown? You know, something tough that we can be proud of?"

At the same time, Van and I ease our heads toward each other, then we turn and glare at her, folding our arms over our chests in unison. "You're not *proud*?" Van asks.

"Come on guys, I didn't mean it like that. I'm so proud of my gay buddies. I'm here, aren't I?" Sarabeth's eyes dart between the two of us, but we stand there, impassive. "I dumped my boyfriend of two years and stole my father's truck to help with a secret gay mission. I can't be any more proud."

We say nothing.

"Okay. Fine," she says as she unzips her hoodie with flourish. Underneath is a nubby polyester shirt—fitting a bit too snug—with a big fat rainbow Care Bear on the front.

"Aw, he's so cute. I remember those pj's," I say, and give her a cuddly hug. "I'm proud of you for being my ally."

"Ahem. We have a mission here, ladies." Van clears his throat and tears out a piece of notebook paper with a crude pencil map of the Goodman's' property. He gives Sarabeth the once-over. "Nice T-shirt." He tries to hide his smile but fails.

"You are the stick art king," I say once I get a look at his plan.

Van puffs up proud. "Thanks. Sarabeth, you drive the truck up to the edge of the driveway with the lights off. Kill the engine and reverse back down in neutral."

"Aw, look, Sarabeth, he actually drew you inside the small truck on the map."

"Adorable," she says all deadpan.

"The slope of the driveway will help the truck roll, then Kaycee and I can push it the rest of the way to the shed door. The metal garage door will be loud as heck. The house is a good hundred yards away, so if we move it slowly, we'll probably be fine, but we shouldn't take any chances. Once we wrench it open, we're going to have to move fast to hitch up the trailer and take off before anyone notices what's going on."

I'm feeling pretty confident with Van's last-minute plan, and it's looking way better than my streamers idea. If everything falls into place smoothly, we should be on and off the property in under ten minutes. We shuffle down the road and survey the shed for a good five minutes. Lights are off at the house, and nothing has stirred.

While Sarabeth goes to get the truck, Van and I use Sarabeth's key to unlock the office. The same office with the couch she and Andrew used to make out on. *Ew.*

"Don't turn on the overhead because somebody from the house might see it," I say.

Van leads the way but stops abruptly. I ram into him. He bounces me back, and I fumble over something that sounds like a plastic trash can. He curses. "Did you bring your penlight?"

"Oh, now you're loving the penlight." I whip it out. The tiny beam shines around the room until I find the office door that leads to the main garage of the shed.

"Hey, if it wasn't for me calling Sarabeth, we'd still be figuring out how to break in."

"Whatever. You're such a glory hog. You know, if I hadn't—"

The overhead lights flip on to illuminate the entire shed. For half a second, I have a mind to scold Van, but the two huge guys leaning against the combine tractor shut me up. Center stage, Andrew stands with his arms crossed over his chest and smirks. A third kid walks over from the light switch panel on the wall, a junior linebacker. The boy who flanks Andrew graduated last year; he's a big dude. I expect Chuck the Buck to emerge at any moment.

Dang it. Obviously Van let our plan slip to the wrong person.

"Oh crap. It's the plaid KKK," Van mumbles to me.

"You got that right." Andrew cracks his knuckles.

"Wait." I stand in front of Van with my hands up, as if I could really stop a two-hundred-pound bull. "We just wanted to make a few changes to the float. No big deal."

Andrew and his buddies chuckle. "Did you hear that boys? No big deal. If you think you can put one piece of that gay crap on my float, you'd better think again."

I'm rethinking the Rainbow Pride warrior stripes we both have on our faces. Why in the world did I ever think we could pull this off?

"It's not *your* float. We all worked on it." It's a pathetic argument that loses wind the second it leaves my lips. This is a lost cause now. Nothing we can say will convince Andrew or his cronies to let us take the float, much less make any changes.

Operation Rainbow dies here.

My hopes that this town could ever grow past a certain mentality die too. My attempts to speak up for the wrongs that have been done toward Bren and her family will now go unheard. All I wanted was a chance to show it doesn't always have to be about violence. That we can all be bigger than that. That it can be about love and acceptance, or at the very least...tolerance.

"Let me ask you something, Kaycee," Andrew says. Something about his sneering causes me to shiver. "How do you decide who's the bitch between you and the dyke whore Bren. Huh?"

I freeze, terrified to say anything.

"If you see that half-bred lesbian again, ask her if she liked my Photoshop skills." Andrew gets appreciative laughs from his plaid cows. "We ran one dyke out of town. No reason why we can't do it again."

My body grows ice cold. I can't tell if it's anger or fear or shock I feel from knowing that someone I've known most of my life could be this cruel. Or worse, that I allowed myself to ignore the tiny comments and actions over the years for fear I'd be found out. I'm at a loss for what to say or even do. If Bren were here, she'd know how to smooth things over, keep the peace, and make everything all right. But she's not here. She's never coming back thanks to this jackass. As much as I want to explode all my anger on him, I know it's pointless. The loss of this night feels like the death of hope. Some people, no matter what anyone does, will never be able to see beyond their hate.

Behind me, I hear the office door open. "Why'd y'all turn the lights on? It's bright as heck out there—" Sarabeth looks up from her phone and skids to a stop.

Andrew stands to full attention. The shock of seeing Sarabeth with us wipes the smug grin off his face. "Don't tell me you're helping these freaks, sugar. Don't do this to us." He makes a move to approach her, but she scoots next to me.

"These *freaks* are my friends. And there is no us. Not anymore."

Andrew jabs a finger in the air. "That was your doing, not mine. What you and I had was good. Don't tell me they converted you to that gay stuff too?"

"Did you get dropped on your head as a baby or something? Do you even realize how stupid you sound? Convert me to being gay," says Sarabeth. "Yeah, that makes about as much sense as converting me to black. They're born that way, you idiot."

Words fly between them. Crappy parts of their relationship that have been a long time coming are flung back and forth. They argue a bit, and finally Andrew says, "Fine, ruin your life with these clowns. When your reputation goes down the toilet, don't come crying to me for a good time. You, that dyke, and her faggot friend need to get your asses off my property."

"What is all this yelling about? I can hear you all the way outside." Chuck the Buck strolls in through the office door.

Crap! I look to Van and shake my head. We are screwed now.

"Oh hey, Andrew. How's it going?" Chuck's eyes go big as he looks to Sarabeth, confused. Now I'm not so sure why he's here.

"I thought we were friends." Andrew seems shocked as well. "You picking their side now?"

"Come on, man. They just want to throw a little pink on it, spruce it up. Why not let them do their thing?"

He's here for us? My heart goes pitter-patter for the big lug. Something always told me he was a softy under all that hayseed plowboy.

"And yeah, I guess I am on their side." Chuck tugs proudly on his pink shirt. *Holton County Pig Catching Contest* is stamped on the front, and a pig's rear end, complete with coiled tail, is on the back.

"Chuck, I said rainbow, not pink," Sarabeth scolds. It's a harsh whisper we all hear.

Chuck throws his hands out. "It's the only gay shirt I've got."

"Just because they're gay, doesn't mean they all wear pink." Sarabeth turns to Van. "Do they, Van?"

"Why am I the expert on gay attire all of a sudden?"

"Are you girls done?" asks Andrew. He steps forward. "You pansies talk shopping somewhere else. If you think you can take this float all by yourself, Chuck my boy, then bring it on." On cue, Andrew's plaid buddies step up to the plate behind him. It's a lot of USDA beef staring us down. Even though Chuck is a linebacker, I don't think he can take them all on.

"Come on, man. It doesn't have to be like this." Chuck sidesteps over to the huge shed door. His hand pauses on the handle just before he rolls it up. A loud clickety-clack repeats until it's completely open. Just outside, Terrance Carver and a few boys from the basketball team sit in the back of Chuck's truck. From the passenger window I see LaShell; she gives me a small wave. The sight of more allies gives me the tiniest hope. I scan the faces of the few kids who came to help—a small group, but I'm grateful for their presence even if we don't get the float.

"Ooh," Van says, sucking in a mockingly painful gasp. "There's like one, two, three, four…nine of us and three of them," Van says to me, not so much a whisper. I nudge him in the ribs. Andrew gears his shoulders back, as if numbers don't matter to him.

"He's got a point," I say. "What are the three of you going to do? Fight us all, girls included?" I make a shaky laugh and pray like the dickens that's not what he's planning. For a moment, Andrew's boys waver, looking to one another as if deciding whether or not this is worth the fight. I seize the opportunity. "Chuck," I call over my shoulder, "hook up the truck."

Chuck the Buck doesn't waste a second. He tells one of the guys to back his truck into the garage, and he readies the hitch.

"We're taking the float. You can't stop us all." I hesitate only a moment before willing myself to move despite my fear. I toss my car keys to LaShell, tell her to follow Sarabeth, and drive my car back into town.

Terrance—like the pit bull he is—keeps a guard-dog watch on Andrew and his buddies while they have a whispering powwow on what they should do. Before they can make their minds up, Chuck and the guys have the trailer hitched and secured.

I look at Andrew. "I'm sorry." I don't know why I'm apologizing. Maybe I feel sorry for Andrew because no matter what, he'll never see the wrong of his part in all of this. Van and I hop into the back of Chuck's truck with a few guys from the basketball team. I know Van's feeling the same need I am, to protect what is ours.

We tear off down the long country road back into town. Chuck the Buck leads the way with our Tennessee Treasures float trailing behind.

Sheets of tinsel tatter in the breeze, and the backdrop of the Grand Ole Opry bends against the pressure of the wind.

I bang on the cab roof. "Slow down, Chuck. Or you're gonna rip Elvis's head right off." He slows just enough to stop Elvis from being decapitated. The stapled-down tinsel sheets no longer flap madly.

A whooping "Yeehaw," screams through the night. Chuck shakes a victory fist out the driver's side window, honking his horn. Hell yeahs and high fives make the rounds in the back. Sarabeth honks her horn like a mad woman behind us. LaShell does the same.

The night sky sparkles with starlight. An exhilarating thrill runs up my spine when I think about what we are about to do. People who I never thought would support me now stand with me. They are taking my cause and making it their own. After this night, Sunshine will never be able to go back to being the same place it used to be, at least not with the youth. We'll spend the rest of tonight converting this float into a thing of beauty. Tomorrow, our voices will be heard. Tonight has been just perfect.

Well, almost perfect.

If Bren were here to see me now, maybe she would forget all those awful things I said to her last. I face toward the side of the truck. The wind whips my hair into a bird's nest around my head, hiding my tears. Van squeezes my hand. I can't hide anything from him.

Who knows, maybe at the end of the school year I'll make a road trip to Boston. See her again. Probably won't ever happen, but I let myself believe for a moment that I would actually drive there…and that she would *want* to see me.

Chapter 23

My eyes zoom out of focus as I stare at the colorful spray paint on my hands. An entire night of no sleep is starting to mess with my consciousness. It's in these moments of exhaustion that I'm weak and let my mind slip to thoughts of Bren. I can almost see her lifting my knuckles to her lips and kissing them. The pain of not having her is too strong. I shake the thought from my head. A vague awareness slowly lifts the fog; I wake out of my revelry. Sights and sounds snap to life like a rubber band.

"You all right?" asks Van.

"Yep, all good." Voices of chatter and a flurry of activity buzz all around me. It takes a minute or two for my brain to get back online, and then I remember where I am: the auction warehouse off Bells highway. It's a property owned by LaShell's uncle. Someplace large enough to work on the float, but nowhere Andrew and his plaid cows would ever think to search.

"Here, drink this."

I accept the Red Bull that Van shoves in my hand and guzzle down the sweet nectar.

"Your mother called a few minutes ago on Sarabeth's phone to check in. You should call her back."

"Thanks." When I knew I wouldn't be home by midnight, I called Mother from Sarabeth's phone to tell her we were pulling an all-nighter to fix the float. Last-minute sabotages have been known to happen in the past. Technically, we were the ones sabotaging—minor details. I think she was so happy I had my friends back, she called off the so-called suicide watch—not that she really needed to worry about that to begin with.

"Good morning, sunshine," Sarabeth says to me. She took off at two a.m. but looks like she's had a full night's rest—hair perfectly smooth, clothes crisp, and a face full of makeup. I don't even want to know what my crow's nest of hair looks like.

"Here. You might need these." Sarabeth hands me a fresh set of clothes and a small tote with an arsenal of toiletries and makeup.

"You're the best." I make use of the unisex concrete bathroom. With cold water on my face and the Red Bull kicking in, I'm already starting to feel more alive.

A few minutes later, I emerge from the bathroom looking and feeling a little less homeless. And thanks to Sarabeth, I have clean, comfy jeans that feel like home. "So, how much more do we have to do?" I ask Van through a yawn.

"Float is done. We should clear everybody out. The parade will be starting soon."

I turn around to see the final product. My breath catches. What took us weeks to prepare, we have redecorated, and rethemed in one night. We, as in my small core of friends, a couple of eccentric art students, a few sci-fi tech geeks, and an outcast redneck or two from the wrong side of the tracks— my new clan of nonconformists. Terrance's basketball buddies helped with stealing the float, but they took off before we redecorated it. They didn't want to be a part of the entire scandal. I guess I can understand that.

236

There was a decent group of people to help out, maybe fifteen of us. I owe every one of them my gratitude. Van and I stand back and admire our handiwork. Thanks to Sarabeth confiscating the leftover supplies from the past years' school events, we had enough to change the float.

The red barn backdrop of the Grand Ole Opry now shimmers with a colorful hodge-podge of metallic tinsels. Elvis stands proud in the field of purple glitter irises—the only thing we didn't change. His once infamous white suit the twins took home and fabric-dyed it in an array of colors. All the musical notes on the Graceland gates have been repainted in different colors with matching glitter trim. Then there's the best part—the gold-painted homecoming king and queen thrones that Sarabeth and I painstakingly covered in clear rhinestones have been spray painted over in rainbow colors.

"Holy pot of gold, Van. It looks like a unicorn puked on the whole thing and made it a giant sparkly rainbow. We done good." I loop my arms around him in a big fat hug.

Chuck the Buck walks up to check out all our hard work, a rainbow afro springing and swaying on top of his head. "More like the unicorn took a dump."

"Ew, Chuck."

"Really?" Van shakes his head.

"Come on, you big dope." I smack him playfully.

"I'm just saying." He shrugs, taking a bite of his doughnut.

"Guess we've got to get this thing moving." I exhale a bundle of nerves.

"Not yet, Kaycee." Chuck releases one of his sharp whistles. It gets everyone's attention. "Any of you losers come through?" he asks the group.

"Sort of," a squeaky voice calls. Pipsqueak Harry steps up in his mascot uniform, the giant wildcat head tucked under his arm. The colorful tie-dyed T-shirt over the uniform's typical jersey is a nice touch. "I heard about what you were doing," he says, glancing at Van—who obviously let the cat of the bag last week, "so I contacted some local business and told them the seniors were doing a service-learning project on equality to educate kiddos about bullying and hate crimes. And that we rethemed the homecoming parade to "Rainbow of Love" and asked for their Wildcat support. Not everybody was on board with the idea, but I think a couple might support us." He shrugs with a smile.

I'm stunned into silence. Harry, who gets picked on all the time for his height—or lack thereof—went out of his way to do something for me? All I can do is nod my appreciation.

Misty speaks up, "And hey, we tried to get the school clubs to get with the rainbow program too."

"But nobody really wanted to help out," Melissa finishes. "Except for the Art Club. A girl named Kera? Kara? Keira?—something—said she'd do a banner for the Wildcat Wall uptown. Her parents own the pawnshop that it's painted on. At least it's something."

They show me the posters they made for their vehicles: *Equality for All*, *Gay Pride Allies*, and *It's Okay If You're Gay*. A few show their support with colorful hair paint, rainbow balloon bouquets, and matching streamers on their trucks. Tawanda tells us how she contacted the primary schools and tried to coordinate a color-themed Equality Day, where each grade level represents a color of the rainbow, but it was too last minute for the school to consider.

"Wow, guys. I don't even know what to say." I look at Van, and even he seems a bit awestruck. All those faces stare back, expecting me to be epic or some shit. "I...I didn't expect this. I don't have the words to say how much it means to me that y'all—" My tears choke my voice.

"Aw. See that, guys, gay people have feelings too." Van hugs me.

I shove him away and smile as I dry my eyes.

"Hey, let's get this show rolling." LaShell claps her hands, ready. "I told my little sisters to spread the word and vote for the seniors' float. If they do, we'll give them the most candy."

"Oh my gosh…candy. Were you guys able to get candy?" Without candy, we have no chance at accomplishing our goal. We wouldn't have the votes. It could make or break our win. We could have made our float out of toilet paper and chicken wire, and so long as we still rained down a thunderstorm of candy on the kids, we could've won this thing.

Chuck looks at Terrance. "Well?"

All eyes fall on Terrance. You could hear a pin drop for the silence that fills the room. It was a last-minute afterthought at ten thirty last night when we realized, in our thievery, that we forgot to steal the candy we had already purchased for the first float and had stored in Andrew's shed.

It's no longer about winning because we're seniors and it's our final year. Something bigger is at stake here. It's hope. Hope that if we make a big enough statement, people in this town will have to start accepting Van and me and every other gay person here for who they are. They will no longer be able to sweep us under the rug.

Terrance sighs a long breath like a deflated tire. "I got four bags."

I squeeze my eyes shut. "Please tell me you mean four giant black trash bags."

"Nope." He picks up the small grocery bags at his feet and drops them on the table.

Hands scramble for the bags, dumping the contents out. There are only a few handfuls of huge movie-theater-size candy boxes and oversized candy bars. I grab a king-size Almond Joy. "Dude, we can't hurl this out into a crowd of children. We're talking concussions here. What the heck? Did y'all go to Big Star? Walmart?"

"Last night we went to Big Star, Walmart, Parkman's Grocery, and every Quick Stop and gas station in Sunshine. We even drove out to the beer store past the county line, and they were cleaned out. Something is up. There's no way the other classes bought that much candy on such short notice."

"Dang it," Sarabeth bursts out, as she flings a candy bar across the table. "That son of a—"

"I was thinking the same thing, Sarabeth," I say. Everyone looks at us for an explanation. "Andrew. I bet as soon as we left last night, Andrew and his buddies hit every store in town and bought up the last of their candy just to screw us over." I plop down in the folding chair behind me, plant my elbows on my knees, and bury my face in my hands.

I hear somebody ask how Andrew could do this when he's a senior too. There's a brief discussion of what else we can toss to the kids since we don't have candy. I cringe when someone suggests Mardi Gras beads.

I can't help but feel that despite having come so far, it will always be like this. No matter where I go or what I do, there will always be naysayers waiting to spread their hate and stop progress. Sure, today we will still make our statement to the town, but winning would have made that statement just a little sweeter. Having to concede this round to Andrew and people like him knots my stomach.

"People," Chuck the Buck says, banging a fist on the table, getting our attention. "We need to figure this out. We're not going to win this thing unless we have candy."

"Did somebody say candy?"

My heart skips a beat. For a second, I tell myself that my mind is playing tricks on me, that there is no way in the world I've heard correctly. But when gasps and cheery welcomes begin to spill out, I know it was not the voices in my head. I jump to my feet, but I don't need to stand to see her. She towers over everyone else.

The few people left move out of the way, and Bren steps up to the table. Her muscles strain from the grocery bags of candy hanging on her arms. She dumps her loot. "There are, like, thirty more bags of the stuff in the trunk of my car." She motions back over her shoulder with her thumb. Her eyes lift to meet mine. Her smile is reserved, something you might pass off to a stranger on the street.

I glance over at Van. He just shrugs. "I called for reinforcements." I can't believe he's gone and done this. I don't know if I should punch him or hug him. He and the others go out to Bren's car to get the candy.

I tell my feet to move and my mouth to speak, but shock and awe keep me still. My heart runs the pony races, pounding my pulse in my ears. I've missed her so much, all I want to do is throw my arms around her. I can't believe she's standing here in the flesh. All those feelings for her come rushing back. They reaffirm exactly what I'm doing here. Thankfully I don't need my brain to function because Bren walks up to me.

"Can we go outside and talk?" she asks, inclining her head toward the side door. There's no warm and fuzzy smile. No soft lilt in her voice, just a straightforward you-and-me-and-words-need-to-be-had kind of tone.

I swallow the brick in my throat and nod my head. This is not going to be pretty. I guess I should be grateful she's taking this outside, to chew me out in private. When I first saw her a moment ago, for a brief second I allowed myself to think she came back because of me, but no, she came back because Van asked her. And to give me a piece of her mind.

The morning sun blinds me. The metal door closes behind us. Bren stuffs her hands into her jeans pockets as if she needs to corral them before she ends up doing something stupid. The way I figure it, I should speak first before she has her say and leaves.

"I...I...I thought you were in Boston."

That's what I say? I haven't seen Bren in weeks, and the last time I did, I totally dismissed her. This is the best I can do?

She opens her mouth to speak. "I'm sorry," I blurt out, cutting her off. "I'm *so* sorry. For everything I said. I just didn't know how to handle the situation. I didn't know what to do or what to say. I acted like a little kid who didn't want to get in trouble again, so crap flew out of my mouth before I could stop it and I—I'm just so, so sorry."

Bren chews on her lip and stares off to the side. I'm just about to give up when she says, "At the time you said all those things to Sarabeth, I believed them. It hurt to hear it." Her eyes meet mine. "Because you wouldn't be the first straight girl to use me to 'experiment.'"

"But I didn't, I'm not—"

"Let me finish."

This whole time she thought I was using her for some heterosexual game? Right now I feel like the lowest life-form on earth. I was too good at my own game of pretending to be something I wasn't. When it came down to it, she believed my lie too.

"Then all that stuff happened to me and my family, and we left. Once we were settled, I tried to call you, left you messages. So when you never called me back, I assumed it was all true...until you called me this week. I didn't want to listen to your message. I wanted to delete it, but I couldn't." She smiles at herself and shakes her head. "And when I heard your voice and listened to you bouncing all over the place with your apology, I could see you and your wavy hair. I realized how much I missed you."

My heart stops beating, and I stand before her, grateful. She missed me. All this time, she missed me. The confession from her could not feel any sweeter.

"I should have known you were acting out of fear. I just wish you had called me back. Talked to me. I just needed to talk to you so bad. I don't understand why you took so long to call me back."

"Ugh," I groan, exasperated. "My stupid phone. My stupid freaking phone. I'm such an idiot. I tossed it out the window—it's a long, pathetic story. Your Instagram disappeared, and I thought you blocked me. Mother locked me off the computer. I had nothing. It doesn't matter now. I'm glad to see you. I'm so glad you're here." The space between us feels like the size of a football field. I tuck my hands in my back pockets to keep from reaching out and touching her.

Bren gives me a crooked smile. It's the most glorious sight I've seen in weeks. I can't help but grin from ear to ear. "Come here." Bren stretches her long arms out to me. I take her hand, and with a slight pull from Bren, I'm enveloped in her arms, comforted by ocean and spice. "God, I've missed you," Bren mumbles against the top of my head.

I squeeze her as tightly as I can, not wanting the moment to ever end. Though she may be here now, she will have to return to Boston, sooner or later. "Wait," I say as I pull myself away from her chest. "How are you here, with your car, if y'all are back in Boston?"

"Mom and I were first, until dad finished up business here. We stayed at my gran's for like a week. But then we sat down and had a family meeting, and we decided the best place for me to finish high school was Knoxville, and—"

I step back with a mix of shock and excitement. "I'm sorry. Did you say Knoxville? As in Knoxville, Tennessee? As in four-freaking-hours-away-from-Sunshine Knoxville, Tennessee?"

Bren laughs. The sound is low and easy and melts me to the core. "I believe the post office prefers just Knoxville, Tennessee, but yes, that Knoxville." She smiles. "My parents thought it would be better for us to go ahead and move there, get to know the area, the people, and settle in, especially since I'm going to be a Lady Vol." Her voice drops to a whisper. "Though technically the UT doesn't call us that anymore."

"A University of Tennessee Volunteer? Wait, you got admitted to UT? I thought you got a full ride to Notre Dame."

"No, I wish. But I got a pretty decent athletic scholarship from UT Knoxville that I couldn't pass up. That's why my dad accepted the job in Sunshine to begin with. Not to mention other benefits that might come from living near Sunshine."

Oh my God, UT Knoxville. Mother and I can't afford UT—nor do I have the grades to get in—but maybe there's a community college nearby, and I could stay at the dorms. There are tons of historical sites in and around Knoxville that I could study—Civil War battlegrounds and the Native American Pinson Mounds.

And just like that, the possibilities of my future start to take shape.

Bren weaves her fingers with mine. "And besides, I kind of left my heart in Tennessee, and I was hoping I could visit it sometime." She pulls my hands behind her back, forcing me forward, right up against her body. Those big brown eyes seem to drink me in. There's a whole lot of *oh please, oh please, oh please* pounding in my chest.

Inches from my face, she stops; her eyes scan my features. It takes all my power to keep my breathing at a smooth, even pace. Somehow my memories of how she felt so close did not do the real beauty in front of me justice. Her brows are sculpted into two perfect crescents. The soft peaks of her lips are filled with the most luscious amount of volume. That hair. *God*, that hair! I want the right to run my fingers through it every day and twice on Sundays. "Man, you are gorgeous." The words slip involuntarily out of my lips.

She bites her bottom lip to hold back a knowing smile. I want to smack myself for looking like a drooling puppy too. Bren clears her throat. "Do you think maybe we can try this again? I hear long-distance relationships never work, but maybe we could give it a try. That is…if you're still into me."

Oh yeah, community college in Knoxville, hundreds of miles from Sunshine, sounds perfect to me.

My body sways into the curve of hers of its own volition. "Oh yeah…just a little." My voice is barely a whisper. I part my lips before she even bends to kiss me. Our lips touch, soft and tentative at first but firmer as the lapse of time apart seems to catch up with us all at once. Her hands slip out from mine and wrap around me.

I don't know how we are going to do this with just weekends and holidays. It sounds more like a child-custody situation than a relationship, but the precious time is worth it. I have no idea even where I'll go to school next fall, but this, right now, is at least something I can latch on to.

Bren's grasp tightens and pulls me up right against her body. Um, yeah, this is way better than the nunnery I had planned.

The metal side door opens. "Seriously, people?" Van's voice stops our kiss, but we just stand there, smiling at each other as if we don't even notice him. "We've got, like, a Gay Pride Parade here we're trying to set in motion. Make a little small-town history. And you two are out here sucking face. Perfect."

We stand there, foreheads touching, unconcerned about the world around us. After a moment Bren asks, "He's not leaving, is he?"

I peer past her shoulder. "Nope."

"You think if we keep kissing he'll get the hint and go away?"

"No way. When Van's not busy being an eavesdrop whore, he's a Peeping Tom."

"I can hear you two."

Bren chuckles against my mouth as she gives me a peck. "I'm not done with you."

"I hope not."

"Ahem." Van clears his throat.

"Vander, Vander, Vander." I walk toward him by the side door. Bren's tight on my heels, hands latched on to my waist. I love that she's feeling the same need to hold on as I am. As if our separation, might break the dream. "What am I going to do with you?" I ask Van as we go back inside to the float.

"I was thinking, since I can't ask Johnny Depp, I'll ask you. Be my queen?" From behind his back, he reveals the most gorgeous copper crown I've ever seen.

"What is this?" I take the crown from his hand. Colorful crystal beads on thin copper wire are woven in an intricate lattice pattern to form the shape of a crown. It's absolutely stunning.

"My idea, but Charlotte's creation." Past his shoulder I see Charlotte Wozniak puffing up proud, her arm around her girlfriend, Jacinda.

"But in the gym I thought…the whole ball and Bren thing…I just assumed that you wanted…"

"Bren?" Charlotte busts out laughing. It's more like hiccups than a laugh. "I was trying to distract the class so you could bust your move, and when you didn't, I gave you a friendly little push."

"Friendly, huh?" The biting sting of the volleyball is fresh in my memory. I'd hate to see how she treats her enemies. "What about Sarabeth and Andrew's crowns?" I ask.

With a bobby pin in her mouth and her hands working the real crown into her hair, Sarabeth says, "You're taking my place on the float and you want my crown too? Hell to the no. Plus I'm not standing up there by myself, no thank you." She finishes pinning the silver and crystal crown on her head. "It's bad enough I'll have to stand on the field with Andrew tonight before the game. Ugh."

Charlotte bends over a shoe box with crushed tissue paper. She pulls out a second handcrafted crown. This one is larger with fatter crystals; less dainty, more masculine. "This one might be a little heavier." She lifts it over Van's head. "But you have plenty of hair for Jacinda to pin it to."

"You made these? This week?" I ask in awe. Charlotte nods. "They're so gorgeous. I…I can't thank you enough." I'm amazed. Camouflage, mullet, and ass-kicker are all I see when I look at her. I'm utterly baffled that someone as hard-edged as her could create something so delicate. What an ass I am. Here I go, not wanting people to judge me for what I am, when all the while, I was judging Charlotte.

Jacinda snap-pops her bubblegum. She steps in front of me with a colorful sash in her hands that says *LGBT Royalty*. Her gum does nothing to mask the stale aroma of cigarette smoke. "I thought maybe you'd like to wear a sash, like they do for the real thing."

Her curled hair is teased up huge and poufy, molded stiff with half a can of Aqua Net. I'm tempted to advise her against smoking with hair that flammable. I didn't realize she had so many freckles, which soften her rounded cheeks like a little kid. Of course the marker-thick eyeliner and hairy spider-leg eyelashes tell me she's not a child in the slightest.

Jacinda drapes the sash over me and makes a slight adjustment to center it just perfectly on my shoulders. She leans in to whisper to me. "You're brave. You know that?" She picks a piece of glitter off my sweater and steps back.

I feel like I'm the one who should be saying thank you to her. Sarabeth pins my crown to my head, giving me words of love and encouragement. Van is over to the side, receiving his own LGBT royalty sash. A smaller sign that says, *Love Everybody*, is shoved in my hand, the rainbow glitter not quite dry. Somebody tells us we've got the huge supply of candy between our thrones to throw to the kids. There's more candy for those who'll ride in the back of the pickup that pulls the float. It's like the world is happening around me, and I'm only an observer. All of this is because of me. Me.

Bren squeezes my hand. "You okay?" She steps into my line of sight.

There's this humbling realization that my plan is coming together. In a few minutes, the whole town will know what I am. I won't be able to hide behind my lies anymore. Something about the absolute truth is freeing. Today will go down in Sunshine's history as the day of the first Gay Pride Parade, and for once, this town will have to face the reality that not everybody fits in the same mold. They will either embrace diversity or suffocate in their own hate. Either way, I've done my job. I look up at Bren. "I'm doing this."

"Yeah you are, babe." Her smile is contagious like a yawn.

I'm sporting a grin that reaches all the way to my heart. "I've never done this before." The words tumble out in a hurried rush of excitement.

Bren leans in close and cocks her head all serious. "What? You mean to tell me you've never been in a Gay Pride Parade before?" She shakes her head and tsks. "Oh, you haven't *lived* until you've been in a Gay Pride Parade." My body rumbles with laughter. She gives me a good luck peck on my cheek before jumping into the back of Chuck's truck.

She's right, I really haven't lived yet.

But I am now.

The float jerks forward and slowly moves toward Main Street.

Butterflies flutter in my stomach. Van reaches over and grabs my hand. "You ready?"

"You bet your life I'm ready."

* * *

Bunches of color dot the crowd like scattered Skittles—just small groups of high school students who rallied in support. Not quite the wave of rainbow color I was hoping for, but a good start nonetheless. From the end of the strip, I can see all the way up to the courthouse. At the top, the juniors' float rounds the corner of the Court Square, and on it, a giant book lies open. But the pages aren't the "I Wish I Were in Dixie" sheet music as they were rumored to be. Instead a giant fluffy quill has scrawled the words, *God made marriage between Adam and Eve, not Adam and Steve* across the pages. It's a big fat slap in my gay pride face. Their float has *nothing* to do with the Tennessee Treasures theme, but their anti–gay marriage statement will surely get some votes.

Van squeezes my arm. "Don't let it get you down, Kaycee. Stand tall."

I smile at Bren who's sitting in the back of Chuck the Buck's truck and find strength in her presence. I lift my head up and pull my shoulders back.

Buckets of candy are packed all around her and Terrance. Sarabeth stands behind the cab of the truck. She winks at me before she turns around, executing a flawless homecoming queen wave as we approach the crowd. Kids scream as fistfuls of candy rain into the crowd.

A couple of businesses participated in Pipsqueak Harry's service-learning project. Colorful balloons and posters brighten the lone Mexican restaurant in town. A few others took a more subtle approach with *No Bullying* and *Stop the Hate* signs in their windows. Maybe the message isn't as loud as rainbows, but their small gestures mark their place in history. A moment in time when their participation changed lives in Sunshine, whether they realize it or not.

A few shops are closed, unusual since it's not a Sunday. The Christian fish symbol and Christ's cross are painted on their doors with the words, *Protect our religious liberties!* The Hannigan Funeral Home that Chelsea's family owns has *Leviticus 18:22* painted in bloodred on the front window. It makes me feel sad for her...for like a half a second. Old Man Jenson hulks in front of his barbershop, scowling at us as we pass. Andrew and his fellow plaid cronies stand next to him with the same face of disgust. Van, Sarabeth, and I exchange glances as our minds arrive at the same idea. In unison, our hands dive into our candy buckets, and we throw fistfuls of candy at Andrew, causing a horde of children to scramble around his feet. I smirk.

Halfway up Main Street, my jaw drops open, and I forget I'm supposed to be tossing candy. The most beautiful thing I have ever seen rolls into view.

The giant brick wall that greets everyone who passes through town no longer features Sunshine's Wildcat football pride, but a different kind of pride.

A magnificent rainbow streams from a huge lopsided heart painted in the bottom corner. The colors wave up and across the wall like flowing ribbons. The Sunshine High School Wildcat's roaring mouth has been repainted into a cartoon grin, no longer terrifying but a big ole pussy cat.

"*This* is the 'art banner' Melissa was talking about." Van yells over the screaming kids so I can hear him. I shrug. His guess is as good as mine. "Can you believe it?"

I point to the top of the two-story building. As we roll around the Court Square, we can see Keira and three of her fellow art students from school waving at us. Paint covers their hands and arms.

"Omigod, that is not some small banner." Van tosses a few more handfuls of candy.

"No, it isn't. But it's amazing." I shake my head, smiling. But holy smokes, we're going to pay something fierce for ruining their football wall of pride. I shake the worry from my head and fling a fistful of candy to the kiddos.

"Kaycee Jean McCoy," Van says, "I'd say we've done good today. Haters be damned."

"Agreed. All I wanted was some colorful streamers on the float. Maybe a show-your-pride banner. But this, this is way more than I ever hoped for." Though in my heart, once we got started, I imagined something explosive, like those Gay Pride Parades in San Francisco. Next year, Kaycee. Next year.

I see my fellow classmates riding ahead with their rainbow-decorated cars, gay pride signs hanging on their car doors. A few months ago, I wouldn't have believed one person—besides Van—would support me. Now a small clan of people, made up of classmates who aren't even gay, has joined our cause. As we move up Main Street, with the support of our friends all around us, I stake claim to my gay pride and vow to never hide from it again. Like Van told me before, there will always be haters. But if I open my heart up to loving and accepting myself, I open it up to beautiful people like Bren too.

As we make our way around the courthouse, Kappy's Diner comes into sight. All dressed in his Sunday's best, Mr. Bobby waves a rainbow flag with his right hand. Standing next to him, holding his left, is Ms. Doris Carver with a matching colorful feather boa draped around her neck. I smile hugely at the two of them holding hands. Next door, in front of Hot Flix, Arthur stands with a big smile. I snap a shocked look to Van, who blushes. Mrs. Betty waves at us like a chicken flapping its wings. She has painted a Band-Aid over the broken heart on their rainbow window.

Next to her store is Mother's shop. I hold my breath.

I'm not sure what I expected really. Colorful streamers in the window maybe? A rainbow flag? Balloons? A sign? But there's nothing on the outside of the building from my mother to show support for her daughter. As the float drives past, my heart sinks. I crane my neck as we get farther away, praying for the tiniest sign.

And just about the time the store is almost out of sight, Mother steps into the window's view real quiet like. A smile spreads across her face, and a shaky hand tosses me a light kiss. We disappear around the corner. I close my eyes and hold on tight to the image.

It's something. As tiny as it was, it's all I needed to feel her love. Okay, so it wasn't a bold window display, complete with rainbow-spewing heart, like the one Van's mom made for Hot Flix's storefront window, but she didn't lock her doors in protest like other businesses. It's middle of the road. I can accept middle-of-the road. Middle of the road means no telling where we might go.

For the first time in my life, I feel like I can truly be myself.

I use the sleeve of my sweater to wipe my tears.

Bren jumps out of the slow-moving truck and hops onto the float. It seesaws from her weight.

"You did it, baby." She reaches toward me like she's about to hug me but then holds back. "You survived."

"Yep, I did."

Bren stuffs her hands in her pockets and creates a fair amount of space between us, the gap signifying we are only friends.

"I'll be having none of that." I pull one of her hands out of its pocket and clasp it in mine.

"But...what about all these people?"

I laugh. "I'm holding your hand, Bren. It's not like we're making out. Besides, cat's out of the bag now. No sense hiding."

The crowd thins as the float turns off of Main Street. The sound of screaming children dies down. I tug Bren a little closer.

"You know, the day ain't over yet. We still have to survive tonight's homecoming football game and the cornfield after-party."

"Cornfield party? You southerners and your traditions." She shakes her head.

"Yes, cornfield party. Don't tell me you've never been to a cornfield party, because you haven't lived until—" The sweetest lips I've ever tasted shut. Me. Right. Up.

Bren pulls back and speaks across my lips. "If I want any lip out of you, I'll just take it."

I smile against her mouth. "I'm counting on it."

Bren peers past my shoulder and points. "Look."

In the distance, at the end of the parade route, is the Wildcats's giant silver-and-blue balloon arch. The juniors' giant feather quill has snagged the arch, making the middle droop and turning it into a big fat heart.

"Love note," Bren says, then kisses me again.

ACKNOWLEDGMENTS

To my incredible agent, Lauren MacLeod, thank you for dealing with my overactive type A personality, for being as passionate about this book as I am, and above all, for believing in my story.

To my editor, Wendy McClure, thank you for your in-depth insight and your spot-on tightening and tweaks. Thanks to Kristin Zelazko, for keeping my characters in charge of their own body parts and allowing me to disindumbedify my story with made-up words. I am grateful to the entire Albert Whitman team. I have found my home.

To the fierce and wonderfully inspiring Ellen Hopkins, thank you for pointing your finger at me at that SCBWI conference so long ago and telling me to "Write that. Write that book. Write what scares you."

To Tim Whittington, who was my Van that one faithful summer, I hope you find your one true love someday.

To my OLBFF Nicole McLaughlin, we made it! I'm so happy we had each other to lean on.

To my indisputably awesome girlies, Kathryn Rose, Rachel Searles, Jessica Love, and Elizabeth Briggs: "Started from the bottom, now we're here. Started from the bottom, now my whole team's here." Thank you for the writing retreat laughter, for being my conference compadres, for your encouragement, love, advice, and support—but, most importantly, for your friendship. I could not have traveled this road without you by my side. Extra chocolate for Rachel, Liz, and Jessica for critiquing those fledgling drafts.

To Ara Burklund, thank you for all our many hikes to reassure and guide me through my publishing journey and for always reading my raw first drafts and seeing my story's potential with enthusiastic support.

To my mother, Steva Banks, you've always said I should write a children's book. Here it is. Though it's not a picture book, I hope I've made you proud. I love you, Momma.

To my boys, Luke and Jackson, thank you for being the beautiful chaos in my life.

And finally to my husband, Chris Elmendorf, you are my love, my soul, and my best friend. Everything you give to this family made my dream possible. I love you, honey.

ABOUT THE AUTHOR

Dana Elmendorf was born and raised in a small town in Tennessee and now lives in southern California with her husband, two boys, and her tiny dog. This is her first novel. Visit her online at danaelmendorf.com.